———————————— ★ ————————————

Jane went into her bedroom, eager to pull off her wet clothes. She reached for the light switch, but her hand groped against the wall and felt something else. A denim jacket. An arm. The arm slammed her against the wall.

She screamed and hit him with her fists, but that did not stop him. Jane took another breath; then, using all her strength, she twisted and turned to look directly into the man's eyes.

"You're not going to get away with this!" she shrieked, and pulled the ski mask almost over his eyes, while kicking his calf squarely.

———————————— ★ ————————————

"...an evocative mystery."

—Pittsburgh *Advertiser*

ALASKA GRAY

SUSAN FROETSCHEL

WORLDWIDE®

TORONTO • NEW YORK • LONDON
AMSTERDAM • PARIS • SYDNEY • HAMBURG
STOCKHOLM • ATHENS • TOKYO • MILAN
MADRID • WARSAW • BUDAPEST • AUCKLAND

For Doug and Nick

ALASKA GRAY

A Worldwide Mystery/July 1996

First published by St. Martin's Press, Incorporated.

ISBN 0-373-26206-X

I think I'll go to the park and watch the children playing.
Perhaps I'll find in my head what my heart is saying.
A vision of a child returning, a kingdom where the
   sky is burning.
Honey, I will be there, yes, I'll be there.

Any world that I'm welcome to,
I say, any world that I'm welcome to,
Any world that I'm welcome to is better than the one I
come from.

—Steely Dan

Form lines, ovoids, U forms, S forms, and the variations of these components are the shapes in which the artist expresses his design concept. When they are assembled in close proximity, the spaces between them create other shapes, and these negative shapes become an essential part of the overall design.

—*Looking at Indian Art of the Northwest Coast* by Hilary Stewart (University of Washington Press)

PROLOGUE

A Rainy Night in Late March

THE WOMAN shut her eyes and concentrated. All she thought about was rolling her head back and forth, back and forth, trying to say no.

She did not want more vodka making the hot slide down her throat.

But he crossed the room, nestled his hand around her neck, and used the bottle to pry apart her lips. She writhed, but his hand was strong. Vodka dribbled down her chin.

He let go of her, and her head flopped back. She rubbed her face instinctively against the sofa. The cheap fabric felt like burlap. The pain was distracting and better than being alone in the black cave of her mind.

She opened her eyes just enough to watch him through her eyelashes. His sweater, his jeans, were intact. Her robe was barely loosened. What was he waiting for? she wondered. What did he want? Even though he had yet to take a drink, he obviously cared more about the bottle than anything about her. His hands were seductive, curled around the neck of the vodka bottle. She remembered wanting, hanging on to bottles that way, a long, long time ago. She closed her eyes completely. She wanted him to leave, and she hoped he'd forget the bottle.

She could not deny that the first sip of alcohol, after years of looking, not drinking, tasted really, really good.

She felt his hand on her shoulder.

"Just a little more," he coaxed.

She moaned and shook her head and opened her eyes. Her eyelids felt like the dull lumps of metal used as fishing weights by her uncle and cousins. She was afraid to look at him and, instead, looked about her room. The room, she corrected herself. Little belonged to her—not the dresser, the bed and its covers, or the rug. Other than her clothes, all that was hers was an old and delicate pink lamp from her great-aunt. The antique could not handle light bulbs of more than forty-five watts, her aunt had cautioned, and its light draped the room in gold and shadows. Such low light was supposed to be horrible for painting, sketching, carving. But she needed something more than light, and during the rainy winter nights of Southeast Alaska, an atmosphere as dim as candlelight dulled details and softened anything she made into beauty. She smiled at the lamp.

"Come on, swallow," he ordered impatiently. He gave her no choice and poured a slow stream of vodka while stroking her throat. The gold glow expanded like mysterious smoke.

"You don't have to do this to sleep with me," she pleaded.

She remembered her terror as she came out of the shower and heard the turn of a key in her lock. She almost screamed but stopped when she saw who opened the door. He had smiled, put a finger to his lips, and held out the bottle of vodka as if it were a gift, all without words. When she took the bottle, he gave her a simple, sweet kiss on the lips. Her fear melted away.

"You don't have to do this," she repeated softly.

He laughed, caught himself, and brought his voice down to a whisper. "I want you this way. You like it, too."

"No more, please," she moaned. "It's been so long. I feel sick...."

"All right, we'll stop," he agreed, quickly returning the bottle to the table. "For now."

He stood, walked toward her bed, and fingered a necklace from the headboard. The necklace was a fine strand of minute black beads. Dangling at the end was a black river stone etched so that it took the form of a chuckling raven.

"You make such pretty things," he commented. "Is this new?"

She nodded. "You may keep it."

"Such pretty things...," he said, as he tucked the necklace into an inside pocket of his jacket.

He looked at his watch and returned to her side, letting his hand fall on her arm. He stroked absentmindedly, as he would with a stray cat.

"Tell me," he whispered again, so softly she thought she imagined the voice. "Does Jane McBride know what you do at the school?"

"Who?" She tried to concentrate on his voice and the movement of his hand. But all she could see was the almost empty bottle.

The thin layer of liquid, not more than a quarter inch, teased in the near light. Even sober alcoholics liked to keep track of how much was left in a bottle. He stroked her harder and harder, and a furious pounding in her head joined the rhythm.

"Jane McBride—the new instructor, the one with the short red hair."

"I never knew her name. She's nice...." She shut her eyes.

"So, you have talked to her."

"No, not really...she asked me questions...."

"And what did you tell her?" he asked pointedly.

"I don't remember," she moaned. "Not now."

"I don't believe you," he hissed. "Tell me."

"Nothing," she said. "Not much. I asked her for some hair. Just a few clips of her red hair. For a mask I'm making. Oh, please, do something, my head is pounding."

"I have something for that," he muttered. He pulled a second bottle of cheap vodka from his backpack and removed the cap viciously. He squeezed her mouth and turned her head. Her wet tangle of hair caught, sending splinters of pain through her head.

For an instant she thought about how her hair would look the next morning. If not thoroughly combed and dried, the strands would look like wrinkled black silk, fallen from a hanger and pushed to the back corner of the closet.

He slammed the bottle into her mouth. She gagged, and vodka splashed. He pulled it out, knocking the rim hard against her front teeth and gums. Before her mouth had tasted like a sour sponge from a filthy kitchen. Now, she tasted blood.

She cried. He wanted something she could not give. What did it have to do with Jane? What had Jane McBride said to him that made him act this way?

The pain in her head roared. Whispers had always lurked inside her mind, constantly reminding her since she was a child that something was not right, that she was different, and that she would never catch up with all the people passing her by. Now the persistent whispers turned into screams of laughter. She remembered the crooked smile of a doctor at Mt. Edgecumbe Hospital after an examination. He'd asked her if she knew what fetal alcohol syndrome meant. She'd shaken her head, and he'd asked about mental retardation.

"I know what I am not," she had answered. He had nodded slowly, held her hands, and explained gently that she was actually lucky her IQ, her situation, her understanding of the world, were not worse.

She had not stopped off at a bar that night or ever again, and the next morning, she'd begun taking birth control pills faithfully. Every night, while painting and carving, she'd held back tears of frustration.

More vodka trickled down her throat. She gave up fighting and he turned out the light. The familiar glow of her room vanished, leaving only a faint trail of moonlight coming in through the window. She twisted and cried in pro-

"Actually, you look more normal than most," he said. "Guess I'm letting you know what you're in for. Where I work, rumor has it they keep Seattle clean by passing out tickets for the Alaska ferries to the so-called undesirables. The inexpensive solution to community mental health problems. I apologize—I haven't been on a ferry in a while, you're the first person I ran into."

"Apology accepted," Jane said. "What made you think I don't live in Alaska?"

"Easy," he said with confidence. "Only newcomers stand out on deck for so long."

She gave him an admiring nod to confirm his observation.

"Not only that," he continued, "I know why you're on the ferry."

"Really? By now, I'd think you would have learned to ask your questions and wait for me to explain."

"I knew it! With answers like 'all of the above' and 'learned by now,' you have to be a teacher," he countered. "The ferry arrives in Southeast Alaska almost a week before the second semester starts—gives you some time to settle in and see the town. When I first saw you I thought you had an uncanny resemblance to Miss Ernie, my fourth-grade teacher. She thought I was a slow learner, too."

"Wrong. About the occupation, that is. One more guess," Jane said as she walked away. "I'll let you think about it awhile."

"Hey, I'm Michael Benoit. Don't make me guess your name."

"Jane," she said. "Jane McBride."

She walked briskly, circling the deck—about one-sixth of a mile. When she turned the corner at the stern, Michael Benoit was gone and so were her tears. He had not commented about her eyes and probably assumed the redness was from the squall. She opened her black mitten and uncrumpled the newspaper article in her hand, grateful he had not noticed and tried to play a guessing game about that.

She glanced at the headline again—CHARGES DROPPED IN TODDLER'S DEATH—just before a gust snatched the paper. Jane tried to grab it, but the article flew with the wind before taking a dive into the ferry's churning wake.

She sighed. Time to let go. Her life was like the wake—any meaning, any sign of what she had worked for and believed in, bubbled furiously and then disappeared, the way the froth vanished before the boat was out of sight.

TWO

JANE MCBRIDE HAD stepped aboard the *Matanuska* as the new director of finance for Katmai Shee Inc. Hardly Fortune 500, the firm was a failing Alaska Native corporation based in Sitka, an island city of eight thousand people. The corporation apparently expected a lot from her—the salary was double that of her previous job in Boston. Fair enough, Jane figured, because she expected a lot from Alaska.

Alaska was the largest and just about the least populated state in the country. According to the latest U.S. Census figures, Alaska's population was young and had more college degrees than any other state in the Union. It had vast, untallied resources and not a whole lot of industry to make use of those resources. Katmai Shee had the potential to make money.

The biggest resource was land. Some was pristine, probably never stepped on by any human being. Some had been shamelessly abused—clear-cut by logging companies, stripped by miners, and oversupplied with shoddy and downright ugly construction. The largest private-land owners were the Indians, through Katmai Shee Inc. and more than two hundred other Alaska Native corporations. That kind of landholding should represent a lot of power, and Katmai Shee should be making a lot of money, Jane repeated to herself for the hundredth time.

She was a meticulous financial analyst and economist. She enjoyed making both money and the most efficient use of resources, for herself and the people who employed her. Success required fierce concentration, which had become impossible in Boston after her divorce. Too many friends and co-workers looked at her with pity. Not good for someone in her field. It was essential that clients trust her instincts and timing, that she direct her junior analysts without having to wonder whether they were second-guessing her. So she decided to find a faraway place, where people would not know that curtness, long silences, and a smile that seemed as enticing as a blank sheet of typing paper were uncharacteristic of a younger Jane McBride.

She thought about asking Benoit about the Native corporations and then decided against initiating another conversation. She had three more days on the ferry and had come to relish an anonymity no longer possible in Boston.

Being alone was not a habit. She was thirty-four, and all the tidy sections of her life had been experienced with other people, never alone. Someone had always been around to reinforce the pleasant memories and obscure the uncomfortable ones. Now she deliberately stepped alone into the next phase of her life. She hoped she could control the future by manipulating the past, choosing which memories to dwell on and which to forget.

She had control, as long as she did not make the mistake of discussing her past.

Staying out on deck helped keep other people away. When the gray sky stopped dumping rain, only six or so passengers walked the decks—from all appearances, strictly for exercise. Jane found herself wishing she could add a beard to her face during her excursions on deck. Somehow a lamb's-wool scarf did not do the job. The moist air penetrated to her neck through her warmest coat, and she could not stay outside for more than an hour.

Inside, strangers did not hesitate to pull chairs up to tables in either the overlit cafeteria or the underlit bar. From a few of the men who traveled alone, she got long looks and resigned smiles, but none suggested a visit to her room. She was not mistaken for a woman who tolerated one night stands.

In Boston Jane had learned to avoid asking personal questions. She'd pointedly demonstrated that she didn't care about other people's lives away from work, and they'd returned the favor, either in retaliation or out of courtesy. She'd come to prefer strangers and three-minute conversations.

The unwritten rules of etiquette on the ferry were nothing like the rules from Boston, though. Fellow passengers wasted no time asking outright intimate questions, while making it clear they knew the answers were none of their business.

After a day Jane ruefully came to learn that a subway train in Boston or New York offered more privacy than the Alaska ferry in the dead of winter.

"Why does the ferry operate during the winter?" she questioned the purser the next day.

"Only three of Southeast Alaska's towns have roads that connect to other cities, so this highway can't stop for holidays," explained Tony, the charming purser, who was quick, short, and in his early fifties. "All of next week's groceries, toys, and liquor for that part of Alaska are on board right now."

"What are the ferries like in the summer?"

Tony rolled his eyes. "Crawling with people oohing and aahing, gawking at every mountain and every damn seagull. Trust me, you picked the right time of year to travel. All Alaskans, no tourists. The only problem with the Alaskans is that they like to pretend they're jaded by the scenery."

"They might be jaded by the scenery, but a lot of them still want to talk about it," she said. "Every conversation turns into a lecture."

He laughed. "Then there's the quiet ones. They're hoping tourists don't notice much more than the rain and the potential for loneliness. They don't want any more people up here trying to dissect the little mystique left in the North."

"I'm not a tourist," Jane said.

"No," he said. "But they envy you because it's new, still a frontier for you."

"You could work for a cruise ship," Jane commented.

He shrugged. "I used to. There's more money to be made on the highway, and people on the ferry expect a lot less. But it's not just that. Me, I love winters in Southeast Alaska, not the Caribbean."

THREE

JANE MADE a point of studying how Alaskans dressed. Once in Sitka she wanted to blend in with the crowd.

If ferry passengers were an indication, she should stop carrying a purse or briefcase and buy oversize rubber boots and lots of jeans. In fact, she'd have to ditch most of the clothes she'd brought along.

"Do people dress differently in town than they do on the ferry?" she asked a young woman sitting alone with a binder full of squiggly-lined charts labeled "Water Depths." The woman's hair was long and blond; her creamy skin looked as if she had never tried to get a tan. Wearing loose jeans, a saggy blue sweatshirt, and serious wire-rimmed glasses, she looked smart and local.

The woman thought a minute. "Depends on the town. Juneau, the capital, is yuppie. The other towns are a different story. Where you headed?"

"Sitka," Jane said, appreciating the direct answer.

"Sitka," repeated the woman, with a coo that could have only been cultivated in Arkansas. "My favorite! The men look just like they do on the ferry, cuddly bears one and all. The women, a tad better—unless they're just coming off one of the fishing boats. That's the streets I'm talking about. For restaurants, going out places, parties, a lot of women dress up. They don't have to, but they like it. Go to the Channel Club in Sitka on any Saturday night, and don't be surprised to see black sequins sitting across from a red-plaid flannel shirt."

The blonde concluded by cocking her head to the windows surrounding the cafeteria. "Rain gear is always appropriate."

Jane thanked her and mentally kissed good-bye to her suits, leather Joan and Davids, and cashmere sweaters. But not with a whole lot of disappointment. Though thirty-four, she was resigned to the fact that she looked more like twenty-five than most twenty-five-year-olds. She was consistently described as a woman who could be more than pretty. The "could" was always emphasized. She scorned makeup and covered her thin, short figure with oversize clothes. Her hair was the brilliant color of an autumn oak leaf in the rain, but she kept it straight and trimmed a no-nonsense length around her ears. Horn-rimmed glasses obscured her hazel eyes. Sure, she could look better, but Jane preferred comfort to beauty.

LATER THAT DAY Jane noticed a strained pitch from the *Matanuska*'s engine. She went out on deck and watched as the vessel neared Queen Charlotte Sound, the largest expanse of open water the ship must cross between Seattle and Southeast Alaska.

The waves no longer looked like petite peaks of frosting on a cake. Instead the boat paused, almost shuddered, before tackling what looked like swollen balloons filled with dirty water. The bow pointed directly for open sea, dead set away from shore. The wind picked up, but the sky showed no sign of storm. The dropping sun kept to one corner of the subarctic sky. No red or gold for this winter sunset, only the worst and best colors of an abalone shell.

She had to concentrate on every step to keep her balance and stay away from the rail. At the stern she almost fell into the arms of Michael Benoit.

"Why are we moving away from the shoreline?" she asked, determined to keep the topic neutral.

"Tacking. It's the fastest way across, and the smoothest, too," Michael yelled back, and used his arms to draw out an obtuse triangle. "The boat will follow a diagonal path to the center point of the sound and return on another diagonal path. That way, we tackle the swells head-on and from the stern rather than from the side. Moving closer to shore would only make it rougher and increase the chance of hitting a rock."

Jane lost her balance for a moment and noticed the second mate out on the bridge. He waved his arms wildly. The engines, wind, and water slapping the hull made his words skip away.

Another man brought out a bullhorn. "Off the deck," the voice roared. *"Now!"*

Michael pulled the door open as the *Matanuska* lurched. Jane stumbled inside. She tensed her feet and spread her legs.

"Congratulations, Jane McBride, you must not get seasick," he said as he guided her down the empty hallway.

"No, not sick," Jane admitted ruefully. "Sea fright—I guess that's what you could call it. I panic about going down. That's why I left Boston by train and why I'm not on a plane right now." She looked out the window. "Maybe that was a mistake."

"An Alaskan ferry has yet to go down." Michael laughed as they both lost their footing and slammed into a wall.

"This won't last two hours," he continued, taking her arm. "And you're with the right person. I'm a psychiatrist, and if it's all right with you, I suggest we head to the bar."

The bar had plenty of seats, unusual for late afternoon. A half dozen or so people clutched their glasses and bottles, even those who did not normally do so. The *Matanuska* rocked hard. Land was a faraway, soft, gray pillow to the right.

Suddenly the boat lurched, and everyone got quiet at the sound of a loud inhuman moan and crashing thud. The engine took on a whine, and the lights flickered.

"That noise—what was that?" Jane murmured as she put her hands to her ears.

"Water knocking against the hull," he said. "It won't last long. Something to drink?"

"Coffee—anything warm," she whispered as the hull groaned again.

Tables and chairs in the bar were not bolted to the floor, and when they started sliding back and forth across the room, most people scurried out. The scene would have been comic, except that Jane was no longer the only one not bothering to hide her terror. Hysterical crying drifted in from another part of the ship.

The bartender handed Michael a cup of coffee and a bottle of Amstel and then removed the cash register drawer. "Help yourselves," he announced, and pointed a friendly finger at the rattling bottles, each shelf secured by miniature fences.

Three people stayed in the bar—Jane, Michael, and a quiet old man whom Michael introduced as Sam Quinn. The three moved to a large booth to avoid getting struck by a table or chair.

The wailing subsided slowly. "Why are people scared?" Jane asked nervously. "Tony said the boat was full of Alaskans. Shouldn't we go where there are more people?"

Michael and Sam shook their heads.

"This is the place to be," Sam said. "Center of the boat is the most stable. The bar has few windows. Enough so we don't feel like we're in a tin can, but not as many as the observation lounge. That's where you can really see the action. People from Anchorage and Interior Alaska head for their rooms and freak out."

"How are you feeling?" Michael asked.

"Frightened and fascinated," she admitted.

"Keep talking," Michael said with a protective arm around her shoulder. "About anything. About the boat, the noise, yourself, or your job. Anything."

Jane could not help but keep an eye on the strip of windows lining the port side of the *Matanuska*'s bar. She was mesmerized by the boat's ability to stay afloat. One moment all she saw outside was sky, and the next, swirling water that looked like liquid iron. The conversation stopped every time the hull took a shuddering hit from a wave. Jane's shoulders tightened.

"Just water on the hull," Michael whispered again. He looked at the clock and went to the bar to collect two more beers. The bartender had drained the coffee.

Mike brought back a small package of oyster crackers. "Have a few—they might help your stomach," he said. "Dinner is going to be a while."

She ripped into the package and mechanically stuffed crisp crackers into her mouth. One slipped and took a tiny slice underneath her mouth. Jane frowned at the taste of blood.

"Damn," she said bitterly, tossing the package to the middle of the table.

Sam spoke as if he were telling a bedtime story. "Remember, fear grows beyond measure in a person long, long before a boat is ready to go under," he said, nonchalantly pouring the rest of his Rainier beer into a glass. The empty can rolled off the table and followed a haphazard path across the room. "Boats of all sizes cross this sound almost every day of the year."

Sam would never stand out in a crowd. Now Jane focused on this short heavy man in his fifties and clung to every word he said.

"This kind of blowup is not uncommon for winter in Southeast Alaska," he concluded.

"How do you know so much about boats?" Jane asked.

"I've owned a few," he said, shrugging. "In Sitka, there's not many people who don't have a boat."

The two men started talking about *Cat Dance,* the newest fishing vessel in Sitka. Conversation, regardless of the topic, soothed Jane, though she would stop listening to glance out the window and catch her breath whenever the water lashed at the hull. Outside, the twilight welded the sky and sea to one color. Water trickled down the windows—not rain, but leftover spray. The ferry had turned and aimed for shore. An emerald green buoy, barely visible in the swells, signaled a channel entrance and the end of Queen Charlotte Sound.

Jane realized she had not heard the dreadful noise for what had to be fifteen minutes. The ferry had found a rhythm with the waves and then resumed a lullaby rock. Michael sensed her sigh of relief.

"You did great," he said with a tone of pride that he must reserve for favorite patients.

Jane scowled at the idea of lying on his couch. His unwavering green eyes made her look away, made her feel dishonest about herself. He thought her tension would fade when the ferry completed crossing the sound. Hah! she thought.

"I need to stretch," she said, excusing herself and going over to the window. She rubbed the ache in her neck and dropped her head. Who was she to judge his ability? She had never been in therapy, and she had been hostile to any suggestions during the past year that she try a psychiatrist.

"Some problems cannot be fixed," she had shot back to friends in Boston. "I want to feel this pain. It would be wrong to make this kind of pain go away." She declined invitations and maintained a cold silence. Her friends gradually stopped talking about what she should do and eventually stopped calling. Friendship between women with children and women without is the friendship of misfits— uncomfortable and incomplete.

She shook her head hard, concentrating on the scene outside the window and the final moments of twilight. A small white fishing boat emerged from the channel and pointed for the center of the sound. Waves washed the deck, but the fisherman didn't turn around.

"Look," she called over to Sam and Michael, pointing to the boat. "Is that guy crazy?"

Sam took the last swallow of his beer and looked at her. "Fishermen cross Queen Charlotte all the time."

"Will they be all right?" she asked Sam, almost in a whisper.

"Queen Charlotte is a high-traffic area," he said. "And this won't be the worst water you'll see. Not if you stay awhile."

The conversation ended when the bartender and passengers returned. The bartender poured fast to keep up with the drinkers, who were laughing but impatient that happy hour had been delayed by two hours.

Sam excused himself, and Michael joined Jane at the window.

"Come outside with me?" she asked.

"Haven't you had enough?" he said with a soft laugh. "Save the deck for tomorrow. How about dinner tonight?"

"Sure," she said, hesitating only slightly. She wanted to prove she could withstand the prying questions about her life from a stranger. If she couldn't handle Michael's questions, she'd resume encounters that lasted no more than five minutes.

"Good," he said. "Right now, I have to check the damage in my room. See you later...."

She pressed her face against the window. Through the streaks of dried salt, she located the lights of the fishing boat, tossed by the surge as if it were a toy—but only for a moment. She waited for the fishing captain to change his mind and turn back and take refuge in the channel. But no. In seconds the *Matanuska* turned in to the dark stillness of the channel. All she saw in the window was her own reflection.

OTHER THAN dinner being delayed by three hours, no one would have realized that anything unusual had happened that day. Conversations were louder, the laughing and gestures of hungry diners more vigorous. But that could have been because of Christmas, too.

Christmas. If someone had told her a week ago that she could forget about Christmas for two hours, she wouldn't have believed it. She did not mention this to Michael.

"You were right," she said over pumpkin pie. "Staying out had to be better than sitting alone in my room."

"You would have felt like someone had stuffed you in a can and given you a good shake," he said.

"The last thing I need," she said, looking down at the pie. "And Sam, what a fabulous man—he knew so much about boats. Too bad he slipped away. I wanted to thank him."

"Sam's another Sitka character." Michael chuckled. "Sad guy. Smart as hell, but depressed. He never forgave himself for getting a girl pregnant in high school. She put the kid up for adoption. It's almost a town legend—when will Sam's son return home? He talks about it more instead of less, the older he gets."

"That's not understandable?" Jane asked, cringing.

"Not really," Michael said somberly. "He has a life, a wife, and two kids. He's hurting people other than himself."

"You never had children," she said, annoyed. She regretted the comment immediately.

He paused and put down his fork as he studied her face. "No," he said gently. "But I was a child, and I know what children go through when they watch their parents suffer and never heal."

He knew. He guessed, and Jane hoped the panic she felt did not show on her face.

"Anyhow, he's different." She changed the subject. "A real Alaskan."

"He's about as real an Alaskan as you get," said Michael with a dry laugh. "Born here—he's Indian, an Alaskan Native, you know."

"That's not what I meant," she said, embarrassed. But she realized as she spoke that Sam was the only Native person she had spoken with on the entire trip. Other Native people were on board, but she never saw much of them.

"So, Natives and non-Natives don't do much together?" she asked.

"I spend a lot of time with them," he said. "But that's because I'm a psychiatrist for the Indian Health Service. But, you're right. For people our age, socialization is infrequent."

"Why is that?" she murmured.

"Only about twenty percent of Sitka's population is Native. This is Alaska, as far west as you can get, and there's still a lot of prejudice." Michael shrugged. "A lot of bitterness. Bitterness comes easy when there's still plenty of people around to remember that the Tlingit only got the right to vote in 1921. That's a couple of years before the rest of the Indians, by the way. The ban on selling liquor to Natives was lifted in 1953. As late as the early 1960s, the Natives still had their own section in the theater, and they weren't allowed in any of the clubs or restaurants, except the American Legion, and that only because most of the men fought in World War Two. There's a lot of old-timers and not-so-old-timers around here who remember that, and a hell of a lot more."

"There can't be a solid line down through the middle of town!" Jane exclaimed. Or the corporation would not have hired her, she thought to herself.

"Of course not. Sure, Natives marry non-Natives—but those couples almost always include one person new to town. And sure, you see little kids playing with each other. Adults work side by side at the pulp mill, the seafood plants, and the hospital. But from what my clients tell me, among the people who grow up here something happens in junior high. Kids who grew up next door and played together since they were babies, all of a sudden look at one another and see something different. Kids start listening to and partially understanding their parents' resentment. I'm talking about both sides.

"So," he concluded, "if you're counting on learning something about Native culture, I suggest you take a course at the college, and not count on learning it at your kitchen table with your neighbors.''

Jane bristled. ''Is that your source of knowledge about Natives, a course at the college?'' she asked coolly.

He grimaced. ''Worse than that. During the first six months of my job I was paraded past every so-called Native leader in Southeast Alaska. Leaders created by white people. I'm the first to agree that some cultural awareness goes a long way for any job, but I also know it takes more than...words. Blind faith that any Native can handle Native affairs better than any non-Native man or woman is not only wrong, it's cruel. It can hurt the Native businessman who's pressured to invest hard-earned profits in local projects rather than safe investments. It hurts the three-year-old foster kid who goes to the most dysfunctional Native family in town before being sent to any non-Native family.''

''You exaggerate,'' Jane said, wanting to blurt out that she had been hired by Natives.

''I wish I did,'' he said intently. ''I desperately needed this vacation after a self-centered clique wrested a happy eighteen-month-old baby away from one white family. The mother of the child had gone to a teacher at school and arranged a private adoption. The teenager fell in love with the way she thought a family should look—the way the teacher and his wife and three kids looked when they shopped in the grocery store or played in the park. Hell, sometimes she'd walk by that teacher's cottage at night and linger. Linda was pregnant, alone, and fourteen, but she knew what was best for her son. She didn't want him growing up the way she had—raped before she was ten by a cousin and a brother. She thought her son was safe, she went back to high school, but a few powerful people viewed the arrangement as an insult. The teacher lost his job, and that little boy is in the home where his mother grew up.''

''She's older—surely Linda has more control now,'' Jane reasoned. ''It won't be long before she can raise him on her own.''

"No. Linda's dead. Suicide."

Jane's breath came out with a ragged cry.

"Jane, I'm sorry," he said. "I'm not trying to hurt you. But I was the one who had talked Linda out of running away to Seattle, and I'm bitter. You can't imagine the pain I see and hear about every damn day on my job. I used to think that I was part of the solution—but there's nothing I can do about it. Most of what I say and do just hurts—when I tell the truth and refuse to make up fairy tales or excuses. And now I wonder whether Natives and non-Natives should try to work out these problems together."

"That's ridiculous," Jane snapped. "Of course you feel terrible about Linda. But you can't give up."

"I boarded a ferry heading north, didn't I?" he said. "I walked away for four weeks, and I'm going back. Oh, I should shut up while I'm ahead, but two beers are more than my limit, and you look like the kind, dedicated sort rather than the carpetbagger. So I'll give you one more piece of wisdom—if you're a teacher, a nurse, or journalist out to do good deeds for the Natives, save yourself a lot of misery. Go home."

"You've given up!" Jane said. "At least I'm willing to try. But it's good to know what people like you are thinking. Because I'll not only be working with the Natives, but for them, too."

"Katmai?" he asked.

"Yes, Katmai Shee Inc.," she said smugly. "Finance director."

He raised his eyebrows and blew a long, soft whistle. "Good luck—you're going to need it."

"Yes, I know that," she said with a determined smile. "The board of directors wants me to turn the place upside down—and I don't think they're so stupid to think they found an Alaska Native in Boston."

"Who the hell hired you?" he asked. "That board won't let you toss the lettuce at the Katmai Hotel salad bar!"

Jane felt something wrench inside her. "Really?" she said, shaking as she stacked her plates on the tray. "I think

I'll be tossing something greener than lettuce, Dr. Benoit. From my conversations with Katmai executives, all they care about is state-of-the-art financial skills. What *I* don't need are bad vibes about the people I'm going to be working for. Do you understand me? I need this job, and it's going to work."

"Jane, someone hired you as decoration, and you better find out why."

She didn't answer. People at the next table were openly watching them. "Good night, Michael," she said, smiling distantly as she picked up her tray and walked away. She almost never left a cup of coffee undrained. But she knew of no other way to end the conversation.

In her stateroom, she threw on her plaid flannel nightgown, turned out the lights, and crawled into the top bunk so that she could stare out the window at the dark pincushion islands and mountains—silhouettes outlined with mist turned silver by the moon. The *Matanuska* would cross Dixon Entrance into Alaskan waters during the middle of the night, without ceremony.

She pulled the heavy regulation navy wool blanket around her with a sigh. Trying to sleep in recent months had been hard enough, alone with the cold touch of her past. She had not expected to feel so edgy about her future.

FOUR

NOT EVEN five o'clock in the afternoon, and the sky was as black as midnight. Jane tapped her fingers on the rail as the ferry eased near the dock. She came out on deck, eager for her first glimpse of Sitka. She stretched to look in both directions for lights of town. All she saw was a trail of headlights surrounding a small wood-frame building.

She tapped her fingers faster.

"That's the ferry terminal," Michael Benoit said softly from behind. He caught her by surprise again. "You can't see town from here. And you won't see all your mountains for skiing until morning."

"What makes you think I like skiing?" Jane said with a scowl, wondering how he'd developed his bizarre theories about her. "I don't ski." He looked surprised, but she didn't want to talk anymore. She turned away. "Time for me to head down."

"I wouldn't hurry," he said, putting his hand on her shoulder. "We're another ten minutes from tying up, and right now there's at least a dozen impatient drivers down there starting cars and trucks. If you go down now, you'll eat a lot of exhaust."

Jane paused. "Oh, I didn't know," she said sheepishly.

"I learned the hard way," he said with a laugh. "Which hotel you headed for? I'll give you a lift."

"No, I don't need one, thank you," she said with a friendly smile. She wanted to avoid explaining to Michael why she knew the street address where she'd be staying but not the woman's name. The woman was connected with Katmai Shee, she knew. During a telephone conversation two months ago, the woman had spoken quickly and softly, in staccato sentences that were obliterated by the static and echoes typical of all Jane's calls to Alaska. When she'd asked the woman to repeat her name, all that had come through was the word *question*.

Jane sighed and resolved to slip away from Michael after the ferry docked. She wanted to complete her journey into Sitka alone, and she was not about to attempt articulating her reactions to a psychiatrist.

Michael continued his offer: "All three hotels are in the center of town. It's on my way."

"I'm not staying at a hotel."

"It can't be far—not in a town with seventeen miles of road. At the same time you get a guided tour of hangouts for Sitka's sociopaths and borderlines—all the places to avoid."

"Michael!" she chided him. "You can forget about me ever confiding in you."

"Not too many secrets in a town this size," he said casually.

"I appreciate the offer. But I have some stops I need to make...." She let the explanation drift. Truth was, she did not have a ride.

"Jane, about the other night, I'm sorry," Michael said. "Don't say no because of that. Seriously, I got cocky. What can I say except that I'm a nice guy with a big mouth." He kept his tone light, but his dark forest-green eyes pleaded with her to understand something more than the words. "We could..."

Jane looked away and held up her hand to stop him. It was an imperial gesture that she had seen used back in Boston. She hated it but knew it got results, stopping the conversation and giving her time to think.

She took a deep breath. "I know you're a nice guy. For now, I just want to go off on my own and form my own judgments. That's all."

She turned, and his eyes locked on to hers. How did he maintain that intensity? she wondered. She felt guilty for looking away, but she had to do it now and then to keep track of what she was saying. Watching him now, seeing him give her a sad smile, she wondered if he realized that he was not trying to figure her out, understand her feelings, so much as wanting to know more about himself.

"I think you understand," she said softly.

They left it at that—with too much said by one party and not enough said by the other. Jane had never lived on an island before and wondered how often she might encounter Michael.

The boat touched the dock. The lines were rapidly tied. Michael continued to stare at her intently, as if he were trying to read her mind. This time she did not avoid his gaze.

"I'll see you around," he said. "Good luck with the job."

Metal slammed against concrete as the crew opened the lower deck. Passengers rushed for the ramp, looking as if they had been released from a cage. Northbound Sitka passengers had the longest ride. Jane walked fast so her legs felt less wobbly, less out of control.

The driver of a turquoise-and-red Totem Cab leaned against his open door. Jane was thrilled to nab the only cab in sight. She hefted her bags into the open trunk and hoped Michael didn't notice in the confusion.

The cabdriver did not move except to light a cigarette drooping from his mouth.

"Eighteen twenty-four Sawmill Creek Road," she said cheerfully.

The cabdriver tilted his head back and looked into the sky before blowing a mouthful of smoke. "We'll wait for more people," he said flatly. His hair was long, black, and greasy, and he was in his late teens. He was too young to inhale so deeply or speak so tonelessly.

Jane glanced at the dusty dashboard. Empty crinkled cigarette packages surrounded a naked doll as fat and tall as a thumb. No ID, no cab company telephone number, no hot line for complaints, no meter for measuring out the fare. She could be in the hands of a deranged rapist.

She almost laughed out loud. She was thousands of miles from Boston, where meeting violent types could be as routine as brushing one's teeth. How many Totem Cabs could there be in a town with a total of seventeen miles of road? She leaned back and shut her eyes.

In minutes the crowd thinned.

"I'm out of here," the young driver muttered as he snapped his cigarette to the ground. He floored the accelerator and turned onto two-lane Halibut Point Road with a squeal. Jane sat up and pressed her hands against the front seat. Instead of looking for houses, totem poles, or Sitka Sound, she stared at the speedometer and then at the steering wheel. The cabdriver held on with only one hand, and that was missing two fingers.

They drove about half a mile in silence.

"Do we drive through downtown?" Jane asked.

The cabdriver shrugged.

"How much extra would it cost to drive through town?" she persisted, annoyed her voice took on a pleading tone.

Jane watched his face as he studied her in the rearview mirror. He was making a decision about her, and his eyes were off the road long enough to read the headlines on the front page of a newspaper.

"You a tourist?" he asked.

She shook her head.

"Twelve dollars to go out to Sawmill Creek. Nothing extra for the drive through town."

"Thank you," she said. The speed dropped from sixty to forty miles an hour, only five miles over the speed limit. Jane turned to her window.

She tried to get a sense of the passing dark shapes, but the driver had started the dilapidated Buick without waiting for the windows to defrost. Jane used her finger to outline a clear miniature square in the steamy window. It was something she hadn't done in a car since she was a little girl.

The cabdriver must have noticed. He flipped a switch, and the defroster came on with a blast of cold air.

Halibut Point Road had no traffic lights, and it was only when the cab snaked a fast right that she saw a cluster of light that had to be downtown. Any anticipation she had of country charm and solitude faded like the frost on the windshield. From first glance, Sitka, the former capital of Russian America, was now nothing more than an ugly huddle of weathered two-and-three-story buildings.

Too many of the downtown buildings were concrete block, with poorly shingled or painted facades. Too many had flat roofs. A lot of the store displays—large crayon-like Christmas scenes sketched directly on the windows—seemed to be done by one person. The mannequins in the windows appeared to be leftovers from the 1950s.

Any spirit of Christmas had come and gone. Only dreary remnants of tinsel and plastic dangled from street lamps. The drizzle was like a heavy blanket, and the sidewalks were empty.

The driver glided the cab smoothly through the commercial district without comment, slowing as they approached the gray-and-white wood-frame church. The church should have seemed small and simple by Boston standards. But the structure had a bell tower and spires five stories high. St. Michael's Cathedral stood solidly in the middle of the main street and was the tallest building in town. Even in the rain and mist, gold Russian Orthodox crosses shone with holiness against the black sky.

The driver twisted the wheel and hit the horn. "Damn," he swore under his breath.

A young woman was stretched out on the street—laughing or crying hysterically. A young man clutched her wrists and feebly tried to yank her to the curb. The drunk woman's hair was half-straight and half-frizzed curls from a cheap perm that was more than a few months old. She wore a limp windbreaker that proclaimed in big letters, white on green, HOLMES BARRETT COLLEGE.

The cabdriver studied Jane through the rearview mirror again.

"Great advertisement for Holmes Barrett College," Jane said. "Should we stop and call for help? I don't mind."

He grunted and pushed his foot on the accelerator. "College kids." He spat the words out in contempt.

Jane swore softly to herself for coming to Alaska without ever seeing the place. Her life was out of control, no less than the life of the woman sprawled in the street. In Boston she had convinced herself that Sitka was as different from the East Coast as one could get. The fledgling corporation was in a state rich with natural resources, but Third World–like in its capability to produce and market its treasures. The shares of stock—which by federal law could not be sold or traded—were poor in value, but rich in culture, land, and politics.

She shuddered at her self-imposed confinement. Sitka might be Alaska's sixth largest city, but like most towns in Southeast Alaska, it was accessible only by air or water transportation. All the city's roads stopped abruptly at water, forest, or mountains. And the rain, she reminded herself. Sitka got one hundred inches each year.

She sighed. Katmai Shee was Sitka's second largest business. Turning a corporation around could boost an entire community and maybe even her own spirits.

Ten minutes later the cab slowed and braked at the bottom of a steep, rutted driveway. A cockeyed sign—1824 Sawmill Creek Road—was hammered to a tree. The driver let the engine mutter while he pulled her luggage from the trunk and dropped it on the gravel. She handed over fourteen dollars, and he hopped briskly back into the cab.

The cab's headlights illuminated Jane and the cottage as he backed out of the driveway. The driver picked up his receiver to radio the dispatcher.

"You can call him now. She's here."

FIVE

THE RED COTTAGE was nestled underneath towering hemlocks at the base of Mt. Verstovia. It had one door and two windows with blue shutters in the front. Soft light glowed through thin curtains. It was simple, like a dream house nestled with a train set under a Christmas tree.

A mountain stream gurgled furiously next to the driveway. Rain pattered in the trees arching overhead. Because of the shimmering fog coming in from the bay, Jane could not see anything beyond thirty feet. That didn't matter. She felt she had found the most comfortable place in the world for being alone.

She knocked on the front door. No answer. She knocked again. There was no car in the driveway, and because she had no key, she gave the doorknob a twist. The door opened directly into a small, warm living room.

Jane shut the door and called out. A pearl-green antique lamp had been left on. The living room was no bigger than twelve by fifteen feet, and Jane immediately discovered the note left on a counter that separated the main room from the one-cook kitchen.

The note was no less cryptic than the narrow slips found inside fortune cookies: ''Make yourself at home. Directions for heat on wall. Blankets on bed. You will need your sleep for tomorrow. Francesca LaQuestion.''

A name! Jane smiled. She looked around at the sparse furnishings. Francesca had to be a young woman, without time to fill a home. Maybe a workaholic. No time for men. No children.

Jane shook her head—she had been around Michael Benoit too long. She didn't want to form an opinion about

Francesca. The home's furnishings gave her absolutely no clue as to what position the woman held with the corporation. She could be anything from a secretary to a manager, but more likely the former, considering the small size of the house.

Why aren't I staying in the hotel? Jane pondered for the hundredth time since she had left Boston. One of the corporation's major working assets was a forty-room hotel in downtown Sitka, which should have been the obvious place for her to stay. Jane yawned and noticed that a used scrap of typing paper was taped to a closed door across the room, with the heavy scrawl "Your room!"

She opened the door and was startled by a blast of cold air. Across the dark room, another door to the outside was wide open. She hurried over and paused to study the property behind the house. The forest literally started at the doorstep, and she could hear the long branches of the trees mutter in complaint against the wind.

Jane slammed the door and bolted it. Then she found the light switch. The room was clean, the bed was turned back. She decided to let her curiosity rest until the morning. Her legs and her head felt like thick jelly after four days on the boat.

The phone rang. Jane dropped her suitcase on the floor and waited for the fourth ring, hoping an answering machine would pick up. The call would not be for her, anyway. By the sixth ring she went back into the living room and stared at the phone. Eight rings. The ringing wasn't going to stop.

"All right," she murmured, hoping the caller was not Francesca or anyone else who wanted to talk for any length of time. All she wanted to do was drop into bed.

"Hello," Jane answered crisply. She heard a noise that was not a voice. "Hello? Anyone there?"

She was about to hang up when she heard a click, and a mechanical voice began: "Jane McBride, by now you must realize it was a mistake to come to Sitka. You must leave at once. Leave Sitka before it is too late...."

Jane slammed the phone down. Some adolescent prank, she decided. Anonymous threats were rarely dangerous. Except the telephone call had not been totally anonymous—she had been addressed by name. She shook her head and succumbed to a wave of fatigue. She would walk into the Katmai offices and start getting her answers tomorrow.

SIX

JANE WOKE with a start from a dreamless sleep, in a space as cold and dark as a refrigerator. Remembering where she was, she pulled the four blankets over her head to warm her nose and cheeks, procrastinating about getting out of bed. She was not prepared for this kind of damp chill. She remembered the blithe comment from a travel guide:

"Coastal temperatures are mild, ranging from forties to sixties in summer and from the twenties to forties in winter." Though ninety-five percent of the people living in the United States would have guessed wrong, Sitka was more like Seattle with puddles and clouds than Fairbanks with snowpiles and icy wind.

Jane waited. She thought she heard a noise. She shut her eyes and listened. A car engine started outside, but inside, the house was silent, except for the insistent pendulum of a clock. The car must have been Francesca leaving for work. Jane crawled out of bed, still wearing the wrinkled clothes she had worn on the ferry, and groaned as her bare feet touched the cold linoleum. She tiptoed quickly into the living room. Just as cold, but she could smell coffee. Good coffee, she decided. The pot was full. It was tempting, but Jane figured she should get the heat going first. She admired the kitchen—neat and organized so early in the day. Even the coffee filter was already washed and in its place next to the coffeepot. She checked the time. Not so early at that, according to the old clock in the living room. Eight-fifteen. She checked her watch. The old clock was right, yet there was no hint of daylight.

Jane turned and saw the blood around the kitchen counter. A large flat white fish with a gash in its side was folded into the stainless-steel sink. The eyes were clear, and a hook protruded from its mouth. Jane willed herself not to gag.

"It's just a fish," she said out loud.

Propped underneath the window was a note: "Welcome. Hope you like the coffee as much as I do. If not, tea in the cupboard over the counter and juice in the refrigerator. F."

As she backed out of the kitchen, Jane remembered the telephone call warning her to leave town and wondered about Francesca. Was she a woman with a peculiar sense of humor?

She shook her head. The call was a prank, and the fish was an oversight. They had nothing to do with each other. Still, it nagged at her that the anonymous caller knew her name. She would come right out and ask Francesca about the call.

Jane decided to begin all the necessary chores of establishing herself in Sitka. Before she could accomplish anything, she had to warm her hands. She kept her fingers crossed that the heater would not be fickle.

"Directions for heat on wall," Francesca had written. Jane found the scrap from a legal pad tucked to the cedar-plank wall. She knelt beside the metal contraption.

"Lighting the oil-pot stove," read the first line. The page was covered in small, careful handwriting, and a pack of matches was taped to the margin.

"Oil pot," Jane growled. "Looks like an old empty can." Worse, the primitive heating system had more directions than a modern appliance. Jane read on.

"Open front panel. Flip switch on side to open vent. Turn knob no higher than two notches. This allows oil to drip into bottom of pot. Light a match and toss it into the puddle of oil quickly. LIGHT OIL BEFORE PUDDLE GETS TOO BIG. MAKE SURE OIL IS LIT."

The last two sentences were underlined with hard strokes, twice. What happened if the puddle got too big? She would have to remember to ask Francesca.

The instructions continued: "You can control how much oil drips inside the stove, but there is no thermostat—it's either on or off. DON'T ATTEMPT TO RELIGHT A HOT STOVE. ALLOW TO COOL BEFORE RELIGHTING."

More fierce underlining.

"Turn knob and switch to off if flame goes out." And finally, "Don't leave heat on when leaving house or sleeping."

"I don't believe this," muttered Jane, who preferred any software program in the world to tinkering around with matches. She returned to her room and clawed through her suitcase for her warmest ragg-wool sweater. She reached for her coat, too. She wanted to be dressed for outdoors in case the damn thing exploded.

Jane lit the match, flipped the switch and the knob. She propped open the large door and tossed the match inside directly over the puddle of oil at the bottom of the can, withdrawing her hand fast as the flame did a seductive blue dance over the oil's surface. She slammed the door to the stove and then stood by the front door to wait for something to go wrong.

Nothing happened, except that the stove's putter reached a gentle rhythm. Moments later invisible fingers of heat reached out into the tiny living room.

Jane looked around slowly, giving the stove only an occasional glance. The rug was thick and dark green. All the walls were cedar, and unbleached muslin curtains were drawn across the windows. The sofa was covered in a dark-green-and-white quilted material and flanked by end tables that were piled with magazines. She wondered if she would ever feel comfortable enough to curl up on the sofa and read a book. She took off her coat and put it on the chair closest to the front door.

Jane paused at the kitchen. The fish was starting to smell. She turned the faucet on—hard and cold. The water washed the blood down the drain. That helped. She opened the refrigerator with trepidation, but it was clean, if overstocked for one person, especially a woman. Jane found half-and-half. She thought about placing the fish inside the refrigerator, but there was no room. She pulled ice from the freezer and emptied the trays on top of it. Once the staring eye was out of sight, the fish seemed much less ominous.

On top of the refrigerator was a white bakery box, with "Help yourself" scrawled across the side. Jane reached inside and pulled out a pecan roll. Ummm, sticky sweet, brown, and delicious.

She returned to her room. Dark brown paneling and too much furniture made the space look smaller than it really was, she decided. The twin bed with an embroidered quilt was pushed into one corner. The room lacked a closet, but there was a rack with enough space for hanging everything she'd brought. A small desk had enough room for the computer she had had shipped here earlier. Because of the sloping ceilings in this room and the living room, Jane knew the upstairs had no more than one bedroom.

The house was one-quarter the size of the home Jane had left in Boston.

"Perfect for your first few weeks," the vice president had assured her over the telephone. Finding an apartment would be no problem during the winter, he'd added, pointing out that she would have plenty to choose from before the fishing and processing crews arrived in town in April.

Jane mulled it over. She'd never opened her home to a stranger before. Had the woman been forced into this? Was Francesca avoiding her? She made a mental note to assure the woman immediately that she planned to start searching for an apartment that day, that she would not even plan on unpacking her suitcase, and with any luck she'd be out in a week. She sighed, though. She would miss the cottage.

Jane sipped the coffee, checked the clock in the living room, and saw it was after nine. She located the telephone. The half-inch-thick book was for all of Southeast Alaska—and more than half the pages were devoted to zip codes, area codes, how to write letters to politicians, and laundry and stain-removal tips. Telephone numbers for Sitka took up twelve thin pages.

As she dialed the Katmai number she fretted that she would seem anxious rather than diligent. She kept on dialing. The first week at any job was hell; anything could be misconstrued by curious co-workers. Jane planned to leave a simple message for the vice president, Cameron Reynold—that she was in town and would stop by that afternoon to introduce herself and collect corporation documents to read in preparation for the job.

But the receptionist took her name and said Mr. Reynold was in. He got to the phone fast. Jane relaxed and leaned back against the soft sofa cushions.

"Yes, Jane, you mean to say you're in Sitka now?"

"Yes, I am, Cameron. I wanted to meet everyone and get to know the town." She bit her tongue. No stupid remarks about how it sure wouldn't take much time to get to know a town the size of Sitka.

"Well..." He paused. The line had static, and the vice president did not sound any closer than when she had called from more than three thousand miles away.

"Good for you, Jane. I have to talk to you. This would better be handled in person, but I don't want to mislead you any more than necessary."

Despite the static, she could hear hesitation. He went on, "I tried to telephone you last week. The job...well, there isn't a job anymore. The corporation is in a difficult period. You know that. Timber prices are plummeting. Overnight tourism is shot. Some nasty murmurs are coming from D.C. about tax write-offs. Some jobs had to be eliminated."

"As I said during our interview, it sounds like the perfect time for hiring a finance director with my experience," Jane retorted quickly. But her stomach turned. She slouched, closed her eyes, and managed to keep the edge down in her voice. "Someone who can analyze the assets, target some for sale and others for special attention."

"I couldn't agree more, Jane. But we have elections for the board of directors in five months. Could mean a huge shake-up in the corporation. Reelection of the incumbents who wanted to hire you is less likely every day. Layoffs don't help. All the pink slips were sent to Natives. Shareholders. To be honest with you, politically we simply cannot hire new personnel at this point, especially a woman who has never set foot in town before."

He paused. Jane waited. She wasn't going to make his dirty little chore for the morning any easier.

"I'm so sorry." His voice sounded sincere. "I would like to say maybe in May, but that would be too much to ask of a person with your qualifications. I tried to telephone, to catch you...."

He rushed through the rest of the conversation about wanting to meet her, about providing severance pay and fare to Boston. Jane didn't argue. She agreed to an appointment later that morning and softly returned the telephone receiver to its cradle.

"Damn," she whispered. She grabbed a quilted pillow and pounded it with her fist. She was not so angry about the job as she was at the idea of returning to Boston; how anyone who knew what she was running away from would pity her. "What a little fool I am," she said, shutting her eyes.

What would she do? she asked herself fretfully. Maybe she could catch a ferry out of town later today and not even say good-bye. The corporation could mail its check. She thought about Michael and Francesca, how quickly she would become an insignificant part of their past, just another newcomer who couldn't hack it and had turned around and fled on the next ferry. Who cared? She sighed.

Deciding to take a walk, she grabbed her coat and angrily pulled her wool hat over her ears and eyebrows. Then she flung open the front door, ready to give it a good slam before jamming her hands in her pockets and taking off.

Jane caught her breath as she stood in the doorway. After lighting the stove, drinking coffee, and calling Katmai, she'd never thought to open the curtains and take a look outside. She had not seen much during her rainy drive the night before, and she had taken for granted that Sitka would be as dreary as Ketchikan, Petersburg, Wrangell, and the other stops—necessary but ugly interruptions along a stunning coastline.

But Sitka was on the sea. The beach on the other side of the road was rocky and wild. The water of the bay flashed teal blue and silver. Perfect puffy clouds filtered deep gold rays of early sunlight down through the big sky. To the left, one end of the bay was lined with a row of mountains, the steep slopes covered in capes of unblemished snow. The sun made a sparkling path in the water, leading directly to Mt. Edgecumbe, an extinct volcano of perfect shape crowned by clouds of silver and gold in the just rising sun.

Jane fell in love with the idea that she was part of Sitka's landscape. She clung to the rail and stretched the way she had done on the deck of the ferry. Her smile was determined.

"This is it—home," she vowed.

SEVEN

FORGET WALKING off steam, Jane decided as she stepped back inside. She had to find a job. Any job. Staying in Sitka was not a ridiculous whim, despite the Katmai mess. She had no reason for moving on, and there was no way she'd head back to where she'd come from.

First, she showered and changed into a wool skirt, mauve cardigan sweater, matching wool stockings, and leather flats. She thought about putting on her expensive wool blazer, then reached for the thermal jacket. She didn't care what Cameron Reynold and the others at Katmai thought anymore.

Katmai Shee Inc. offices occupied the third and top floor of the Katmai Hotel. As she walked the hallway, Jane wondered which office was Francesca's and which would have been hers.

Cameron Reynold didn't make her wait thirty seconds. He shepherded her into his office, a pleasant room with an oak desk, leather chairs, and a view of downtown Sitka nestled against the mountains. Jane preferred the view from Francesca's home.

Cameron must have noticed how her eyes lingered on the view ''The future of Katmai Shee,'' he murmured.

Jane sat back, crossed her legs, and folded her hands together. She had no trouble keeping her smile wry. Though he was in his fifties and handsome, Reynold was sheepish and overly polite.

He immediately shoved a check across the desk. ''For travel expenses, and some extra, for all the trouble,'' he said, struggling.

"It better be good." Jane made a point of not leaning over and snatching the check right away. "I left a job with Peabody, Janus, and Grant in Boston, and I can't exactly waltz back. Do you change your mind about employees often?"

He laughed. "Turning new hires away? No. We have too much trouble getting them. Spending money frivolously? Every day."

She laughed, too. At least he was honest. She reached for the check, prepared to demand more. She looked down and hoped her expression did not change. Seventy-five thousand dollars. She would have been thrilled with one-tenth the amount. What kinds of expenses and trouble did he think she had? Any student in Budget 101, let alone a finance director, would have been horrified about a corporation throwing money after services no longer needed.

But it wasn't Jane's problem anymore, and showing gratitude would be ludicrous. Then she noticed the check wasn't signed. She raised her eyebrows.

"It's yours," he continued, "as soon as you sign this letter, giving your word you will not file any legal complaints. No other catch."

Jane read through the two paragraphs of the letter three times. The words were simple and forthright, but she had trouble seeing anything besides the figure $75,000. She thought about seeking an attorney to look it over, but people at this corporation changed their minds fast. Even if she did want to pursue a court case, all she could hope to win would be travel and expenses.

"I'll accept this," she told him, tapping the check against his desk. "But I want a letter detailing that the change in plans had absolutely nothing to do with my qualifications and credentials." From her experience with attorneys and personnel directors, Jane knew that the statement would be as good as saying the change of heart had nothing to do with the price of pie in Kansas. The bottom line was that they didn't want her, and she had demonstrated poor judgment in believing them enough to quit a good job and trek up to Alaska. With any luck she'd never need a letter—she'd be crazy ever to mention this debacle on a résumé or during a job interview. But any statement was better than nothing, she figured.

Cameron buzzed his secretary and quickly dictated a second letter over the telephone. The typewriter started the instant he hung up the telephone. The details were taken care of, and the silence was awkward.

"Cameron," she said bluntly. "Why the change of heart? What really happened?"

He took a deep breath and looked out the window. "You want to know what really happened.... I suppose that's the least you deserve. Everything I said on the telephone is true. The upcoming election for the board of directors has turned this place upside down. Two members of the board—a fringe minority would be putting it kindly—proposed that the corporation set out to establish a world-class ski resort. Three members are adamantly opposed. The remaining four members are undecided. At my suggestion, and I thought it was a worthy one, the director of the personnel committee searched for and hired a financial analyst, someone who could be neutral and quantitative about the whole damn affair. You. But the two board members who want the ski resort screamed foul and pulled out all the stops to rescind the decision. You're non-Native, you're young, from the East Coast, and your résumé neglected to mention skiing." He shrugged. "Those two board members created enough pressure to force off any hire until after the election. And then they want to hire a corporate director of tourism—specifically a skier."

"A skier!" Jane scoffed. "You know as well as I do that it's better to hire a manager than a doctor to run a hospital, and it's better to hire an economist or finance expert before choosing an investment, especially one as risky as a ski resort."

"You know that, and I know that," Cameron said with a wry smile, "but I serve at the whim of the board—and that's an understatement."

A knock at the door terminated the conversation. Cameron called in the secretary. She handed him the letter, and he signed and handed it to Jane without reading it, as if he were tired of the sorry affair. Jane watched him sign the check. The woman left and closed the door.

"Nobody ever mentioned skiing to me," Jane pressed. "What's the big secret?"

"The board wants to keep the plans quiet. The state is getting ready to put in bids for the Winter Olympics eight years from now. Different events would be held at different sites throughout Alaska. The resort proponents think Katmai would have the time and a head start on putting together a decent proposal for all the skiing events. They want to limit the competition. Officially there are no plans for a ski resort, only rumors. The discussion has been limited to closed executive sessions of the Katmai board."

Jane rolled her eyes and pocketed the check. "One other thing," she said as she stood. "Who knew that I was arriving on yesterday's ferry?"

"I didn't," he said. "Only Francesca, I believe. She's the director of the personnel committee and arranges such matters."

And Michael, Jane thought to herself. Why would either one make the threatening telephone call? Neither one had a good motive.

"Is Ms. LaQuestion in now?" Jane asked.

"No, she doesn't have an office here. None of the board members do."

Jane nodded. "I look forward to meeting her."

"Again, I regret the inconvenience," Cameron said, smoothly dismissing her. "I bid you farewell and the best of luck."

"But no." Jane cocked her head and gave her most sparkling smile "I plan to stay in town for a while. I don't know whether it's fortunate or unfortunate, but I got attached to the notion of living in Alaska. I'm not ready to pack up and leave.''

''I don't know what you'll find here,'' he said in a voice lacking enthusiasm, ''but I recommend our fine hotel.''

He pointed his finger, as if she would be staying in the next room. Was that a hint that Francesca wanted her out right away? Jane couldn't be sure. One could never trust company executives when it came to their opinions about individuals serving on the board of directors. With her, he talked and acted as if he sided with Francesca on the hiring decision, but he could easily shuffle the words around and make the ski-resort folks walk away happy. He probably didn't have a real opinion and merely wanted to maintain a truce.

Cameron escorted her down the hall past the receptionist's desk. The woman sneaked a peek at Jane's face—what did she expect to see, distress or joy? Jane deliberately remained expressionless.

''You'll be finding yourself desperate for something to do by the end of the week,'' he said with another laugh.

''I'm resourceful.'' Jane smiled mysteriously as she fingered the check stuffed inside her pocket. In more ways than one, she thought. He would not have confided in her if he had guessed she would do anything other than take the first plane out of town. Her candor and unthreatening stature, along with the ability to get people to talk—more so than her dexterity with numbers—was what made her a superb financial analyst. Analysts relied on information, and she could always ferret out a bit more than her competitors. Now that she was not working for Katmai, Cameron was part of the competition.

His wave was cheery and his face relieved as the elevator doors closed. Was he trying to drop a hint that she was an embarrassment? To herself or the corporation? Jane smiled serenely. She was determined to change her life. Sitka was the place to do it, and she could handle a little embarrassment.

She visited the town's four banks, compared rates, and had a short-term account set up within the hour. Then she celebrated over lunch—a cheeseburger and stale barbecue potato chips. She had to ask twice before the waitress brought her a glass of ice water with lemon. Jane toasted, discreetly lifting the glass toward the view of the bay.

EIGHT

THE NEWSPAPER OFFICE followed lunch on her mental list. The thought that she would need to search the classifieds in Alaska had never crossed her mind. The kind of job she was qualified for was never advertised in classified sections, even in big-city newspapers. At any rate, the newspaper still would be the best source of information about which businesses in town were up-and-coming.

Michael had talked about the newspaper during the ferry trip. It was rarely more than sixteen pages long, typically eight, and packed with local news. An article on new policies of the town dogcatcher would take precedence over an article outlining reasons for a presidential veto. The paper was family owned and run, from the father-publisher down to the daughter-papergirl.

The *Daily Record* had a small circulation but would have cleaned up in awards for sales or reading per capita, if such awards existed. Only a few households in Sitka refused to subscribe—families distraught because a son's arrest for drunken driving was duly noted or because the sports' editor neglected to mention a daughter's winning volleyball serve. Still, no Sitkan could stay angry long, because Lindsey, the wife of the editor, kept meticulous score on such matters and made a point of smoothing over relations a month or so later by assigning a feature on the son's business or strategically placing a photograph of the daughter at the prom. Temporary boycotters could not resist borrowing copies from neighbors or paging through issues at the library. The newspaper's indispensability was ensured by the fact that it was the only source for comprehensive television listings. And television was half addiction, half necessity for Alaskans during the dark, rainy winters.

"Yes, even you will succumb to television," Michael had promised solemnly.

She laughed as she remembered his voice—measured and low. Michael had been nervous, and comments about people, about herself, had come out of his mouth like pretzels tumbling from a bag into a bowl. Michael was the only person she had really talked to so far. And she knew he had to be popular and successful, largely because he thrived on gossip, another addictive pastime for a small town.

So far his descriptions of life in Sitka were accurate. He not only lived in the town, he made it a case study. And if his assessment of the newspaper was correct, she might eventually find a job. Vacant apartments, eligible men or women, impending bankruptcies, and upcoming contracts or jobs could be gleaned, he promised, if not from the classifieds or legal notices, then by reading between the lines of what might otherwise seem mundane but very thorough and very local features.

Jane walked into the hot, disheveled, and surprisingly modern lobby. About thirty feet behind the reception desk a printing press roared and spat out newspapers—skinny ones. About a dozen people laughed and talked, as if they were at a party, but their arms moved like those of robots. The receptionist looked up from her three stacks—newspapers, fat red fliers, and the newspapers stuffed with the fliers. She had been in the middle of counting a stack with inky-black fingertips and was miffed at the interruption.

"Red? Red!" From around the corner came a howl that could be heard over the bedlam of machinery and people. "It is the week after Christmas, and don't they realize that people are sick of red! What about brown? Or purple. Or gray! That's a color that would stand out this time of year."

The receptionist rolled her eyes and looked at Jane, as if asking her to step forward and express an appreciation for red. A woman with thick brown curls popped into view and then disappeared again. Jane heard a scolding whisper.

"Don't worry, Lindsey," the receptionist drawled. "She's not from Borden's. You're not, are you?'

Jane shook her head and looked at the desk. The flier was for Borden's Pharmacy.

"Cin-dee," the woman named Lindsey pleaded, and then flashed a big smile at Jane. She had to be in her forties, but she had the happy, bouncy stride of a teenager.

"Is today's paper ready yet?" Jane squeezed in her request quickly.

Another head popped out from around the corner. A man who could have been the grown-up version of Dennis the Menace. His hair looked like grass dried in the sun. Late twenties; not very tall, chalky skin, except for some freckles sprinkled on the nose; and small blue eyes framed with almost invisible blond lashes. Not good-looking by any stretch of the imagination. But if he knew that, he didn't let on.

He spun a newspaper down the counter, where it stopped directly in front of her. "Watch your hands—hot off the press." He relied on the minimum number of words and stressed every one. Jane wondered if he was consciously trying to imitate Clint Eastwood.

He held up blackened hands. The left sleeve straggled, and ink smudged the beige-and-baby-blue flannel. Jane pointed it out.

He shook his head. "Should have worn my red-and-black plaid. What kind of business would insert a flier the Monday after Christmas in this town?"

Jane picked up her newspaper and folded over one corner to check the last page number. Six—and only a tiny ad down at the bottom of the page.

"A shrewd one that doesn't like a lot of competition for its advertising," Jane shot back with a smile. Then she slid the price of the newspaper, thirty-five cents, across the counter and started to leave.

"Hey, you can't just walk out of here and leave us in suspense," he said, dramatically putting his arm on the door.

Jane stepped back and looked at the receptionist. Were they all crazy here?

But the receptionist drawled an exasperated, "Bob..."

"What do you mean?" Jane asked.

"This is a newspaper office in a small town in the dead of winter," he exclaimed, removing his arm and eyeing her up and down. "You could be from the Internal Revenue Service here to audit the mill, from Fish and Game to announce some new regulations on halibut, from the postal service to investigate the feasibility of home delivery, from the Bureau of Indian Affairs to announce cutbacks, or from the EPA to sniff out the woodsmoke and threaten our wood stoves. Or, best of all, you could be here from the U.S. Forest Service to start surveying Gavin Mountain—for the ski trails!"

"I look like I work for the government?" Jane asked, looking down and trying to figure out what it was about her clothes that made him talk this way. "And if I did, what would you do about it?"

"Write a story!" he said as he whipped a skinny notebook from his back pocket. The word *Reporter* was emblazoned on the cover. "Take your photograph!"

"You're a reporter?" she asked in disbelief.

"*The* reporter, these days. Bob Denson at your service. Believe me, you'll have fewer questions to answer and fewer explanations to make if you let me take your photo for tomorrow's edition and tell me what brought you to town."

"Really?" Jane asked, and she could not help laughing. "Actually, you couldn't be more right about that. People could just telephone and make appointments for interviews. I wouldn't have to waste résumés. I'm sorry, but I'm just here to find a job."

The corners of his mouth turned down, and he averted his eyes from the giggling receptionist. He shoved the notebook back into his pocket and jammed the pen into his shirt.

"A job?" he said. "No prospects? You are either a very brave or very crazy woman to arrive in Southeast Alaska in the middle of winter and expect to find a job. I mean, in the spring at least you can get on the slime line at the seafood plant." His eyes panned down from the glasses and pearls to the skirt and expensive shoes. "But somehow, you don't look the type."

"No," Jane said with a little shake of her head. "So, you're telling me there are no jobs in town."

"No, I didn't say that—all depends what you do," he said, the tough-guy routine returning.

"Finance," she replied.

"Hmmm, there are possibilities," he said with raised eyebrows. "Want to talk about them tonight over a beer?"

She hesitated, and he saw it.

"Just beer, and maybe some leads," he said seriously. "No better person to talk to about a town than a reporter, right?"

"It depends on the reporter," she murmured, and watched as his face fell. "All right, all right," she said. "As long as you promise not to add me to your list of gossip items."

"Deal," he said, looking at the clock and moving backward. "Give me two hours. The Sheffield at four. I need a photo for tomorrow's paper, and light is fading fast." He was around the corner before she could say anything. The receptionist shook her head, but her smile was warm.

Jane opened the door again and paused. It sounded like a riot outside. She watched a dozen children push and holler about who had been at the set of doors first.

"Paper kids," Cindy called out. "They get mean when the paper's late." She bellowed. "Hey, you kids, get away from that door and let this woman out!"

One jumped back and knocked down a small boy with tousled black hair. The little boy clutched his legs and started crying. Jane went to the child, took him by the shoulders and helped him to his feet. His brown jacket, at least two sizes too large, was thin for the damp air, and there was a gaping hole in the left elbow. Jane knew these kinds of tears were not from the tumble, but from a day or even a life of frustration. She whispered in his ear, and he shook his head fiercely, then smiled. Jane pulled a dollar from her pocket and slipped it into the tiny, dirty fingers.

"I would have bought my paper from you," she said. "Next time, I'll keep my eye out for you."

He ran to the door, waving the dollar in triumph. The other children giggled nervously and packed up against the doors again, trying to wedge their bodies close. Jane didn't want to leave, but she didn't want to frighten the boy. After all, she was a stranger. She waved good-bye and brushed away a tear, not looking back as she walked away.

NINE

FOUR HOURS LATER, Bob and Jane lingered over empty glasses.

"Some kind of amazing courage you don't take the first plane out of here," Bob said as he played with his glass. "Think you can stick it out until spring?"

She nodded slowly. "Yes. At least that's what I think today. I won't lie to you. My answer wouldn't have been the same last night. I had doubts before the job vanished, and after Reynold told me, my first thought was to hop back on the ferry and not say good-bye to anyone.

"I was miserable. Then I walked outside, and instead of feeling stuck, I felt . . . free. Like, if I had to, I could climb a mountain and build a cabin and take care of myself, and life would go on regardless."

She looked out at the sparkling lights of the harbor. "There is something about these mountains and the sea. They can't be forgotten. Do you know what I mean? You glance at gorgeous pictures of faraway places. But when you get there, you discover how the photographer emphasized the right things and blocked out all the wrong things. That's not a problem here. This landscape still overwhelms the people and what they have done to the land."

Bob nodded and chuckled.

"Sitka looks better to me every minute," she said. "It's enticing."

They both looked out the window. Through the darkness the snow on Mt. Edgecumbe appeared a bitter shade of violet. The harbor was a tangle of fishing boats and shadows.

"Does every house in town have a view?" Jane asked.

"Ninety percent," he said. "So, you're in love with the place from the start. But will that last? Chances aren't so good if you don't find a job, a lover, or a hobby in the next week or so. You have to keep busy to avoid going crazy in Sitka."

"You can go crazy anywhere," Jane countered. "Besides, I'm not utterly useless. I have experience. Somebody in Alaska should be able to take advantage of me."

"Especially in Alaska," he agreed.

She laughed and took the last ice cube from her glass.

"But don't get too cocky," Bob drawled. "You have to prove you're reliable. Around here that could take six months. And the people who do know what you're talking about, they won't like the competition and won't appreciate the change in the status quo. You're lucky you know an insider at the paper. I can always give you a head start on any classifieds."

"All six of them."

"Don't laugh. That's what makes Sitka. Seventeen miles of road, no traffic lights, no golf course, no high school football, and a handful of classifieds in an eight-page daily newspaper. But speaking of classifieds, there's something I wanted to ask you. You're sure that Reynold offered you that job with Katmai?"

"Of course I'm sure," Jane said indignantly.

"How did you find out about it?"

She shrugged. "I responded to a classified in a trade journal for finance advisors about two months ago. I was interviewed over the telephone by Reynold, the controller, and a board member. Someone contacted my references, and a week later a board member telephoned and asked me to head north. Francesca called the same afternoon and invited me to stay with her. The connection was terrible and all I got was the address. There was no confirmation by mail."

"Strange," he said. "I'd have to double-check in back issues, but that job wasn't advertised in the *Record*. Maybe there's a story in you yet...."

Jane smiled. She was a story for Bob all right, especially if he knew how much Katmai had just handed over to keep her from complaining about losing the position. The sum would have hired a junior analyst for two years! The pay-off was fair from her point of view, but not from that of the Native shareholders. But for the time being, Jane would keep to herself the information about her check for expenses. Certainly until the check cleared. She'd promised in the letter she signed that she would not take legal action, but that didn't prohibit her from taking the story to the media.

"Maybe they knew there wasn't anybody in town," Jane said. "They wanted fresh blood."

"Not likely. It's standard practice for employers in town to advertise every position in the newspaper—at least once. Local hire is a touchy subject in Alaska. About the only time they don't advertise jobs is when the employer doesn't realize what they need until a new person with qualifications walks through the door. But as long as he or she has a local address, that's all right."

"Maybe that will happen to me." Jane sighed.

"A woman came to town for a biologist job with the state. Her husband—he had a master's degree in psychology or sociology—had trouble finding work. The guy was down and didn't know anybody, and they were about to call it quits. Somehow his wife's boss convinced him to try out for a play with the community theater group, something to keep him busy for at least two months until the boss could replace Kathy, the wife. The husband played Renfield, Dracula's crazy sidekick. So, he got into the part and let it rip—grunting, groveling, and gulping bugs. The hospital administrator offered him a job the next week—researching the need for a mental health unit in town. The hospital decided the guy did such a great job with the Renfield part, he had to know something about schizophrenia."

"That's not fair," Jane said, incredulous.

"Employers are not that different from casting directors for a theater, especially in a small town. They have a good idea of qualified people and make their minds up fast. It's tough coming to Sitka cold and hoping to find a job. The place is not that big. The town has exactly three reporters, about a dozen doctors, four dentists, three phys ed teachers, three accountants, two grocery store managers, one psychologist, one veterinarian, one pet store, one art gallery, one dry cleaner... You get the idea—a lot of ones. There's not a whole lot of room for competition. The best tactic for you is to find a niche, one where you won't step on any toes. Sitkans have been known to turn into yapping, whining dogs when someone approaches their turf, pit bulls when the newcomer has a lot on the ball and stands to compete."

"Now you're telling me to act stupid!" Jane teased.

"No, here's your tactic. Let people know a valuable commodity just hit town, and let them fight over you. If you get desperate and it shows, it's all over. Employers will wonder what's wrong with you."

"People are going to wonder that anyway. The Katmai fiasco.'

Bob shook his head. "No sweat. That won't surprise anyone. Stuff like that happens around here. Katmai is... I'm still trying to figure the place out myself. Ironic, though, the hottest plans for development going on in Alaska, second only to drilling oil in the Arctic National Wildlife Refuge, are right here in Sitka behind the doors of Katmai Shee Inc. They're trying to keep the ideas under wraps, but they could use some hotshot analysts more than any other business."

"Skiing," Jane said, shaking her head. "Somehow, I just can't visualize it. Not in this town. Not the way I saw it last night, all the rain."

"There's plenty of snow up in dem der hills," Bob said with a laugh. "Anyone who's hiked in the winter around here can tell you that."

"Maybe." Jane smiled. Any analyst knew every development project had more than one critical factor. There was also more to running a ski resort than snow. But Katmai was not her baby anymore, and she kept the thought to herself.

"As for you, get the word out—you like it here, you want work, but don't let on how good you are. Tread carefully. Don't step on toes. I have a feeling you're good, real good. Most of the people in finance positions got their jobs when Alaska was begging for professionals, before computers became standard. These guys are fixtures, and that can get irritating for a hotshot from the big city. That's you."

"Worse than that, my degrees are from Harvard," she said. "That's not for your gossip column, either."

"Lindsey's department, not mine," he snapped. "And don't think you're the only one. There's enough of us here to start a full-fledged alumni chapter."

"Sorry," Jane said softly. "Guess I'm letting off some steam . . . after what happened today."

He grinned. "No problem. Meanwhile, you have time to go out and see the town. How about we try that some night?" he asked as he pushed his glass around.

"Too early for me," she blurted. Stop there—no need for explanations or excuses, she warned herself.

"That's novel," he said, unperturbed, as he returned the conversation back to easy patter. "By too early, I take it you mean you want to check out the men before making any hasty decisions. Want me to spread the word around?"

"What?"

"You seem pretty adamant in general—I can spread the word around," he said. "Lots of guys are going to be hitting on you. Eligible men outnumber the eligible women by three to one in this town. I bet there's a dozen men after you already, and you don't even know it."

"I doubt that," she said. "I haven't met a dozen men yet."

"That doesn't mean they don't know about you," he said.

"This conversation makes me wonder if I'm cut out for small-town life. I feel so...exposed."

"Get used to it," he said.

"I haven't met Francesca yet, and I'm nervous enough about that," Jane said, moving the conversation to safer territory. She wanted to hear what Bob had to say. He was young, a kid brother kind of guy, but he was practical, and she didn't have to worry about him looking for different meanings to her questions. Besides, she could not avoid gossip. Gossip was Sitka's favorite activity, and if she was going to play, she wanted Bob on her side. "So, what's she like?"

"Widow. Presumed widow, that is. Her husband disappeared on a hunting trip. Body never found. She's in her early forties and gorgeous. On the board of directors for Katmai."

"So she's Native?" Jane asked.

He nodded and kept on. "Up for reelection in May and could lose her seat. A television reporter, mediocre compared to yours truly, but worthy competition. She has a son. Named Bojack. He used to be bad news. But maybe he straightened out in the last year since he got a real job. Or maybe he got smarter.

"But enough. You can form your own opinion. Look over there, she just walked in. I'll introduce you. But let me add one word of caution," he said as he stood and waved to a woman in the doorway. "Don't be surprised if you feel the need to start searching for other accommodations. Soon."

TEN

THE WOMAN approached the table slowly, the way people do in movies when they know everyone in the room is watching. She was short but stunning. She grabbed the hair that swept down her back and twisted it over one shoulder as if it were a brilliant, if annoying, black rope. A dozen or so carved silver bracelets clanked together on both wrists.

"I am in the unusual but pleasant position of introducing two roommates," Bob said as he stood. "Jane Mc-Bride, Francesca Faith LaQuestion." He turned and waved his arm once. The bar was packed, but a waitress immediately came to the table and took the order.

"Thank you for the place to stay, the coffee, everything this morning," Jane began nervously. "And I already started working on finding an apartment. I guess you know...I won't be working at the corporation after all." Jane stopped rambling. Francesca looked uncomfortable.

"The case of the vanishing job," Bob drawled.

"The corporation will be in...a state of transition until after the elections." Francesca took time to choose words carefully. "I apologize for that confusion." Her eyes were like melted bittersweet chocolate, and she looked at Bob sternly. "I trust you're not here to take notes."

"Don't worry," he said. "I've had too many beers for that."

"Thanks," she said coolly.

"But that doesn't mean I don't have a few questions. Why wasn't Jane's position—ex-position, I should say—advertised locally? I thought that was standard practice for Katmai."

"Oversight," Francesca retorted. "Call and ask Cam about that."

"You know he wants to talk to me as much as he wants to talk to an IRS auditor. All right, all right—let's declare a truce while we discuss Jane's predicament. But you can't say I never warned you, Francesca, how tough it is riding two horses at once—reporter and corporate official."

"An unfortunate necessity in a small town." Perfect teeth showed in her smile, and her quiet charm returned. She turned to Jane. "So you plan on staying, at least for a while." Her smile was genuine, not one of a woman who would deliberately leave a dead, bloody fish as a twisted welcome message.

"I'd like to," Jane said. "I looked forward to the job and Alaska, and now there's no good reason for leaving."

"Then it's settled—stay with me," Francesca said, clanging an armful of bracelets on the table. "Indefinitely."

Briefly, Jane wondered how long it took before a person could ignore so many bracelets. Then she quickly examined the near future. On the negative side, Francesca was connected to the corporation from which she had just been dumped. On top of that, she had a problem kid. On the plus side, Jane knew the woman kept a clean house and was not a big talker. Francesca's work would give Jane time alone in the cottage by the sea, time to find out if she were meant to live the life of country mouse or city mouse. Jane could not help but smile at the thought of Michael Benoit's face when he found out that she'd be drinking coffee and washing dishes in a Native woman's kitchen every day.

Most important, the invitation was being offered not out of pity, but out of eagerness. Jane had lots of recent practice at sensing that out. No, Francesca really wanted her to stay and might even need something. But Francesca had poker eyes, and Jane could not be certain what that need might be. If the need was too much, she could always leave.

Living with Francesca could be better than living alone. Jane made up her mind fast.

"Thank you," she said simply.

It was late when the two women returned to the cottage. Throughout the day Jane had focused on the loss of the Katmai job and the need to find some other suitable position in Sitka. As the long winter night wore on, Jane kept remembering the threatening call. The open door and the dead fish could have been coincidental oversights, but there was no mistaking the call. People who carried out mean pranks eventually tried to catch a glimpse of their victim, to witness the fear and confusion. Jane decided she would not give any person that satisfaction. She refused to show any worry and wouldn't discuss the phone call, not even with Francesca. But she could make some casual inquiries. So far, she could assume the person knew when she was coming to town but probably did not know the Katmai job had been snatched away. Eventually she would discover and confront the culprit.

"I didn't know what to do about the fish in the sink this morning," Jane mentioned. "I threw some ice over it."

"Fish?" Francesca asked, pausing on the staircase. "Bojack must have been by. He goes out almost every day and drops off some of his catch now and then. He must have been in a hurry." She turned around and headed for the kitchen.

"Oh, look," she said, holding the freezer door wide open. "He came back and cleaned it. He must have realized you were here and sleeping and didn't want to disturb you."

Jane opened the refrigerator. The freezer contained at least ten neat packages—white lumps of halibut, cleaned and fileted. Bojack, Jane thought. Again, she reminded herself that the fish could have been a simple mistake. But having a hint of who wanted her out of town comforted her. She couldn't forget the voice on the telephone, and she would recognize it when she heard it again.

ELEVEN

JANE SAT HUNCHED in front of the computer monitor. It was before seven a.m. She set her alarm early each morning, getting up just before Francesca left for work and thwarting any more surprise gifts of fish. The room was dark except for the gray-green glow that cast strange shadows. The only sound was the soft hum from the disk drive. She knew what it felt like to be alone in a capsule, drifting aimlessly through outer space.

The blank screen irritated her. One would think more than a few sentences would emerge from the fifty computer spreadsheets surrounding the desk. She had collected the data for an article on forecasting real estate values. But the proposal that had been so crucial in Boston now seemed pointless. She tapped the keys hard to switch into another file, to reexamine the letter that accompanied her résumé. To get the right kind of job, the letter needed to be daring. The three paragraphs were incomprehensible, but she could not logically explain why an experienced financial analyst was unemployed and wanted to stay in Sitka.

"Hell, anyone who lives here should know the answer to that," she said.

She typed in a new date for the letter: January 4. She didn't like the aftermath of Christmas and had always disdained resolutions. But resolutions or not, who could ignore the general mood of self-evaluation that came with the new year? In the past she threw herself into projects with vigor. Now she couldn't get past the date on a letter.

Bob was right. Sitka was wonderful, but only for people in love, whether it was with a person, a career, or life in general. She thought about switching files again and typing a letter to some old friends in Boston. But friends would wonder why she didn't mention Katmai. Explaining why she had become attached to Sitka would be easier once she found a job.

A cracking noise came from outside. Jane pushed her chair back to the window. After a few moments of listening and hearing only silence, she moved the curtain slightly and looked out into the forest. She did not want to startle the animal that made the noise. The forest was a cluster of dark anonymous shapes that did not move. Light filtered through the trees from the kitchen window. She held her breath and waited. The noise, maybe a large stick breaking, had not been made by a bird or squirrel. Possibly a deer or even a bear, she thought. She pulled the curtain back even more and looked at the far end of the house—the battered garbage can was standing, and its lid was intact, a large rock on top. Bears rarely came to town, but if one did, he wouldn't pass up an easy meal from a garbage can. Something bright blue was caught in the brush not far from the garbage can. Jane squinted. Yes, a scrap of blue cloth.

The phone rang. Jane caught it before the second ring.

"I knew I could count on you being a morning type," Bob said breezily. "Meet me for breakfast before I take off for the police station. I have a lead on a job for you."

"Where?" she asked.

"Katlian Café. In forty-five minutes." He hung up.

"The job, not the restaurant!" she shouted, but the receiver buzzed at her.

It was exactly 2.3 miles from Francesca's home to downtown Sitka, and to meet him on time she had to leave right away. She switched off the computer and searched for her old shoes. They would stand up to rain that could come at any time. With three fast strokes, she brushed her hair away from her eyes and forehead, then grabbed ten dollars off the dresser. She paused and opened the curtains wide. No bear, she thought with a laugh.

She checked the window again. Birds twittered and moved about. The creek showed an occasional sparkle as it curled its way down the mountain. The garbage can and rock were safe. Jane looked again at the brush. The blue scrap was gone. The forest was full of shadows. Either her eyes had played a trick on her or the wind had blown it away. She looked about—even the tiniest branches were motionless. She told herself that bears didn't wear blue, shut the curtains, and left quickly, jogging along the beach side of the road.

She slowed when she was about a quarter mile away from the house. She felt as though she were out in the middle of the night for a stroll. Sawmill Creek Road hugged the shoreline, and Jane kept her eyes on the lights of the town and the few fishing vessels preparing to leave the harbor. She glanced at her watch—traffic would soon rush by for the first shift at the pulp mill. But for the next mile, not a car passed. Jane walked faster.

"You won't see a bear in town, unless it's along Indian River or in the national park," Bob had mentioned once. "Maybe in your backyard if Francesca's sloppy with the garbage. Don't leave any garbage out on purpose, though, that's illegal."

He had discussed bears so casually. Jane started jogging again, even though the January air hurt her lungs. She stopped only when she had passed the park and reached the front walk of a home with lights. Less than ten minutes later she was inside the steamy restaurant.

Katlian Café was squashed under a hotel that would have been labeled a single-room occupancy setup in Boston, Seattle, or New York. Fishermen stayed at the Katlian when they wanted a change from living aboard or needed some privacy for a steady girlfriend. The café had six tables, ten counter seats, decor that included lots of chipping paint, and one objective—passing out clunky white plates overflowing with wholesome bland food, fast.

Bob wasn't there, so Jane waited at the counter for a two-seat table to open up. A copy of the *Daily Record* had been left behind. ''Police Blotter'' caught her eye:

A golden retriever was impounded on Katlian street at 8 p.m.
A resident reported that a toolbox and tools, worth $100, had been stolen from his truck about a month ago.
A black mixed-breed dog was impounded on Lincoln Street at 9:40 p.m.
An intoxicated man was reported on Sawmill Creek Road at 10:50 p.m. Police escorted the man to his home....
A Labrador-collie mix was reported missing from his Harbor Drive home at 11 p.m.
Police also responded to four domestic disputes.

A crimeless town, she thought, and laughed, a combination of relief and embarrassment over how she had run nervously away from the cottage from imaginary bears and intruders. The noise had probably been made by a stray dog. Still, in the restaurant, as everywhere she went, she listened to voices, trying to track down the man who made the prank phone call.

A table cleared just as Bob swung open the door, his hat pulled low and his shoulders hunched. He grunted hellos toward patrons at the other tables, and then he sat down noisily. Jane could not help but notice how other diners gave her a closer look before returning to their pancake stacks and eggs. A waitress in a pink uniform slammed down two thick white mugs and sloshed coffee into them.

''I'll be back,'' she said.

''Great, Flo,'' Bob said, playing with the menu.

''Next time you have news in the morning, drive on over, and I'll cook you whatever you want,'' Jane muttered.

"This place has great home fries," Bob protested. "The food tastes just like my grandmother's cooking, not that anyone except my grandfather liked that. Besides, what would all those mill workers say after seeing my car parked in Francesca's driveway at this time in the morning?"

"I can believe that." Jane scowled and picked up the menu, a handwritten Xerox copy, protected by a greasy plastic cover sheet. "Last week, the drugstore clerk knew about my Katmai job and asked when I'd be leaving. You should have seen her face when I said I thought of Sitka as the perfect winter wonderland and had no plans to leave."

"Long wavy black hair?" Bob asked.

Jane nodded.

"Ugh—" He grimaced. "No surprise about that reaction. I went out with Judy a few times. She's probably jealous."

"If I'd known, I could have eased her mind," Jane said, studying the menu. "Who are you trying to make jealous in here?"

"You," he whispered, and then he leaned back and laughed.

"I'm a little old for you."

"Anything goes in Sitka."

Other than raising her eyebrows, Jane ignored his comment. "About this job," she said. "I hope it's worth my walk this morning. You could have told me a little more on the telephone."

"I don't know if it's what you're looking for," he said. "But the finance director at Holmes Barrett College quit. He's left town already. It happened suddenly. No notice, no good-bye party, from what I heard, so they could be desperate. The ad is going in today—one day only. You should check it out."

"Don't worry, I will." Jane nodded. She looked at her watch. She could not call before ten. "I should go to the library—read up on the college."

"Here's a clip file from the *Record*. Copy what you need and give it back tomorrow. The school was started for Native kids by a missionary. Now it offers four bachelor's degrees and a handful of associate degrees."

"Thanks," Jane said, patting the file. "Surprise—the *Record* comes to the rescue of the woman with nothing but time on her hands. Back in Boston I could spend half the morning drinking coffee and reading the newspaper."

"Don't laugh," Bob said shortly. "There's some serious stuff in the *Record*."

"Certainly not this part," Jane said, laughing, pointing to the Police Blotter. "From the sound of this, dogs are Sitka's biggest problem."

Matching orders of scrambled eggs were slammed down on the table, though Jane had ordered a smaller portion.

"Don't you dare laugh," he said, stabbing his potatoes. "Most of my major battles have been fought over those ridiculous inches."

"Battles?"

"The Blotter is a constant source of argument. Half the people in town will do anything to avoid mention, and the other half want to know every dirty detail. Any change results in dozens of letters and calls. Once I eliminated the times from some of the more embarrassing items, domestic disputes, and that sort of thing. I figured, if there was no arrest, let the couples do their own explaining to their neighbors about why a police cruiser pulled up in the middle of the night. People howled. Lindsey stuck up for me. But it wasn't easy."

"The things one has to worry about in a small town," Jane said in disgust.

"I know, not exactly Pulitzer material," he said.

"There have to be stories buried all over this town," Jane mused.

"I don't know," Bob sighed. "I can't believe anything stays hidden from the *Record*, not for long. Somebody sees a commotion at the end of town, and I can expect about twenty phone calls. Everybody likes to think they're a reporter—and the *Record* accommodates them."

"Maybe I'll give you a call someday," Jane said with a laugh. "And maybe it will be from Holmes Barrett College."

"I'll keep that in mind. You and Francesca getting along?" Bob changed the subject, busy buttering his toast.

Jane nodded. "Great, so far. I have yet to meet Bojack. What's he like?"

"Young. Difficult. Tries hard to be cool and not care about much. Yikes! That sounds like me!"

"So, he's not mean to Francesca or...dangerous?" Jane asked, avoiding eye contact.

"Nah," Bob said. "A troublemaker, but not dangerous. Shouldn't you ask Francesca about this?"

Jane was embarrassed. "It was a question. Please don't mention that I asked. Francesca doesn't talk much about him, that's all. Not that I see her much. We get along wonderfully for two people who see each other five minutes here and there. She's off to work as I get up in the morning and not back till late. She's dedicated."

"To what?" he scoffed. He picked at a dried drop of egg on the table. "Not journalism. She has a distorted sense of objectivity. She not only belongs to every Native organization in town but holds office in most of them. She talks about Native potential and leadership but doesn't think a Native group could survive in this town without her. And she doesn't blink an eye about being on the board of directors at Katmai—sometimes she uses inside information for her TV reports, and other times she holds back. Like the skiing. She knows plenty. The Katmai board refuses to release a word. Francesca soft-pedals every negative Native story that comes her way. What it comes down to, she's nothing but a flack. It's pathetic; she could do a hell of a lot more for everyone in this town, especially the Natives, if she devoted all her attention to either the Native politics or her job. But she can't play it both ways."

Jane reached over and pulled his hand away from the spot of egg. "Maybe the rules are different in Alaska," she said, softly. "Or in small-town Alaska."

"Or maybe Francesca is a spoiled little princess," he snapped. "I mean, literally, she's the great-great-granddaughter of some chief. What I don't understand is why you're so quick to defend her. She comes off as perfect, but don't forget that she's damn good at hiding a lot. You don't know her, and from what I've heard, your job fiasco started after she jumped the gun, told another boardmember to call and tell you that you were hired. She figured the other directors would be too embarrassed to send you packing, but they called her bluff, jumped all over her, and canceled the job."

"Who told you that?"

"A source. Someone who's not happy with Francesca, is all I can tell you. The same source has passed along some other juicy tidbits that Francesca knows nothing about. All I can say is that, after those Katmai elections in May, this town is going to be hopping like a fish on the line, and Francesca may have more time for real journalism."

"Don't be hard on her," Jane said. "My Katmai job is gone. But I'm not complaining, and I can't blame Francesca. I do know her. She did not deliberately set me up." She could not help but blush, thinking about the check. Bob still didn't know, she thought guiltily. No one had a poker face that good.

"Like I said, it's only a rumor Cameron refuses to confirm, but I believe it. It makes sense. Don't be offended. I've known her awhile, and she's my competition. Great journalism requires competition. And it's tough for me to treat her seriously."

TWELVE

SOON AFTER she got home, Jane telephoned the president of Holmes Barrett College, Henry Ellsley, to schedule an interview.

"New in town, you say? I must warn you that we have qualified staff also submitting applications. I want to meet you, but I also don't want you to be disappointed. Ummm, it's unusual for people with your qualifications to come to town without some sort of prospect."

"Yes, it is," Jane said firmly. No need to go into detail now. The pause was long, but she refused to budge.

"All right," he said finally. "Tomorrow at ten-thirty, then. My office."

"I look forward to meeting you."

THE NEXT DAY Jane fretted about what to wear. More than anything else she wanted to command respect and look like a Sitkan. Easier for men that women, she'd observed.

She had not seen Francesca in the past three days, except on the nightly television news. Every night Francesca wore solid-color wool sweaters. The other half of her outfit was never visible to viewers, but Jane knew from experience that it could be anything from a corduroy skirt to faded jeans. Now Francesca wore a thick red bathrobe and sat in the kitchen, staring out over the bay while she drank her coffee. The sun was just rising, casting pale pink light around the edges of the dark mountains. Jane explained about the interview.

"Who are you meeting with?" Francesca asked.

"Henry Ellsley."

Francesca pretended to gag. "You're too good to work for him. It's no secret what I think about Henry Ellsley."

"Why?" Jane asked.

Francesca slowly combed her fingers through her hair to push it away from her face, the kind of gesture a beautiful woman could get accustomed to using to detract attention from what she didn't want to talk about. "He's power hungry, and he sees Natives as a group waiting for a leader. The chief of the Wannabe tribe. He's desperate to do Native politics, but he's not a Native. Not officially. What's ironic is that he's probably at least a quarter Tlingit, on his mother's side. The family did too damn good a job of covering that up back in the 1940s and 1950s."

"When it was as socially acceptable to be seen with a Native as it would have been to serve skunk cabbage at a dinner?" Jane said.

"Something like that," Francesca said as she twisted her dark hair and returned her gaze to the bay.

Jane regretted the flip words as soon as they left her mouth. How easy to put down prejudice of forty years ago. Francesca was too circumspect to ask the obvious question aloud: Would Jane have moved in with her back then? But she remained quiet and poured more coffee for them both. Jane had not lived with Francesca two weeks. Their encounters still required momentum. Unnecessary questions or comments could kill a conversation.

Francesca waited until Jane returned the coffeepot to the counter and relaxed on her seat.

"It wasn't cool to be Native until 1971 and the Alaska Native Claims Settlement Act," Francesca said matter-of-factly. "That wiped out more than two hundred tribes' claims to both the oil fields and proposed route for the pipeline. In exchange the Natives got almost one billion dollars and more than ninety percent of the private land in this state.

"That cash and land were distributed through corporations, more or less assigned with the tribes—like Katmai

Shee. To be a shareholder at Katmai, you had to be born
before 1971 and prove you had one-quarter Native blood.''

"You would think he could prove it," Jane said.

Francesca lowered her voice, but bitterness was apparent. "If Ellsley's mother had gone before the tribal elders
with any shred of evidence, they would have gone back into
the tribe and collected their one hundred shares of Katmai
stock and one hundred shares of stock from the regional
corporation. A lot of people came out of the woodwork that
year.

"But that old woman was stubborn. She snickered that
the corporations would go bankrupt in less than ten years,
that the money would all go back to the government and the
liquor stores. She had her wealth and landholdings, after
marrying a non-Native merchant in town and wearing him
down with her cruel words and ways. She claimed she
wouldn't be bothered with handout land from the government. She died in 1979, and if she left any evidence, Ellsley
hasn't found it...."

She stopped. "You don't want to hear all this before the
interview. You need a job, and you asked me a question. But
I have to admit, I can't wait to hear what you have to say
about Ellsley."

Jane looked up, puzzled. She remembered what Bob had
said about Francesca not trusting others to make ethical
decisions. What would she think if Jane got the job? Jane
did not want to trade impressions of Ellsley with Francesca
if she went to work for the man.

"What should you wear? ... Ellsley always wears a suit.
One of the few men in town," Francesca said thoughtfully.

"I brought two," Jane offered.

"Wait a minute," Francesca said. "He's one of the few
men in town who wears a suit every day. Maybe Ellsley
wants to corner a certain image all for himself. He's that
type."

Jane went into her room and returned with a deep purple, severely cut suit in one hand and a gray pleated skirt

with a pale blue sweater in the other. "Which do you think?"

Francesca waved off the suit and gently fingered the powder blue cashmere. "Dress comfortably. Signal you're in step with Sitka. Despite the pleats and cashmere, this looks Alaskan. Let him be king of the suits.

"Needless to say, don't mention that you live with me," Francesca said as she carried her coffee upstairs. "It looks like it's going to pour soon. Get dressed fast, and I'll give you a ride downtown."

"YOUR CREDENTIALS SEEM . . . impeccable," said Henry Ellsley, frowning at her papers before him on the desk. Behind him was a huge window that showed only streams of rain and fog.

Jane forced herself to stare at Ellsley. He was stiff, and the rain behind him was distracting.

He wore pinstripes, a pressed white shirt, and a pale yellow tie. He was in his forties, short, no sign of gut through the suit. Not bad looking. But he was insecure, and from a fast survey of the offices she passed with him on the way in, she guessed he preferred being surrounded by unattractive and tentative people—an older woman with gray hair and a heavy young woman with dull eyes forlornly studied a computer manual. Another man, about Ellsley's age, bald and dumpy, constantly nodded, too eager to please the boss. Ellsley undoubtedly enjoyed the inane questions and the barrage of attention. If these people were the inside competition, she could have a chance at the job. During the interview, Jane listened, hoping to appeal to Ellsley's insecurity.

"Impeccable," he repeated with a deeper frown. "But people who have not lived here for long, who have not been part of the unique cultural environment of this town, let alone this college, find it difficult to adjust, scale down. The college is small—fewer than five hundred students. Every employee must be fully aware of the cultural background of these students and willing to contribute to their overall development.'

She swallowed to keep her annoyance from showing. She pointed out the positions on her résumé with smaller firms. He nodded and continued to study her paperwork, as if he were looking for problems to jump out.

"I am willing to learn," Jane said firmly. "Granted, I have never held a finance position for a college before, let alone a college that targets a select cultural group. However, I have worked with endowments before, large endowments, and I believe my track record in low-risk, inflationproof investments should be of help to Holmes Barrett. In addition, my real estate management skills—"

A woman knocked on the door and handed Ellsley a folder. Plain and stalwart in her navy blue polyester, she studied Jane unabashedly. This woman, too, could be competition, Jane thought. Fast judgments were big mistakes in Alaska, where individuals often had lots of education, money, or talent and not always ample opportunity to show it off. Jane tucked her rubber-booted feet under the chair. To have worn anything else on such a rainy day would have been ridiculous, and she was not about to carry a little bag with fancy shoes for a meeting not expected to last more than an hour. The woman shut the door hard, as if to signify that Ellsley had wasted enough of his valuable time on Jane.

"Most informative," Ellsley concluded. "You will go far, Jane, with your background. I have other candidates to interview and expect to make a decision later this week. Again, your experience is most impressive, and you will hear from me."

Outside, the rain smacked against the window; Jane found it difficult to concentrate. She stood and initiated the farewell handshake. His grip was firm, and the words sounded all right, but inside she knew that the job would not be hers.

THIRTEEN

JANE PULLED her hat down hard over her ears and angry thoughts. Ellsley had hardly asked any questions. It was obvious he did not want to meet her and learn more about her. She had been the major annoyance of the day for him. She pushed the door so hard, it bounced on its hinges.

Mistakenly, she went out the wrong door in the administration building. Instead of going back inside, she stubbornly sloshed through puddles and mud to get around to the front of the building. She sure didn't want to run into Ellsley or any of his staff. She imagined them standing around his desk, all pleased about the new hotshot in town having to leave Sitka in disappointment.

"But you're wrong," she said out loud. "I am staying."

The administration building was one of twenty or so on campus, one of nine that circled a sloping green field overlooking the street and the harbor beyond. The rain had not let up, and she was alone on the path. Clouds tumbled in more violently than the waves. She didn't know if it was the scene or her anger after the interview that made her feel dizzy and strange. She thought about Ellsley again and kicked a puddle. A spray of water shot across the path.

Jane tightened her parka around her and slowed her gait. Expect rain in Sitka, she had been warned repeatedly. No one mentioned that she might enjoy the stinging drops on her face, the fresh smell of sea hitting earth, and even the trickle down her neck that made the rest of her body feel warm.

She would laugh with Francesca about what a jerk Ellsley was. To Bob, she would mention only that the interview went poorly. Neither of them had to know that Jane suspected Ellsley had a secret dislike for her. They would think she was paranoid.

As she neared the end of the path, she noticed a small building of octagonal shape. A sign read "Holmes Barrett Museum," and Jane followed the arrow.

She pushed open the heavy doors and found herself alone in a lovely all-white Victorian-style lobby. A long hallway connected the octagon with a larger building next door, the college's library. Jane peeled off her dripping coat, paused before a sign detailing fees for the museum, and looked for a staff person. No one was around to collect her three dollars.

Jane coughed. Still no sound.

So she entered the octagon. Delicate cases and shelves lined the eight walls, and in the center of the room was an oak display case, massive, old, and also octagonal. Each side had a stack of thin drawers.

Jane slid one drawer open and found inside an array of stone-cutting implements along with a tiny yellow card. "Tsimishian, from Nass and Skeena Rivers, circa 1790," read the card. The print was uneven, done on a clunky typewriter fifty or more years ago.

Usually Jane felt uncomfortable in a museum, and it was apparent that staff of this museum assumed its visitors knew plenty about the history behind the collection. But alone in the octagon, her imagination played. She saw one tiny knife with a carved bone handle and thought about carrying it for a day, using it for everything from shaving spruce for a basket to splitting open a succulent smoked salmon.

She closed the drawer slowly and walked around to get a feel for the room and the kind of people who worked on the baskets, capes, furs, beadwork, ivory, stone carvings, and masks from all over Alaska. Hundreds of artifacts were in the museum, and there was little room left for history or documentation other than the small, faded labels, tersely listing tribes, villages, and dates.

Rain still pounded on the roof of the museum, but miles away, over the ocean, the sun pierced the clouds. Jane did not notice. Instead she discovered the delight of an old-fashioned museum, cramped and unsophisticated. The lack of documentation stimulated her creativity. She was caught up in the world where people relied on these strange, ornate objects every day and where it was up to her to discover how and why they were used.

She moved closer to one case. Catching her attention, back in one corner, was a pair of stern, tragic eyes in one carving. The piece was wood and particularly battered. The body was a raven, but the eyes were human, and they scolded her with their sadness.

The raven was the handle of an elaborate ladle, now retired next to masks, boxes, containers, and beadwork, united in front of a sign that read "The Tlingit and Raven." Jane knelt to get a closer look. Its carved black wings were tucked tight against the length of its body. Its maker had taken special care to detail the feathers. In the sunlight Jane thought she saw a distinctive Z show through the etching along the wing. Had that been the carver's name? Would the mysterious Z have been proud or dismayed about the utensil being put behind glass, no longer handled by busy hands to serve food that had been cooked over the heat of a fire?

Jane felt she had found a secret treasure. Inside the crowded case of a museum that was hundreds of miles away from any major city, the ladle captured the appreciative glimpse of maybe one of every thousand visitors.

"And me." She sighed aloud, disgusted because she was not working and because she found it impossible to consider her freedom as leisure.

"Lucky you," came a low voice from behind her.

Jane jumped away from the case.

"It's a perfect day for visiting a museum, and you have the place to yourself," said the man as he came nearer. His hair was black, straight, and almost long enough to be tied back. Unlike most men, the long hair didn't detract from his good looks. He had distinctive angular high cheekbones and deep blue eyes.

"You caught me talking to myself," she said, blushing. "I hope I didn't startle you. Were you here all along?"

"No, I was in the library, talking with the staff over there. It can get lonely here in the winter. It makes up for the crush of tourists in the summer."

"You work here," Jane said, fumbling through her pockets. His clothes were rugged and suited the hair and eyes—an olive cotton sweater over a chambray shirt and worn corduroys. She could imagine him climbing a mountain with ease. He was casual and confident, so unlike Ellsley. "Here," she said as she handed over three neatly folded bills.

"Ignore the sign," he said, shaking his head. "I don't bother collecting this time of year. Not too many people come through, so I might as well give the locals a bargain. Have you been looking long? Did one piece strike you in particular? You were so intent. One of the rare visitors who stays more than ten minutes."

"It's charming here," she said, smiling. "What a lovely place to work. But I have to confess I did stop to get out of the rain. Do you think visitors would stay longer if they knew more about the people who made all of this?"

"Are you an art historian, a curator?" he inquired, leaning against the case. He was tall. Her head would fit neatly underneath his arm.

"Hardly," she said with a nervous laugh.

"That doesn't mean you can't have a closer look," he said with a warm smile. "If you're not an art historian, maybe you should be. You're certainly looking at the right case."

He pulled a ring of small keys from his pocket and opened the glass door. Jane did not mention which piece had made her linger at the case. His hands reached over the ladle for an old mask, with a skeletal motif, that was in the center of the shelf.

"This is one of the most exciting pieces in the museum," he said reverently. "It belonged to a shaman, not long after Russian trappers were settling in the area. The mask was presented to him as an offering, by a household begging that he cure an ailing girl. The shaman mixed some potion for the child, and then he donned the mask to dance away from her bedside, outside among the trees and spirits that surrounded the Tlingit camp. Suddenly, a woman screamed. People ran and found her crying. But it was a scream of joy rather than pain, because the fever of her niece had subsided. The shaman did not know that and danced deeper into the shadows. The mask was later found at the base of an immense cedar tree. Villagers claimed to see a raven take off from the top branches of the tree and head for the mountains. The shaman was never seen again, so the story goes."

The mask—with crazed, almost human eyes and a sharp birdlike beak—was old, with paint rubbed off. Jane was silent as she held it awkwardly.

"Why did he run away?"

"Maybe he heard the scream and fled because he feared his medicine no longer could stand against what the Russians had to offer. Maybe he really was Raven, the creator who was a trickster, according to the Tlingit."

"The Tlingit art is my favorite. How did they find time to do this kind of detailed work while surviving in the wilderness?"

"The people lived in a world of plenty, and they had abundant leisure time. The carving skills of the Tlingit were the highest of any indigenous people in the world. Their art was complex, like their social system. The Tlingit were unlike any other Indian tribe in the United States: every person knew his or her rank. Households collected wealth—art, food, slaves—and for special occasions would throw huge celebrations that lasted for days. Potlatches. Depending on the mood, the hosts shared their good fortune with a hundred guests or more, or they destroyed everything before their very eyes." He studied the mask for a moment in silence and then gently returned it to its place. "Anything else you would like to see close?" he asked as he locked the cabinet.

"No, but thank you," Jane said. "Are you the curator?"

"The curator and the museum's only employee during the winter."

"I always think of curators as old and gray."

"Not in Alaska. Doctors, lawyers, accountants, and curators end up with more responsibility than they would ever get in another part of the country. Invariably, after a few years, they take the experience and run south. But not me. I got my job before I finished my master's thesis—that was five years ago."

No regret in his voice. Jane envied that.

"And what about you?" he asked. "Visiting?"

"That's a good question." She laughed. "At this point, I wish I knew. I moved to town, but the job I thought I had fell through. So, now I'm searching for another job, and I hope I can stay. In fact, I just came back from an interview on campus."

"Really?" He seemed pleased. "We could be co-workers soon. What job?"

"Financial director."

"I'd have to file my budget request with you. I should be more discreet."

"Don't count on it," Jane said.

"Not enough experience?"

"It's not that," she said, hesitating to tell him more. She looked outside. The rain had stopped, and sun cast brilliant long rays to the water and shore. The light made tiny specks of dust inside the museum shine silver. Ellsley and his job didn't matter much anymore."

"I'm sure the interview did not go as poorly as you think," the man murmured.

"Believe me, I'm not getting this job." Jane shrugged. "Henry Ellsley and I did not click. Oh, he looked my résumé over, but he didn't ask any questions and acted disappointed because he couldn't find something wrong. It was like he was afraid of someone with experience. I should be more discreet myself. The walls in this town have eyes and ears. I thought living in a small town was supposed to be simple. So far it's been anything but."

He reached his hand out, put two fingers under her chin, to give it a gentle lift. The skin on his fingers was rough. But she didn't mind what she would have normally regarded as an intrusive gesture.

"Don't look down. Small towns aren't so bad. Get familiar with a few rules, try not to break them too often, and life can be wonderful. By the way, what's your name?"

"Jane McBride," she answered softly.

"I'm Daniel Greer. And the next time we meet, Jane McBride, you will have a job."

FOURTEEN

JANE HAD ONLY one key on her ring, and that was for Francesca's box at the post office, where they had to pick up their mail each day. The two doors of the house had locks, but Francesca explained she had purchased the home without ever seeing the keys. "No need for them out here," she insisted. Jane thought about offering to purchase some new locks but decided against it. Francesca was a better judge of how much to trust the town after living there all her life. The doors bolted from the inside, and Francesca smiled as Jane faithfully checked the bolts each night.

Now Jane was grateful she would not have to stop and open the door. The sun was strong when she left the museum, but when she was halfway home, clouds crept out from behind the mountains. The rain came down like bullets.

Jane was cold and miserable when she trudged up the porch stairs. She stopped in surprise to see the front door ajar. She remembered waiting in Francesca's red pickup truck that morning and studying some of Bob's material on the college. She had not paid attention when Francesca left the house.

We were in a hurry, Jane thought as she pushed the door open.

She went right to the stove, and her hands shook from the cold as she lit the match. She propped open the large door and confidently turned the switches. She tossed the first match inside. It bounced against the stove wall and went out. As she pulled out a second match, she heard a noise.

"Francesca!" Jane went to the bottom of the stairs and called. "You home?" No answer.

She went back to the stove and hesitated before lighting the second match. How big is a big puddle, and what happens when you light a big puddle? she wondered. Francesca never hurried in lighting the potbellied stove, and she never had problems. The puddle was about an inch deep. Jane shrugged and dropped the match. The flame instantly covered the surface.

Jane went into her bedroom, eager to pull off her wet clothes. She reached for the light switch, but her hand groped against the wall and felt something else. A denim jacket. An arm. The arm slammed her against the wall.

She screamed and hit him with her fists, but that did not stop him. He only grabbed for her breast with one hand and controlled her wrists with the other. So Jane breathed deeply and went limp. And she forced herself to count to ten in her head—slowly. His hand reached up underneath the sweater. But his other hand also loosened its grip around her wrists. He was nervous, and Jane counted to five, again slowly. Her attacker let go of her wrists so that both his rough hands could claw underneath her sweater. Jane took another breath; then, using all her strength, she twisted and turned to look directly into the man's eyes.

"You're not going to get away with this!" she shrieked, and pulled the ski mask almost over his eyes, while kicking his calf squarely. She didn't stop shrieking at the top of her lungs, and she tried to yank the hat off again.

At the same time, the sound of clanging metal came from the living room. Smoke filled the first floor, and the house felt as though it were falling apart. The deafening sound overpowered her shrieks and terrified her into struggling even harder to free herself.

She wasn't sure it if was her sudden switch from limpness to power that disoriented him or the bedlam. But he let go of her and lunged out the back door. Jane did not stop her bellowing while she ran after him. He was much quicker, and rather than running to the highway, he ran up the driveway and into the trees. No way she'd follow him through the forest.

Jane sat on the porch and caught her breath a moment. The pounding subsided, and the smoke that smelled like kerosene drifted away. The puddle must have been too big, she thought ruefully as she buried her head in her arms. Thank God, she thought. She should telephone the police immediately. But she wanted to see her room. She tiptoed into the house and listened to the stove, praying it would not explode. Instead the pot stove was gurgling normally. Jane went to her room, turned on the light, and let out a cry.

The bed was torn apart, the computer was knocked over, and papers were scattered. Her small boxes of computer disks had been emptied, and she found two cracked in half. Hundreds of pages of data destroyed. Her suitcases had been emptied, and her clothes were scattered on the floor. She wanted to sit down and cry, but she also wanted the culprit caught.

Shaking, Jane telephoned Francesca, told her what happened, and asked her to telephone the police. Then she took off what had once been her favorite sweater, threw it in the garbage, and prepared herself to sort out the mess.

FIFTEEN

JANE SPENT the next three mornings straightening out belongings and throwing away what was in shambles. Her clothes were easy to sort, iron, and fold.

Her computer equipment sustained the most physical damage. More than fifty disks were bent or cracked—data and program disks alike. Her monitor was shattered.

But what hurt the most was that the intruder had found all the books she'd sent to Alaska. He'd thrown them into a pile, tearing anywhere from two to twenty pages out of each. In the massive macroeconomics text he had found her four photographs, the only ones she had brought with her. Each was torn in half. Jane taped the pieces together, trying not to let tears fall on images of happier days.

Meanwhile, the intruder had overlooked her jewelry box and some folded bills that were in the side pocket of one of her suitcases. Two detectives from the police department investigated and tried to collect fingerprints. They suspected that Jane had caught the vandal by surprise, before he'd had a chance to ransack the rest of the home.

The short detective had called and asked her and Francesca to come down to the station. Jane checked the clock. After three hours of cleanup, she had enough time to walk to the post office and collect the mail before going to the police station.

As usual, P.O. Box 2216 contained a two-inch stack of catalogs, advertisements, bills, and letters. Jane reorganized the pile and examined the labels. Everything was Francesca's except for the two-day-old *Wall Street Journal*. Even so, she did not mind collecting the mail. Such a simple chore was a novelty for her and a good excuse to get out of the

house. At the same time, Francesca thanked her profusely.
For a reporter, avoiding the post office meant avoiding a
bombardment of news tips, questions, and complaints. Jane
could linger in the bustling lobby in relative anonymity. All
around her groups of friendly people stopped for conversation. She envied them their small token of daily social activity. She had yet to run into any acquaintance.

Jane decided to experiment with different times so that
she might encounter Daniel Greer. She wanted to know
more about him but was in no hurry and would not ask Bob
or Francesca. Both would immediately try to guess at her
motive and speed romance along. Or advise her on all his
faults. She thought about returning to the museum, but that
would be too soon and obvious. Daniel had already commented that she showed more than average interest in Native art.

"Hi, Jane," a familiar voice called out. "Settling in?"

Michael Benoit took the stairs three at a time, with his
parka open and flapping in the wind, defiant against the
chill.

"More or less," she said, clutching the bundle. That
many catalogs could get slippery.

He shoved his hands into his pockets, adding to the coat's
misshapen look, and studied her face. "Sitka must be
treating you well," he said. "You look happy despite all
that's happened. I read in the paper about the break-in at
Francesca's. How are you holding up?"

"It seems like a bad dream now," she said. "We almost
have the house cleaned up. Francesca thought it might be
retaliation against her for a news story. Maybe the Katmai
elections. But we have no idea."

"Anyone who knows Francesca knows that kind of tactic will only goad her on," Michael said.

"We're meeting with the police this afternoon, and we're
hoping they have some leads. The guy raided the refrigerator and my room. The police checked for prints, but he wore

gloves. I surprised him before he grabbed the television and CD player or my money. But why did he smash the computer monitor? The rest of the computer hardware is all right. The monitor is the least expensive part to replace. The software hurt a lot more. He destroyed everything."

"You have copies?"

"Some, not everything." Jane shook her head with a sad smile.

"But you're not devastated?" he asked, amazed.

"I finished what I left behind in Boston, I have yet to start anything in Sitka," Jane said, shrugging. "All I lost were data for an article that I probably would not have finished anyway. So, I'm a free woman.... Oh, I shouldn't be so flippant. Truth was, I was terrified that day."

"Get some good locks on the doors?"

She nodded. "I hope Francesca can get used to using a key. Now tell me, what else have you heard about me?"

Michael grimaced. "The screwup at Katmai and the college making the major mistake of not hiring you. Not the first time Ellsley made a dumb move, but then I'm not always consulted...."

Jane had only heard about the decision the previous afternoon. "Word gets around fast. But that's no big surprise. So don't expect me on your couch yet."

"Jane," he said in exasperation. "I have enough patients—I don't need to solicit clients in front of the post office. I have one couch, and it's at home. In front of the fireplace and the TV. You don't have to be a client to talk with me. Most of my patients make a point of avoiding me in public."

"That's good. I wondered whether I should be embarrassed about standing around the post office with you. How did you find out I didn't get the job at HBC?"

"Dan Greer told me who got the job. Allen Wilson. That dud's been working with Ellsley for years. So don't feel bad. Dan asked me if I knew about any finance jobs at the hospital for a woman new to town. I knew he had to be scouting for you."

"Thoughtful of him," Jane said, attempting to be nonchalant.

"So you've met Dashing Dan."

"I met Dan at the museum. He's pleasant, and he doesn't gossip. You should try it sometime."

"I'm a friendly gossip. Dan gossips—you just don't know him yet. Gossip is an essential force in every small town, and men do it as much as women do. Hell, Bob makes a living at it."

"Bob is sweet, safe, and like a brother," Jane said. "Go easy on me, Mike." She turned to walk away but gave him a warm smile.

"I'm glad you're staying in town," he said. His voice was low and sad.

Jane waved and felt sorry for him. He was friendly. But he was a psychiatrist, and he could get her to talk about parts of her life that she wanted to forget. Maybe she would call him for lunch. Someday.

As she headed for the police station, she thought again about the call she had to make to Ellsley. He had called the day before and repeated what he had said at the conclusion of the interview—that he needed a finance director with regional experience.

He'd then asked if she had a forwarding address.

"I'm staying in town," Jane had said, hoping he could sense her smirk. "You have the telephone number." He'd coughed as he'd said good-bye.

Two hours later the telephone had rung. Ellsley again.

"I've done some thinking. We can't let a person with your qualifications slip away. There's an opening for an instructor in the business department. This semester. It starts in February. Would you consider teaching?"

"I'm not an academic." She'd hesitated.

"You have a master's degree," he'd replied.

"I'll give you my answer tomorrow."

"Hope you can join us," he'd said tersely.

After he had hung up, she'd looked at the receiver. Ellsley was obviously not thrilled about her joining HBC.

Now she thought about the job. Not what she wanted, not what she was qualified for, but an excuse to stay in Sitka for four months. After the meeting with the detectives, she would go home, telephone, and accept the position. But she worried about Ellsley and his eccentricities.

Most of all, she pondered, why would a finance director need more experience with the local culture than an instructor who would be working directly with students?

SIXTEEN

"SO, YOU GIRLS LIKE a cup of coffee?" the detective shouted from a back room. He was a big man, with dark, wavy hair, and should have been handsome but was as gawky as an adolescent. He didn't wait for an answer but returned with two paper cups that looked ridiculous in his huge hands.

"Thank you," Jane murmured. She almost dropped the cup on the desk—the black coffee was unbearably hot through the cheap paper. Jane noticed Francesca nodding her head, directing the detective to place her flimsy cup on the desk—of course, she was a reporter, she had been to the police station before. The detective walked to the desk across the room.

"Detective Morris, is there any new information?" Jane asked politely.

"Charlie, he's my partner, he should be along any minute. Then we can go over the details. Francesca, you don't have to hang around if you're busy at the station...."

"It's my house," Francesca said harshly.

Detective Morris looked like a puppy who had been kicked. He started shuffling through some papers on a desk across the room and a folder fell to the floor, scattering what looked like receipts around the room.

Jane glanced at Francesca and quelled her own attempts at pleasantries. Francesca looked like a stone, but her dark eyes were angry. The man was sexist, but that didn't bother Jane when the cause was social ineptitude rather than deliberate meanness. She leaned over in her hard wooden chair and picked up a few of the receipts.

There was nothing to do but wait. Not a lot of money went to the police station, Jane thought. Besides the chief's office and the jail, the police station had two cramped rooms that were bleaker than a bus station, with dirty green walls and metal desks in shades of brown and army green. A gritty layer of dust covered every surface. A plastic window—maybe it was bulletproof, but certainly not scratch-proof—separated the dispatch area from the outside entrance, with its waiting space of exactly three feet by four. No pictures adorned the walls, no reading material was at hand. The two windows had drawn shades.

A back door slammed, and from a dark hallway that passed the jail came the short detective. In contrast with Morris, his sport jacket fit well, and the knot to his tie was snug.

"Sorry I'm late," he said crisply. "A vagrant was helping himself to food from the Sindoyas' kitchen while the family was out black-cod fishing. Turns out they might give him a job. Morris fill you in?"

"I was waiting for you, Charlie," Morris said, lumbering over from his desk. "You put the papers in your desk."

"That's right, that's right." Charlie deftly unlocked the bottom drawer. He pulled out what looked like a plastic bag with crumpled papers from the garbage and placed it on the desk. "Have you noticed anything of value missing from the house since we were last over?" he questioned.

Francesca and Jane shook their heads.

"That's unusual. Too unusual to be a fluke. The guy was not an ordinary vandal. He came in the front door—which was unlocked—stopped in the kitchen for a snack, and then passed valuables in the living room. He heard you enter, but didn't take off through the door to the outside that's in your room when he had the chance. Instead, he waited and attacked you. He targeted your room, Jane McBride, and for the most part, material relating to your work—the books, the computer equipment." He opened the bag and handed some papers to Jane.

"Maybe he was interrupted before he could get to the rest of the house," Francesca interjected.

"Possible." Charlie nodded. He turned to Jane. "You recognize these?"

"My spreadsheets," she said. "For an article I was writing...."

"You can pull them out," he said. "We dusted for prints, but the paper's too crummy for that. And, sorry to say, the case isn't big enough to send them to the state crime lab."

Jane nodded, but she wondered if the case would have been big enough had she been raped. "Where did you find these?"

"No place that can be tied to anyone—a trash can downtown."

"Any computer disks? I'm missing at least twelve."

"Afraid not."

Charlie read from the scraps that were left. "Land type A, land type B, land type C.... What's this all about?"

"It's a work sheet for an article I'm ... was writing. I developed a forecasting tool for real estate prices. You plug variables into the work sheet—the price of land, zoning and use, acreage, projected inflation, and interest rates, anything you want, really. With the touch of a button, you can project revenues from the property, five, ten, twenty years from the start of development.'

"You lost me," Charlie said. But Morris leaned over Charlie's shoulder, and Jane could tell by the way his eyes moved back and forth over the numbers and column listings that he knew something about computers and was interested. Francesca stood and leaned over the desk to examine the document more closely, too.

"The theory behind the formula is that real estate holdings—whether those in a community or those held by a company—are interrelated. What happens to parcel A affects parcel B as interest rates and inflation and other factors change and intermingle over the years. The work sheet is a huge decision tree, and minor adjustments—a percentage point in an interest rate or a couple of acres—can make a tremendous difference. Complicated decision trees always present a lot of surprises. They allow the user to test out the potential of different properties with more than thirty variables over a twenty-year period. A human with a calculator could over days perform the calculations of one scenario. This program offers dozens of scenarios instantly, with the touch of a few buttons.''

"Hmmm," Charlie grunted. "It doesn't look all that complicated.'

"These printouts show the end results. Behind each number on that paper is a lengthy calculation. In essence, you're only seeing the answers.''

"Are these red marks yours?" Morris interrupted.

Jane shook her head.

"Someone was interested in this stuff," Morris pondered. "This all the pages to the document?"

"No," Jane said, remembering how she had them arranged on the floor. "There were seventy pages in all.''

"Why the hell would anyone want this crap?" Charlie said, staring at Jane.

"I don't know," Jane said. "The actual computer disk with the forecasting tool is somewhat valuable. A company in Boston is developing some software based on the tool for real estate developers and, eventually, for specialized industries. We've copyrighted it and expect to sell programs for at least ten thousand dollars each. But this printout is worthless.''

"Is that disk missing?" Morris questioned.

Jane laughed. "No. The person who robbed the apartment didn't know much about computers. He destroyed the monitor, the least important part of the setup. And his efforts to destroy my software were a waste. First, any person who depends on a computer always stores a copy of crucial software and data disks in two different locations. I placed copies of all my important material in a safe-deposit box the day after I moved here. Second, he forgot to look inside the disk drive—I was in the middle of working on the article, and the disk with the forecasting tool was still inside.'

"Are these calculations about properties in Sitka?" Morris interjected.

"No, these are numbers for a fictional company, simply to illustrate the features of the forecasting tool for the article. It's just one set of answers for one scenario."

"Could someone mistake them for numbers applying to Sitka?"

Jane looked at her work sheet. "I suppose. For this calculation, I used some exaggerated variables to make the article a bit more humorous...."

Charlie raised his eyebrows.

"Sitka is full of exaggerations," Francesca murmured.

Jane looked at the work sheet again. "Yes, I don't see why not. There are no labels on the work sheet to indicate otherwise."

Morris had taken the lead with the questioning, and now he shut his eyes. The other three remained quiet, giving him time to think before another question. But he opened his eyes and looked at his partner.

"That's all I have for now. Charlie?"

"All right. Francesca, we're almost through here. I just want to ask Jane a few questions about the attacker. You don't have to stick around."

"Jane, you don't mind if I stay, do you?" Francesca asked.

"Of course not," Jane replied. "Please."

Francesca looked back at Charlie. Her face showed no expression, but there was an almost triumphant glow in her eyes.

He sighed. "All right. You mentioned during our first interview that the guy didn't say a word to you, that correct?"

"Yes," Jane said.

"Did that seem unusual?"

"I didn't think much of it, it happened so fast," Jane said. She knew she must look guilty of withholding information. She could not stop thinking of the odd phone call her first night at Francesca's home. She kept waiting for Bojack to telephone Francesca, so that she could hear his voice. But he never called, at least not when Jane was around to pick up the telephone. Now she couldn't bring up the call. Francesca would be hurt that she had never mentioned it. "I suppose so."

"Okay. I have a random photo lineup that I want you to look over, Jane. See if you recognize any of them as the guy who grabbed you. Come this way, please."

Jane and Francesca followed him to a table in the corner of the room. A line of eight photos were in place. All were mug shots of men who were less than thirty. All had long dark hair. Jane was sure most were Native. She took a long look at each. She tried to focus on the eyes in each photograph. She looked again. None of the faces were familiar.

She shook her head finally. "I'm sorry. I don't know. he wore a ski mask, and I can't be sure...."

"God damn you, Charlie Dansby," Francesca hissed.

Jane was startled by her vehemence.

"It's random, Francesca," Charlie said with a growl. "We have a job to do here."

"Are you through with us?"

"For now, yes."

Francesca whirled and strode out of the station. Charlie and Morris stared at her, their jaws set, as if she were an adversary.

Jane paused, shrugged. "Thank you," she added feebly. "Please let us know if you find anything else." She hurried after Francesca, following her to the pickup in the parking lot.

"What's the matter?" Jane asked after she had climbed in and slammed the door.

Francesca leaned her head on the steering wheel. "Why couldn't you say it wasn't any of them? Why couldn't you?" She was on the verge of tears.

"Because I couldn't!" Jane insisted. "All I saw was the guy's eyes. I might have an idea of his height, if I stood right next to him again. That's it. What else could I say?"

Francesca pushed her hair back nervously, and she looked out the windshield, toward the mountaintops that loomed over the grungy police station with its coat of paint over the stucco peeling away in the rain.

"Nothing, I guess." She sighed. "The third photo from the left. They stuck in an old photo of Bojack. My son."

SEVENTEEN

CLASSES AT HBC started in ten days, and Jane would teach two—Introduction to Microeconomics on Monday and Wednesday afternoons and State and Local Finance on Tuesday and Thursday mornings. The courses would be easy; the college had standard textbooks and guidelines, and she was prepared. Still, she spent three days in the college library sifting through old newspapers, finding articles about Native corporations and rural Alaskan towns, extracting cases and examples that relied on the most elementary principles in finance and economics.

She went to the registrar's office to make final arrangements about the classes. While waiting to pick up supplies she had ordered, she flipped idly through the pages of an HBC class catalog.

Maybe she should take a class herself. Teaching would not be nearly enough to satisfy her need to remain busy. The selection was not great; the only options of any interest to her were courses in fisheries, natural resources, and art. Jane scanned the descriptions, and AR-248 caught her eye: "Seminar in Traditional Alaska Native Art—Study traditional art forms, including wood and ivory carving, beadwork, painting, and weaving. Students work on individual or group projects under the guidance of instructor and guest lecturers. Prerequisite: Instructor approval, following interview."

Neither the instructor's name nor the room was listed. Jane asked the clerk at the desk about the art department.

The woman gave Jane directions to the Gavin Building— "Stay to the right, and go all the way back, through the trees." She finished sorting through forms accompanying

Jane's supplies and added: "Sign up early. Registration, with all the students, is a madhouse."

Jane did not mind the unexpected walk into the forest at the far end of the Holmes Barrett campus. After three days of driving winter rain the path was not muddy. Instead it was packed clean with layers of hemlock, spruce, and cedar needles, washed again and again by the rain to a soft lumpiness, like an old carpet. Overhead, dark branches whispered and swayed against a pearl-gray sky.

Jane marveled how she enjoyed the search for the art department. One of the comforts of a small town was that a person could never get too lost. In Boston she would not have bothered investigating a course in which she was only remotely interested.

Gavin was a cedar-slatted building hidden among the trees. No other building was in sight. Jane went inside, but there was no office for making inquiries. The hallway of the first floor was quiet and dark—all the doors were unlabeled. She tapped lightly on one and tried the handle. It was locked. She thought she heard voices and stood still. Nothing.

At the other end of the hall was a staircase. Pebbles were stuck between the treads of her boots and scraped loudly as she walked upstairs.

The second floor was dark, too, but at the end of the hall was a set of double doors, partially open.

Jane walked quietly down the hall and peeked inside. The room was as wide as the building and had two walls of tall thin windows. Lining the wall facing the door were three shelves of masks, totem, and animal carvings—more than two dozen unfinished faces glared, smiled, laughed, and cried at her. She opened the door a bit to see more. Scattered throughout the room were unfinished boxes, sketches, stretched leather, and regalia, as well as older artifacts that appeared to have been dissected. A massive workbench, covered with scars, dominated the room. Huddled at the far end of the workbench were four women, each with various lengths of black hair. All sewed diligently. On the center of the table was a shabby beaded pouch. Unfinished gleaming replicas of the pouch were clutched tightly in the hands of each woman. One woman murmured something as she reached for the pouch and studied a section before returning it to the table and resuming her stitches. The motion of the four needles was fast and constant. The women stabbed their needles through the holes of two or three glass beads at a time and then stitched. Stab and stitch. Stab and stitch.

The art studio reminded her of an economics final. No bantering, no variety in the student work, no obvious pleasure. Jane decided to forget the art course. She started to turn away but hit her foot against the door. The four women stopped sewing and looked up at her.

"Hi, I was trying to find someone who could give me more information about a course," Jane said. "AR-248."

The women looked at one another. But not one spoke.

"The seminar in traditional Alaska Native art? Can you tell me who teaches it?" Jane felt foolish. The women still did not speak. They looked at her as if she were green and from Mars. Then the woman with the longest hair smiled like a happy little girl. The smile was strange coming from a person who had to be at least twenty-five.

"Hiiii," she said, drawing the word out with pleasure. When she raised her face the track lighting on the ceiling highlighted a few pockmarks along her high cheekbones. She was almost pretty, except that her head was small for all the long hair, and her face was misshapen, like a clay statue that had been distorted or flattened before going into the kiln. Her eyes were small and kind but with a distant look.

"Hello," Jane said, her voice getting higher in pitch with her nervousness. She looked at the other three for their reaction, but their eyes were downcast and their faces blank, as if they did not speak the same language. Were these students? Would any of them be in her classes at the business department?

A door slammed, and a man came down the hall toward the classroom. He was wiry, not much taller than Jane. All his movements, especially those of his eyes, were fast, and he caught her off guard.

"Yes?" he said briskly. The women returned their gazes to the beaded patches in their hands, stabbing beads and stitching them into place.

"I wanted information about one of the art courses," Jane asked awkwardly. She was no longer eager to study art. "The seminar on traditional Native art."

He stared at her. "Please follow me. These...students are at work right now." His voice was clear, each word enunciated sharply with disdain.

"I didn't realize," Jane said, hurrying to follow him. "I thought classes didn't start until February."

"Makeup work from last semester." He stopped abruptly in the hallway, and Jane almost stepped on his foot. "New in town, aren't you?"

"Not very," Jane said, defensive and annoyed at his cockiness. "I thought I might enjoy a course. Who is the instructor, please?"

"Daniel Greer, the curator of HBC's museum. I wish I could accommodate you, but AR-248 is the art department's most popular course. Limited space means we have to turn away full-time students, let alone people from town. I assume you're not a full-time student."

Jane shook her head.

"We wish we could help you. I apologize."

"Don't," Jane said, regaining her composure. "The students must come first, and I understand that. Thank you."

He nodded and walked away briskly, leaving the impression that she had interrupted important business.

As Jane went down the hallway, she could not help but feel that she was walking away from trouble that she had caused. She leaned against the rail and shook her head. That notion was ridiculous, a feeling left over from Boston. When she reached the stairs, she glanced back at the workroom. The young man had returned and was watching her. He had been so brusque that she'd forgotten to ask his name. Not now, she decided, running downstairs.

She shoved the heavy door to the outside and paused. From upstairs came the slam of a set of doors, followed by a tremendous clatter, maybe the sound of breaking glass. She thought she heard a shout. Then all was quiet, except for the constant chatter of the red squirrels and the croak of a lone raven.

EIGHTEEN

JANE'S WEDNESDAY CLASS ended at three. She detested the afternoon class more than the students did. They looked as bored as people waiting in line at the bank.

"Opportunity costs—in a market with constraints, the costs of resources do not have to be measured by money alone. Instead, the costs can be measured in terms of the value of alternative uses," Jane explained to the class, trying to keep the frustration out of her voice. "An example would be the student who chooses to party and dance the night away rather than study for the next day's final exam. That decision carries opportunity costs."

Some students laughed and rolled their eyes. Others kept their faces blank. Jane asked for other examples. The class had ten more minutes, and the room was steamy. Not one student raised a hand. They never did.

"All right, you win," she said. "Let's call it quits. But for Monday, please read chapters four and five, and also, please write at least one page on an example of some opportunity costs that you have read about or experienced. Include a brief analysis of how you might compare the opportunity costs of action versus inaction."

Jane would be grateful if half the class complied. The students filed from the room silently. Not one ever stayed after class to talk or ask questions. She was just as glad. She was tired of pretending to be a professor. She was lousy at it and felt for her students.

Microeconomics could be as much fun as solving a puzzle or sorting out clues in an old-fashioned mystery. But only if one understood the simple math behind the concepts. Jane managed to avoid introducing production functions, diminishing returns, marginal analysis, and other difficult concepts during the last half of the class. Still, students walked out of the class when she failed to accompany concepts with entertaining examples. She offered a tutoring session for students desiring more intensive math workups of various problems. No one came.

Jane erased the boards, gathered her belongings, and walked down to the boat harbor, not far from the college campus, and along the dock toward town. After four days of rain, the evening sky was thick with clouds but rainless. The boats were black silhouettes against the winter sky. A yellow streak stained the twilight. She kicked a twig off the dock. Was it a mistake to teach in order to stay in Sitka? Did people have to make mistake after mistake before they fit comfortably into a town, into a family, and into a job? Did she really have any other choice?

Her life was pretty here but useless, she decided. During the last few weeks she had been alone a lot, with more than enough time to think and plan. But she had no idea what to do next. Opportunity costs. Her life was full of them. Living in rural Alaska left her out of the mainstream and gave the impression that she was flighty and not serious about her career. Spending time with Bob could destroy any chance of getting to know Daniel. Walking away from tragedy in Boston meant that she had to resolve the pain inside her alone.

She loved Sitka, but she had no stakes. She had never felt close to the land itself before—not simply the natural beauty, but how the beauty shaped the spirit and independence of the people she met. In Boston her ties came from a meaningful career, community service, or raising a family. Pretending that the rest of her life had never happened was getting too damn hard. She couldn't get close to anyone.

Jane felt lost. She sat down on a bench at the end of the dock. A tear fell and then another. The water lapped and gently pushed the boats, barely straining the ropes that kept them tied in place. No one was around to notice as the sky turned dark and the yellow light disappeared.

A familiar noise came from the grass that separated the street from the water. Jane stiffened and turned. The street and sidewalk were empty as far as she could see. Of Sitka's four harbors, Crescent Harbor sheltered more sport boats than fishing vessels and was relatively deserted in the winter. Jane listened but heard only the occasional tap and creaking of the boats. She was sure she had imagined the cooing babble. Darkness cast its spell on the harbor. The coming night gave intense new meaning to the most mundane noises. She shook her head, then stood to leave—and caught her breath at the sight of the figure approaching the harbor: a lone toddler bundled in a blue snowsuit.

"No," Jane whispered. Why was a toddler wandering near the docks at this time of day? She glanced up and down the street. A car drove by.

"Mama, Mama..." The child started to cry. "Mama..." He looked at Jane on the dock and started to run toward the water and her, the legs working hard against the constraints of the snowsuit—his arms up and reaching out.

Jane scanned the docks. No one else was in sight—the child recognized her silhouette as a woman and hoped she was his mother.

"No!" Jane screamed and tried to put some sternness into her voice. "No. Stop there! Now."

"Mama?"

"No, I am *not* your mother," Jane admonished, her voice choking. She swore to herself. The nearest ramp to shore was fifty feet down the dock. If she tried to run down there, the child would probably fall into the water trying to chase her. She studied the shoreline. The dock was no more than twenty feet from shore, and an assortment of skiffs, most covered, were lined up in the shallow water in between. She might just be able to jump to shore from the longest skiff without getting her feet wet.

"Wait there, good baby," Jane said sweetly as she stepped onto a nearby long white boat. It bobbed back and forth, and she easily caught the sides and stepped to the end nearest the shore. A few inches of water had collected at the bottom, and her pumps got wet.

"Mama, candy?" the little boy said as he tired of waiting and moved closer to Jane and the water.

The five or so feet to shore looked as though it might as well have been twenty feet. Jane would never make it without getting her feet wet. She slipped off her pumps and tossed them to shore. The toddler bent to examine one and landed hard on his bottom.

Jane held her breath and jumped, landing with a splash in water about eight inches deep. "Owww!" she hollered as she ran splashing the last few steps to shore. Instant numbness overcame her feet, and she almost fell to the ground. She tucked one leg up into her skirt and then another, while the toddler watched in delight.

"I can't stand it," Jane panted. "The water's freezing!"

"Cold," the baby said as he crawled to her. "Mama."

Jane shuddered. "But I'm not your mother," she said, stooping down, trying to let her wool skirt cover and warm her feet like a tent. "Come here, little sweetheart. Whatever are you doing here alone? Do you know your name?"

"Hom-hom," he replied promptly.

"Well, come here, Hom-hom," she said. She was sure it was a boy, almost two. She wrapped her arms around him and the bulky suit. He hugged her back, closed his big brown eyes, and nestled his small face into her shoulder.

"We can't stay here," Jane said matter-of-factly as she hefted the baby up. She kicked around for her shoes. It felt as though she were jamming wet boards into the once pliant plum suede. "What will I do with you? Should we look for your mother, or should I take you to the police station?"

She walked to the street. She was not used to carrying thirty pounds of child and snowsuit. The toddler tightened his arms about her neck, but she didn't complain.

A woman darted out from behind the harbormaster's shed, about twenty yards away. "What are you doing with my kid?" she shouted sharply. She strode over to Jane and pulled the child away. Her hair was bleached, her skin was red and rough, and she smelled of stale beer. Jane realized with shock that she was a teenager.

"What am I doing?" she said. She could not believe the young woman's audacity. "What am *I* doing! He almost fell into the water! Where have *you* been?"

The woman ignored the question and spoke to the baby. "See this woman, Thomas? She's a stranger! Bad Thomas. Bad boy! You must not talk to strangers." She gave Jane a thin-lipped smile, raised her hand, and slapped the baby hard. Thomas began to wail.

"My God!" Jane said, reaching for the woman's arm. "Don't hit him for something he's too little to understand!"

The woman shifted whimpering Thomas to her right arm, dangling him like a sack of potatoes. She was short and tough and showed no fear as she looked Jane up and down.

"It's never too early to learn to avoid people like you. Social workers! What do you know about being a mother? What do you know about kids?" she said with contempt. "Tell me what it's like when you have one of your own." The woman laughed and walked away, leaving Jane shivering and alone in the dark.

Ten minutes later a black pickup pulled into the harbor parking lot. Jane did not see the woman talk to the man at the driver's side window for a few minutes. He handed over twenty-five dollars with a laugh and then drove away.

NINETEEN

JANE WALKED to town. Her stockings squished with every step, and her feet were so numb she had to concentrate on when exactly they touched down on the pavement. She couldn't afford to sprain an ankle. She kept her pace slow and even.

Her cheeks burned as if she had been the one whose face had been slapped. Her shoulders shook, but not from the cold. The hateful girl had spoken as if she knew about Jane. But that was impossible.

The woman was simply bitter, and youth and bitterness did not mix well. Jane ached for little Thomas. His mother's haste to escape her own childhood left her little empathy for the baby.

Jane wanted to kick herself for confronting the woman, accusing her of not watching the child. The woman was angry—she couldn't hit Jane, but she could hit Thomas.

She paused outside the *Record* office and, through the window, watched the staff hard at work, stuffing advertisements into the thin papers. She pushed the door open, and the overheated office had all the sounds of a rowdy family.

"I was hoping your class would go a little late," Bob yelled over the sound of the roaring press.

"Are you kidding?" Jane asked. "Want some help?" She tossed her coat onto a chair and pushed up her sleeves, relieved she didn't have to talk about Thomas and his mother.

"You can have my place," Bob said, making room for her. "You do the stuffing and then count out the newspapers into stacks of twenty-five."

Lindsey, with red cheeks and her hair in wisps, came around the corner, lugging what had to be more than two hundred newspapers. "Why, you dear thing. We wouldn't dream...," she stammered politely.

"Come on, Lindsey, she'll feel funny standing around watching us all work," Bob argued, heading upstairs to the newsroom.

"Really, what that boy will do to get out of stuffing newspapers," said another woman. She was plump and attractive, with thick blond hair. "Hi, I'm Gail."

"Don't feel like you must do this, dear," Lindsey said as she bustled away.

People came into the lobby to purchase the newspapers. They put their change down on the counter, smiled at the staff, and unfolded the paper to scan the headlines before leaving.

No one noticed her wet feet, and Jane enjoyed the banality of the task, the race against the roar of the press. It was like taking a shovel to dirt. One's output was measured constantly. To anyone who came through the door she was another part of the usual scene at the *Record*. In less than twenty minutes more than 2,500 newspapers were stuffed and ready to hit the streets.

Bob entered as she finished her stack.

"Done," Jane said, imitating surrender by holding up her grimy hands.

It took six minutes of rubbing and strong soap to get her hands clean.

"Can I use a phone?" Jane asked. "There's a call I'd like to make...."

"Fair compensation, I'd say." Bob pointed to a desk.

Jane looked up the telephone number for child welfare and spoke with a social worker on duty. The woman asked for the name of Thomas's mother and then explained that she could not help.

"How many bleached-blond teenage mothers of boys named Thomas can there be in Sitka?" Jane queried.

The woman was silent for a moment. "I'm sorry," she said. "I wish we could help. If we had a name or an address..."

Jane swore to herself. She should have followed the woman, she thought.

"Keep an eye out for her," the social worker advised. "If you see her, give us a call. And don't fret. We can't intervene unless the child is injured or there's a pattern of abuse or neglect going on. And if that's the case, she's going to get caught."

Jane thanked the woman, hung up, and joined Bob.

"Drinks or dinner?" Bob asked. "Your choice."

"Whatever is closest," Jane said. Her feet were still damp.

"The Sheffield it is, then." Bob was seven years younger than she, but he helped her with her coat. It was like a younger brother pretending to be grown up. He was immature but sincere. He would never have been her friend in Boston, but she could talk to him about almost anything.

They sat at the Sheffield bar for more than two hours, time enough for Jane's feet to dry. Michael Benoit stopped by to say hello. Bob invited him to have a seat. Jane could not help but be annoyed. Why did they never run into Daniel? Or Francesca's son, for that matter? She had been in town for almost two months, and she had yet to meet Bojack or hear his voice.

The group went up the street to have dinner at a legitimate Chinese restaurant, where the food was spicy and amazingly authentic.

"This place has been a survivor," said Bob. "There are only six to ten restaurants operating in Sitka at any one time. When a new one opens people flock to it, and the owners think they've got it made. Then the newness wears off, people forget about the place, and before you know it, one night you walk by and your favorite restaurant has bit the dust."

Bob commented more than once that Jane was unusually quiet. After dinner and listening to a local group play music in a café, she telephoned the TV station. Francesca said she was ready to leave. She had left her pickup truck at a parking lot not far away.

"I can ask Bob to pick you up, and he'll give us a lift to the pickup," Jane offered.

"Let's walk," Francesca replied. "It's not raining, and I'll meet you on the way over."

The night was clear. Jane looked up and, despite the glare of a nearby streetlight, saw some stars. A few clouds had tucked themselves around Verstovia, Gavin, and Harbor Mountains like the wings of a bird who had gone to sleep for the night.

Francesca was waiting at the corner of Lincoln and Lake Streets, and the town was quiet as they left the shopping district.

"Do you ever see much of Ellsley?" Francesca asked.

"Never," Jane said. "So far, though, people at the college speak highly of him."

"Hmm. I should be more objective when it comes to him. He has brought that college out of bankruptcy. He made HBC a pleasant haven for students. He hired my son."

"Your son works at HBC?" Jane said in surprise.

"Yes, in the art department. Bojack's fortunate to have a paying job in the field."

Jane nodded. She wondered how many times she might have passed him on campus. She remembered the abrupt young man in the art building.

"Without a doubt, Ellsley had a constituency among younger Natives," Jane said.

Francesca grimaced and walked faster. "But not among the older people. They can't forget his mother."

"Why would Ellsley want to be listed as a Native?"

"I wish I knew. He apparently believes the Native corporations could wield a lot of power in Alaska.... God knows the potential is there, but he's not the person to trigger it. Anyway, he'll never really become part of the tribe. People are especially harsh about admitting new tribal members because no provisions were made to issue shares to any Native born after 1971. Those children are becoming adults, and they're resentful.

"But now I suspect he's behind a movement to force a vote on easing some of the rules, splitting the stock, and issuing new shares. There's a lot of support because it would be a way to get some shares into the hands of the people born after 1971. But there's also a clause that would change the way people are accepted into the tribe. People could be enrolled after collecting one hundred signatures of tribal members. Ellsley has that many shareholders on his payroll. He—or anyone else who has many Native people dependent for work—would have no problem at all. He also wouldn't mind seeing shareholders in the Native corporations being allowed to sell their stock. That's been a bitter fight. Who can blame people for wanting to get whatever they can for the stock now—and manage that money their own way? But most people fear that selling would be like giving our land away before we understood its potential. It took years for choices to be approved, and Katmai still does not have its entire land allotment. All that makes development like a ski resort inevitable."

"Does the corporation have any other plans for using the land?" Jane asked.

Francesca shook her head slowly. "Oh, there's talk about making deals with out-of-state firms for mining exploration. A few thousand acres are clear-cut every year for the immediate cash. Meanwhile, Ellsley is in constant contact with outsiders, soliciting funds for scholarships and suggesting joint ventures. Sitka's waste incinerator served as a pilot project for a German firm, and there's a Norwegian company that was able to begin an aquaculture research program—fish farming, mass production of tasteless, pintsize salmon that would drive down the price of troll-caught wild king salmon. You can imagine how local fishermen feel about that. But the college makes the perfect entry point for any corporation hoping to do any kind of business in Southeast Alaska. And more shareholders grumble about why Katmai doesn't hop on a gravy train like a ski resort. The guise of academia lends credence to the most ludicrous of ideas.''

"It wouldn't surprise me if corporations all over the world have an eye on the land held by Native corporations,'' said Jane. "Such huge tracts of private land are rare.''

"Exactly,'' Francesca agreed. "And ownership by Native people is a plus.''

"Why's that?'' Jane asked.

Francesca shook her head. "Sometimes I'm not so sure. I like to think I'm a link between the elders who remember discrimination and cruelty and the children who want progress. My term on the board of directors is up in May. I'm not against using the land, like Ellsley and some others would contend, but I want people to think in the long term. Meanwhile, opponents for my seat on the board label me as selfish for my efforts to keep cash in Katmai's reserve fund, rather than approving big dividends. In the big popularity contest that's going to count against me.

"I'm not thrilled with the corporations—the whole messy system set up by the government for distributing the settlement funds. But the corporations exist. Besides the heritage, it's all we as tribes have at this point. If the corporations are weakened, everything is lost.''

"Surely some people must agree that the land could offer substantial long-term benefits,'' said Jane.

"Some do,'' Francesca said. "It's anybody's guess whether there are enough people who will vote that way in an election, though. It all comes down to what people think about the resort. I wanted to get off the board after this term. But some of the elders begged me to run. They're afraid the land will get sold, that control will disappear. They pleaded with me to speak up against huge shareholder dividends and risky investments like a ski resort that could mean eventual bankruptcy and a forced sell-off of the land.''

Jane was silent for a moment. Had Francesca tricked her into coming to Sitka, as Bob suggested? Was her kindness, allowing Jane to stay in her home, a ploy? The silence was uncomfortable. The pause demanded that Jane offer some sort of assistance. But she couldn't. Not yet.

"Francesca, what happened with the job? When I interviewed with Cameron Reynold, he was eager for a financial analyst. What happened?"

Francesca stopped and looked at Jane. They were alone on the dark street. "I convinced him that we needed an analyst. I chair the personnel committee, and I've always handled new positions that way. Before I knew it, the board called a special meeting. A motion was passed—no more employees would be hired until after the May elections. Cameron had no choice but to back out of the commitment with you. He could be looking for work any day himself."

"And my check for seventy-five thousand?"

"Damage control." Francesca shrugged. "It was a compromise between the factions. It saved Cameron and me some embarrassment, and the others were sure you would be on the first ferry out of town."

The story was no different from Cameron's, and it sounded reasonable now that Jane had spent a few weeks in Sitka.

"Well, I don't mind doing some work for the money. Do you have any data on the landholdings of the corporation?" Jane asked. "Acreage? Prices? Potential assets?"

Francesca nodded. "I have some of that at home. Jane, would that computer program on real estate prices—the one you spoke about at the police department—would it work for Katmai?"

"We could try it out. I'd have to dig up some information on ski resorts. That's a phone call away. But, Francesca, you have to remember, the forecasting tool can't predict the future. It can only present scenarios on how the value of the Katmai property holdings might change, depending on a wide range of variables. Some Katmai has control over, like the use of land, and others like interest rates are beyond Katmai's control. The computer performs the calculations. Humans, you and I, must choose which variables are appropriate, depending on alternative land use, and develop three or four likely scenarios."

"If I only knew the alternatives. Who knows what someone like Ellsley and his cronies at Katmai have up their sleeves? It's what I had hoped you could provide, if you were finance director. But..." Her voice drifted sadly. She continued walking. "Maybe I'm wrong. Maybe I'm just resentful. But that's not what I feel in my heart."

"No, I have the same feeling, and that's why I'll do what I can to help you." Jane paused and then probed, "What does Bojack think about Ellsley?"

Francesca did not answer right away. "Confused. He's not happy with how Native affairs have been handled by people like me. Who can blame him? Over the years he has watched friends drink more and grow morose. Many dropped out of school and at best found mediocre jobs, so they qualify for unemployment every two years or so. Some of his childhood friends went to jail for petty theft and disturbances and intoxication. A couple died from drug overdoses and accidents. Bojack and his friends watch as young doctors, lawyers, engineers, and teachers move to town, into positions of influence. And the people who have lived here all their lives have no influence at all. They grow old and lose hope. Losing hope for yourself is not nearly so awful as losing hope for your child.... That's when something dies inside.

"My childhood was no different. But I have held a position of power during the past eight years, and I can't say I've changed much. I wasted a lot of time on petty matters, and I could have done more. He knows that."

"That kind of change takes years to see," Jane said softly, tightening her fingernails into her palms. "People sometimes do more than they realize, and you know that you have done more for Bojack than he's aware of.''

After a few moments Jane asked, ''You don't see much of him. Have I made it more difficult?''

Francesca stopped again under a streetlight. Her eyes were wet, and she touched Jane's arms. ''No,'' she said intently. ''No. We had problems long before you came. I want you to stay with me. Not because of the stupid elections or for the corporation. I want you to know how much it has helped me, the fact that you're staying with me. It had gotten to the point where I hated living alone. I should have said this before, but I have as much to thank you for as you do me.''

They stood there like that for a minute. Jane searched Francesca's eyes and knew the message came from the heart.

Francesca dropped her arms, and they started to walk again.

''I was livid when Bojack got the job at HBC. I was sure Ellsley did it to infuriate me and turn Bojack against me. Before you came, I caught myself hinting to Bojack that he return home to live, and that would not have been good for either of us—but it would have been crazy to think I could have stopped the drugs, the other problems I probably don't even know about. He does not need a mother looking out for him. It's something a mother never gets over, though. I still want to hold him in my arms and shield him from the world. Nothing has ever been so hard for me as letting that boy have his independence and coming to terms with the fact that he is a man who understands consequences. It's sad, we more or less had to disown each another to separate. He made mistakes, got into trouble. It was an attempt on his part to make me stop caring. I threw myself into work at the station and the corporation for the same reason. Bojack and I have known our share of love and anger. No in between for us.''

Jane took a deep breath, full of regret that she would never have the chance to get to know her child as an adult.

The two women approached the shortcut through the HBC campus.

"We have talked a lot by telephone the last few weeks," Francesca continued. "Maybe I'll invite him over this week, so you can meet him. You know, I don't feel like going home yet. Let's go to the park over there..." She pointed to a tiny playground where Lincoln Street dead-ended. Inside the fenced play yard, a metal pony, frog, and elephant had empty eyes.

"I love to swing," Francesca said, laughing and starting to head that way. "Especially late at night when no one is around to see how silly a middle-aged woman can be."

Jane froze. "No," she said, her voice shaking. "I can't."

Francesca turned and stared. The look on her face was vulnerable and self-conscious, like a child reminded by a parent that she was too old to enjoy playing with dolls or making a mud pie. The two women had become so close, with a friendship as easy and spontaneous as that of two children, with impulses and emotions rarely felt by adults. Francesca wanted to celebrate the forging of a friendship with a swing in the nighttime air. She didn't want the magic of the night to end.

Jane had to give some reason, and she felt short of breath. Her insides felt cold and slick, like the metal slide waiting in the park. "It's late," she said feebly. "I can't. Please understand." Without waiting, she headed for the shortcut through the HBC campus.

The conversation lagged as they trudged up the hill. The night was moonless and quiet. Jane looked at her watch. Almost midnight. They fell into step again, and Jane was grateful that Francesca did not ask questions.

The quiescence of the night ended abruptly as Francesca and Jane left the campus. A woman cried out; shouting profanity, and the sound of breaking glass followed. The two women stopped and looked at each other.

"That's Conway, one of the girls' dormitories," whispered Francesca. Sirens and flashing police lights came down the street.

"Let's get out of here," Jane said nervously. The sounds of police at work during the night brought on memories of helplessness.

"No, wait," Francesca said.

Two officers dragged a struggling young man from the building. The man swung wildly at the tallest officer. The other officer threatened but held off from hitting the man with his club. A woman with unruly hair and bare feet ran out of the building, crying.

"Leave him alone, please!" she screamed. "He's my brother! He came all the way from Hoonah. Why can't you leave us alone?"

Lights flickered on throughout the dormitory, and a few faces peered out from behind the curtains. Both officers were white, the other two were Natives.

The man kicked and fought the officers. Blood dripped down the side of his face from a gash above his eyebrow. One of the officers slapped his face. That subdued the man. The officers supported him on either side and led him to the car. The woman dropped to her knees and buried her head in her hands to cry. Another woman opened the door and tried to pull her inside.

"He was staying for a few days.... There was no trouble...," the woman cried as she was led back inside.

Jane walked away, and Francesca caught up with her.

"Tomorrow's police story," Jane said lightly.

"For the newspaper, maybe," Francesca said. "I don't have time for every fracas in town." The testiness in her voice was pronounced.

Francesca quickened her pace to unlock both doors of the pickup, and Jane thought she saw the sparkle of a tear on the woman's cheek. But when Jane slid inside, any sign of tears was gone. The night was over, and they drove home in silence.

TWENTY

JANE GOT HOME in time to watch Francesca's news program. Francesca's sweater was blood red, vivid against her flawless skin, black hair, and dark eyes. She seldom looked at her notes. She told the news as if it were a story, and her voice was musical, warm, and deep like a low, soft song played on a piano. Her gaze was as direct as if she were in the living room, discussing a decision that would affect everyone there the rest of his and her life. That's what bugged Bob about her.

"She's too damn serious," he said. "Can't she lighten up? She's a good writer and has a great tone. But she overuses it, and it loses all relativity. A Fourth of July fish fry sounds like murder, and a fire that kills a family of six sounds like a Pioneer Home concert."

Still, Jane thought the station was lucky to have an anchorwoman as eye-catching and talented as Francesca. The station had only one cameraman, and film clips were spotty during the half-hour newscast.

Jane read quickly through the paper while the news was on. Almost all of Francesca's news was there, but Bob's stories were terse, pointed, with more numbers and detail. Jane glanced through the *Record*'s Police Blotter, unusually long for a weekday. Then she tossed the newspaper aside to make dinner.

If she had no other meetings, Francesca typically arrived home about fifteen minutes after the end of the newscast. Jane started making salad to go with some crab that had been given to Francesca by her son. Bojack consistently borrowed his mother's skiff at least twice a week. With a subsistence permit from the state, he could leave two traps in the water and pull fresh Dungeness crab from the ocean bottom every couple of days.

Francesca boiled the crabs in a huge pot and then packed the crabmeat into plastic containers. Jane considered the white crabmeat to be pure luxury.

Vegetables, and not the crab, were a delicacy for Francesca. For her the sweet Dungeness was just another staple from the sea, available almost every day, a side dish for salad. Francesca craved vegetables every night and told Jane about the winters before the oil boom, before the Native corporations, when the ferries did not run so frequently and vegetables were rare.

"When I was a child," she had said once, "A plate of fresh green peas was a treat. I remember staring at the lettuce in the stores. More often than not it was wilted and brown around the edges, and my mother refused to pay for it."

Jane was slicing avocado to arrange over the top of the salad when Francesca opened the door.

"I am glad that newscast is over," she groaned. "It should not be so hard to find thirty minutes worth of news in this town."

"It sounded fine," Jane said, smiling. For all the rancor and competition between Bob and Francesca, they voiced the same complaints and zeal for their jobs. If only they could know each other better, they might come to understand that the difference in their styles was a benefit for the town and not a deficiency in one or the other's reporting skills.

"...not much here, how about it?" Francesca asked, standing by the open refrigerator.

"I'm sorry, what did you ask?" Jane said quickly. "I was daydreaming."

"What do you want to drink with dinner?"

"Ice water is fine. Francesca, you didn't go to Holmes Barrett, did you?"

"No, I went to the University of Oregon. Five of us went together. Safety in numbers, we thought. Three returned to Sitka before the school year was over. The other one became my husband. I would have never finished without him." She filled two tall glasses with ice and then tap water.

"You must miss him," Jane said, accepting her glass.

"I never thought I could survive without him."

"And Bojack, where did he go to school?"

"He went to HBC," Francesca said with a sigh. "His father worked there. It was wonderful to have Bojack close to home, but I still regret that he did not spend some time out of Alaska. Living away, even for a little while, would have made him understand Sitka better, maybe appreciate it more."

"He's not happy here?"

"He's young," Francesca concluded. "What young person is ever happy or satisfied? And who am I to complain about him? He has a job, a good job. He does not talk about it much, but I think he enjoys it."

"What exactly does he do?" Jane asked.

"He's an instructor at the art department and helps Ellsley as student services coordinator—organizing different activities at the dormitories. He talks about getting a master's degree. But he'd have to leave town. The older you get, the harder it is to leave. I'll be down in a minute." She ran upstairs to change.

The dormitory. Jane remembered Wednesday night and the man with the bloody face being dragged by the police from the women's dormitory.

Jane went over to the sofa, picked up the newspaper and turned to the Blotter, studying late Wednesday evening:

...Harborview Restaurant reported the theft of cash from a register at 9:30 p.m.

A black mixed-breed dog was impounded by police from Marine Street at 9:52 p.m.

Police quieted a loud party in the Nicole Street area at

10:02 p.m.

A minor traffic accident on the 1500 block of Halibut Point Road was investigated at 11:56 p.m. No injuries were reported.

Police removed an unwanted, intoxicated guest from a 280 Lake St. party at 1:30 a.m. . . . .

No mention of the man, the fight, the college. It was as if the scene had never taken place. Francesca returned to the kitchen and set the table.

Jane kept quiet about the absence of the incident from the Blotter. No point in asking Francesca. She telephoned the police each day for actual arrests or major investigations and never bothered with minor incidents. On the other hand, Bob stopped by the police station each day in person and examined the Blotter page by page.

Jane would invite Bob over for breakfast tomorrow and ask him.

TWENTY-ONE

"THIS IS DEFINITELY not your home," said Bob, twisting around on the stool at the counter and surveying the living room. He took off his jacket and let it drop to the floor.

"Hook's over there," Jane said, pointing at the coatrack. "What do you mean this is not my home?" she said as she stood guard at the stove, lightly stirring the scrambled eggs.

"Too bare. Not feminine enough. I can see you with wainscoting, knickknacks, dried flowers, prints, pillows, that kind of stuff."

She bent her head and looked at him over the rim of her glasses. He gave an apt description of her home in Boston. "I arrived with a couple of bags and had six boxes shipped by mail," she said lightly. "Hardly enough room for the items you describe."

"Funny, I thought only a man could do it."

"Do what?" She slid the frying pan off the stove with a clatter.

"Pick up and leave everything behind." He reached over and poured more coffee.

"Oh," Jane said, refusing his bait. He watched her face while she kept busy with the toast.

"But this isn't Francesca's house, either," he continued. "At least not what I expected."

"And that is?"

"Maybe more art, Indian stuff. Some prints, something for the walls," he said, looking around the cedar walls. "Her husband was an artist, and so is her son. I thought I'd see more of their things."

"I never asked," Jane said, leaning over the kitchen sink, looking out at sparkling new snow on the mountains and the dark clouds collecting on the horizon and moving fast toward town. "Anyway, who needs art with views like this?" She paused. "She might have some of his work upstairs. I've never been up there."

His eyes got round.

"And we're not going up there now, or you never get an invitation to breakfast again."

She put down the two plates of eggs and ham. "There's something I wanted to ask you—did you do the Blotter yesterday?" she asked.

"Sure did—it's always me, unless I'm out of town or sick. Why?"

"When Francesca and I walked to her truck the other night, after dinner with you, we saw the police break up a fight at one of the HBC dormitories. The police dragged a guy out, bleeding, and put him in the cruiser. Looked like an arrest to me."

He stabbed an egg. "I wouldn't see that," he answered. "Juvenile stuff—no juveniles go into the paper. I don't even want to know their names. Nothing uglier than an angry parent."

She shook her head. "This guy was not a juvenile. And his bleeding looked serious."

He shrugged. "You know the guy?"

She shook her head.

"Some kids can fool you," he said.

"You don't ever print much on the college, do you—in the Blotter, that is."

"A lot of them are juveniles," he said. "The freshmen cause the problems. Anyone who makes it past the first year learns how to avoid trouble. What were you like as a freshman?"

Jane ignored his question. "Could you check on it, make sure there wasn't a mistake about the age?"

He put down his fork. "Sure I will. But, believe me, nothing will come of it."

TWENTY-TWO

SATURDAY WAS COLD and overcast, but no rain. After breakfast, Francesca convinced Jane to telephone Michael Benoit.

"Jane, I thought you might call one day," he started, "but the last thing I expected was a request to drive up Harbor Mountain in the middle of the winter. I don't mind the drive. The Jeep can handle it. The weather is alright. But I have a hunch we're not sight-seeing. Would you two tell me what this is all about?"

"When you get here." Jane turned and looked at Francesca. Earlier they had debated whether or not they should ask Michael to help and how much to tell him.

An hour later he pulled up in Francesca's driveway and honked the horn of his Jeep. Jane climbed into the back, leaving Francesca to sit in front with Michael.

Michael raised his eyebrows. "We might have to park and hike a ways. Do you have decent boots on?"

They showed him their feet and laughed.

"We called you because you're the only person we know who skis," Jane began.

"Jane spoke with some consultants in Colorado to find out more about ski resorts, the economics and characteristics of the more successful resorts," Francesca said.

"And we thought together, the three of us, we could look around at these mountains for a comparison," Jane said.

"Find out once and for all if a ski resort is feasible," Francesca said. She put her hand out on the dashboard as Michael took a hard right turn onto Harbor Mountain Road. The Jeep bounced into a rut, and he put it into low gear, taking a steady, easy pace up the only mountain in

Sitka that had a road etched into its side. Jane stared out her window into the surrounding forest, heavy with cedar. Sudden changes in elevation forced a lot of switchbacks, and she noticed numerous culverts that redirected streams under or around the pitted road. At one point the road traveled parallel to a rock ledge overlooking Sitka Sound. Under the overcast sky thousands of trees on the lower half of the mountain looked like blue-green velvet. Above, the mountaintop was invisible, submerged in swirling, wispy clouds.

"I'll do what I can, but I'm not sure I can help that much," Michael said, both hands on the wheel. "What's the deal? Katmai would use its land for the resort?"

Francesca shook her head. "No, Katmai doesn't own any acreage with mountains. Katmai would either choose these acres as our remaining land allotment owed to the corporation by the federal government under the settlement act. Or, we could trade other holdings for potential ski sites, including some of Ellsley's land, left to him by his mother."

"What about leasing the property from the forest service?" Benoit questioned. "That's how most ski resorts operate."

"Two-thirds operate on public land," Jane agreed.

"Just between us, I can tell you the corporation doesn't want to take half a step into this," Francesca said glumly. "Katmai will either own the resort outright or have nothing to do with it at all, I'm afraid."

Michael nodded, keeping his eyes on the road. He kept the speed at about fifteen miles per hour once they had passed the snow line. A few times the wheels hit a snowdrift or small patch of ice and spun uselessly. Michael put the vehicle into Reverse and then tackled the road again, changing his angle of approach by a few inches.

"You know the army had a makeshift ski lift here during the war, don't you?" Michael asked.

Francesca nodded. "Supporters mention that at every meeting. But skiing has changed, like everything else. That slope would be like a telegram to today's fax."

Michael laughed. "So, what did you find out, Jane, in your call to Colorado? What goes into a successful ski resort?"

"A lot of things that Sitka does not have," Jane said.

"But the mountains certainly have plenty of snow and a long winter season. That's got to help a lot."

"Snow's important, but it's not everything." Jane's voice was authoritative and efficient, as if she were explaining technical charts in a boardroom rather than riding in the back of a Jeep through Alaskan wilderness. "Number one requirement—proximity of a major market, a major population center. Accommodations, not a few dozen rooms, but hundreds, have to be in place before you worry about the mountain—hotel rooms, condos, vacation homes. Ski areas with large numbers of beds enjoy the highest profitability. The most popular ski areas tend to be clustered— they can team up on accommodations and marketing. Community support is essential. Except for the community support, which is tenuous at best and could change dramatically once any digging or construction begins, Sitka has some serious shortcomings.

"The features of the mountain come next. The greater the difference between top and bottom elevation, the better— for a long smooth trail. I'm not an engineer, but this looks like rough terrain. The average ski area has more than five hundred miles of developed slopes and trails. Smoothing it out here could cost . . . millions. Even if it is smoothed out, it needs to be covered with vegetation that protects against wind and erosion. Then you have to worry about the length of the ski season, lights for night skiing, and snowmaking equipment. An astronomical investment in fixed costs before even one skier slides down the slope.

"Finally, other amenities must be available—cross-country skiing, ice skating, sledding. Sure, there's plenty of snow in the mountains, but we all know what it's like in town during the winter. I haven't lived here long, but we've had one night of snow and at least a dozen of rain. Solid rain. A ski resort? It's a hell of a gamble.''

Michael whistled. ''You don't work for Katmai, but you did your homework.''

''Yes. But I wanted to check out the sites firsthand, take a few photos, and send them to friends who know more about skiing than I do, people who can judge better than I.''

Thirty minutes later the Jeep's tires whined as they pushed aside snow. Michael found a wide section of the road and turned the vehicle around so that it pointed downhill, ready to take them back to town.

They climbed out into a brisk wind and air that was fifteen degrees colder than the air at sea level. The women began trudging up the remaining two hundred yards or so to the summit of Harbor Mountain.

''Wait,'' Michael called. ''I have something to make this adventure a bit easier!''

He unlocked the back of the Jeep and pulled out three pairs of snowshoes. He helped them buckle them on. The snowshoes were awkward until Jane remembered to keep her legs far apart with every step.

Once above the tree line, the three hikers were vulnerable to the whipping wind and snow, and they kept their heads down as they climbed the steep slope that led to a snow-covered summit. Visibility was poor. The extinct volcano across the bay and the town were obscured by the storm. Jane tried to catch her breath slowly. Rapid intake of the cold air hurt her lungs. She watched with envy as Francesca took long, steady strides to the top.

''There's more than enough snow here,'' yelled Michael. He pulled a ski mask over his face. Kicking around in the snow, he uncovered some green brush. ''See this?'' He pointed. ''This is the top of a tree. Scrawny, crooked things that are about eight feet tall. And that's a picnic shelter up there.'' He pointed, and Jane saw a corner of wood sticking three feet out of a snowdrift.

"So, Michael," she said, moving close to him so she would not have to shout. "What do you think? You want to do your skiing here?"

"I've seen better," he said, clapping his hands together. "I've only been up here once before during the winter. The sky was blue, the wind was down. My guess is this type of blowup is more typical."

Jane nodded. "Before investing the sums of money required for a ski resort, someone would have to come up here every day, for at least two years, and graph the weather conditions. I'll write down our impressions, include some photographs, and send them off to experts. I can't imagine anyone would say putting money into these mountains for skiing would be a sensible investment."

After turning to scan the horizon inland, Michael suddenly bolted away from her, waving his arms and screaming Francesca's name. Jane followed him at a much slower pace but couldn't understand his alarm. Francesca was in sight and bobbing along slowly in the snow, almost like a cat stalking a bird. In a few steps, though, she was out of Jane's sight, just over the crest of the hill.

Jane watched as Michael ran clumsily over the flat sections and relied on the slippery material of his insulated ski pants to slide down the drop-offs. Then he was out of sight. Jane swallowed, ignored the cold wind, and trudged on.

As she reached the other side of the small plateau, she looked down and saw Michael holding Francesca's arm, guiding her along the tracks they had made with their snowshoes, backing away from a cliff that dropped three hundred feet or more.

When they reached Jane, he removed his arm from Francesca and covered his face. "That gave me a scare. Stay away from the edges along here. You can't be sure what's solid ground—the snow could be just a hunk stuck onto the side of a rock, or it could cover a rotten tree limb." He looked at Francesca. "You fall down there, and your body won't be found until spring."

Jane shivered. "We've seen enough of Aspen of the North. Let's get out of here." She scanned the snowy expanse, certain it was part of the reason Katmai had yanked her job away.

"Don't hurry down," Michael cautioned. "Head down sideways, or even backward, on the steep parts. Grind your feet in the snow with every step—if you pitch forward, nothing but those trees will break your fall."

Climbing down was far more strenuous than climbing up. Francesca and Michael laughed and zigzagged down the slope like kids. Michael made two snowballs and managed to hit Francesca on the back with one. Francesca didn't bother to make snowballs but scooped handfuls of snow and flung them at him. Jane concentrated on her steps but still fell to her knees three times.

At the Jeep they stomped their feet and brushed the snow from their coats.

"We were up there for almost two hours," Francesca said, removing her mittens and rubbing her hands together. "I'm mixing up some hot cocoa the minute I walk in the door. Sound good?"

"Can't wait!" Michael said, turning the heat up a notch after a few minutes. He kept tapping on the brakes as he drove downhill, and once he came to a complete stop. "I don't want to hurry on this road," he explained, turning to look at both Francesca in the front and Jane in the back. "The grade changes abruptly. You can find yourself going at a breakneck speed in seconds."

As he spoke, the Jeep went into a skid and started to go down the hill sideways. Michael gripped the wheel and pumped furiously on the brake pedal. "Hang on!" he yelled.

Jane gasped. The overlook was less than twenty-five yards ahead of them, and if Michael didn't get control of the vehicle, they would soon pitch over the cliff. Michael swore and twisted the wheel completely to the left. A combination of the sudden move and a rough patch caused the Jeep to slam sideways into a patch of trees on the other side of the road. Jane's head banged against the window.

"Get out, quickly!" Michael said. The three of them scrambled out and then surveyed the damage.

"Damn, I loved that Jeep. There was no other way I could straighten it out...." He looked toward the edge of the cliff.

The Jeep was stuck in a ditch, its front completely caved in. Jane walked to the edge of the drop-off—the cliff was more than two hundred feet tall. They were lucky to be alive.

"Good work, Michael," Jane said.

Michael nodded, but he continued to pace, studying the patch of ice the Jeep had hit.

"That was quick thinking to get us out of that accident," Francesca agreed. She folded her arms and shivered.

Michael looked up. "That was no accident," he said, calmly pointing to the road. On the snow were two long oval patches of ice, starting at the curve just before the overlook and ending at the cliff. "This ice wasn't here when we drove up the mountain. If the water was from any kind of run-off—and it's too cold for that—the ice would make a stripe across the road as water traveled downhill. These patches are over the tire marks, deliberately placed so the next car down would take a sail.

"Some prank." He shook his head. He opened the back and pulled out a small bag of salt, which he sprinkled over the ice. "That will help for now. Well, this vehicle's not going anywhere. Let's go. We have a long walk home. And we have to warn the police. This is dangerous."

The three of them walked down the mountain in silence.

TWENTY-THREE

THROUGHOUT THE week, Jane prepared a packet of information on Sitka and sent copies to consultants in New England and Colorado. Francesca started planning a series on the ski resort plans and spent long hours at the television station.

The following Saturday, Jane decided to spend the morning shopping downtown and the afternoon at the college for uninterrupted time on the computer. Replacements for her ruined software and monitor had yet to arrive.

Downtown Sitka was crowded on Saturday, and Jane could shop any weekday, but the day was bright, the temperature tolerable, and she enjoyed watching people, especially in Sitka, where she began to recognize strangers and could observe people in more than one setting.

She stopped for a cup of coffee and a fat cranberry-nut muffin in the coffee shop, tucked in an alley behind the fire station. Then she went to the bookstore to collect an order and browse. As she came out she paused, wishing she had a camera to photograph the white spires and gold crosses of St. Michael's Cathedral.

"Hiii..."

The familiar voice startled her. Standing beside her was the strange woman from the art room. The beader stared up at her and waited. Jane was not tall, but the woman came only to her shoulder. Her hair was long, clean, and pretty, but the flat appearance of her face still caught Jane's attention. She wore oversize jeans and a long brown jacket that probably was boy's clothing from a thrift store. Little was feminine about her except her eyes, hair, and earrings, long strands of amber and red beads, intricately woven together. Some of her hair had become twisted in with the beads.

"How did your beading turn out?" Jane asked politely.

"Gone. I hate sewing beads. I'd rather carve." The woman shook her head like a petulant child, and more of the black strands caught in the earrings. She stepped closer and reached out for a strand of Jane's hair. She stroked it gently and let her hand drop.

"I like it," the woman said simply. "Please, give me some?"

"Why?" Jane asked with a nervous laugh. She could not figure out why, but something about the woman frightened her.

"Few clips," she said, making the motion of a pair of scissors with her fingers. "For a mask. My mask. I want red hair on one half and black on the other."

"I will try to remember to save some the next time I get it cut. Should I drop it off at the art room?"

The woman giggled and then stopped. She spoke English clearly enough, but something was undoubtedly wrong with her.

"What's your name?" Jane asked gently.

"Nancy," the woman said again with a giggle, and then she turned the other way and ran down the street.

THE COLLEGE WAS by no means large enough to provide every instructor with an office, let alone a computer. Jane's department had only two computers—one in the office of the dean's secretary and another in the adjoining office that was shared by all the business instructors. The computer in the secretary's office was linked to the mainframe for the entire college.

As Jane anticipated, the business department was empty on Saturday. Every noise she made seemed to echo. She sat quietly at Lila's desk and turned on the computer terminal. She entered in her department's code and promptly forgot about being alone.

A short directory came up. Lots of items under "Text," a few under "File," and nothing under "Stat-Prep," "Voice Mail," "Work Sheet," or any of the more complicated features.

She entered her own code, quickly typed two letters and then a short exam for her finance class. She was about to turn off the computer when she thought of the new finance director. She was curious about his work. She tried to call up "Personnel," but the computer required a more specific code to open those files.

"Don't be ridiculous," Jane said to herself. "There won't be anything about him or me. Not yet, anyway."

She studied the directory for administration and was relieved to find files in the work sheet programs, such as Lotus and Javelin. Not nearly as many as she would have started. She wanted to study the work sheet format and see how much the new finance director had on the ball. Her finger tapped a few times through some meaningless codes. The directory for administration was long, but many of the files could not be entered without a secondary security command code. Jane's own code was FACJMM, short for faculty and her initials, and she played around with ADM for administration and various initials. She kept tapping, searching the directory for a file that could be opened, and experimented by tapping out HCE, Ellsley's initials. When she combined Ellsley's initials with the file name "Est," the computer made a gentle chugging sound as the file was located and flashed on the screen. Jane expected to see a screen full of estimates or cost projections.

But the work sheet was blank. Strange, Jane thought. A work sheet file was made up of hundreds of squares, designed for long lists of numbers and calculations. An analyst could fill in each block with either a label or number and create lists, formulas, tables, and more. Someone must have erased the file but not the file name, Jane thought. But no, the prompt at the bottom of the page indicated not much memory was left for the file. Jane idly tapped to check the bottom of the work sheet. The file moved sluggishly, as if it were packed with information.

In the middle of the work sheet—in column A—were parts of words, meaningless, like a section of text that had been chopped off. Jane pushed a button to widen the margin of column A. With each tap more words showed. Each window could store a lengthy number or line of text. But when the program was turned off, the work sheet automatically reverted to the one-inch margin, or eight taps of the space key. The person who opened the file could use a column to type text at least eight inches wide, or sixty-four taps of the key. Jane widened the margin to a full page, and at the far left of the page she found the signature line for Henry C. Ellsley.

The letter buried in the computer work sheet read:

Dear Mrs. Chekesh:
Nothing symbolizes or preserves the greatness of the Tlingit culture more than the art of the people. The administration and staff of Holmes Barrett College—especially in the museum and art department—have dedicated their careers to studying Alaska Native culture and encouraging our students to use tradition to influence the modern world.

As you plan for the end of your time in this world, we would like you to keep the commitment of Holmes Barrett College to the Alaska Native people in mind. Do not allow the valuable artifacts of your family to escape into the hands of those who cannot appreciate the greatness of the Native culture. Plan ahead by placing your family's precious heirlooms into the care of professionals with the skill to protect them and allow generations of young Alaska Natives—the future of this great land—to be inspired. Over the years, the college has collected and preserved ceremonial masks, rattles, paddles, and even everyday utensils. Student craftsmen prepare high-quality reproductions so that pieces can remain with the families.

What your village, your family, has to offer is vital for preservation of the culture. For more information about the Holmes Barrett estate planning program, please telephone my office and ask to speak to me. I will look forward to working together with you to preserve the integrity of Alaska's Native heritage.

Jane tapped her finger to look farther down column A of the work sheet. About fifty lines later she saw data—Indian names and addresses from Angoon, Ketchikan, Nome, Juneau, Fairbanks, Burrow, all over Alaska. Some had other notations. "Mask, baskets, ivory" were listed after the name of Danny Ratuchik, Nushagak. Jane moved to the bottom of the file and whistled softly. It had more than 1,200 entries, a lot more items than the small octagon of a museum could ever begin to hold. The letter was undated. She wondered if it had actually been sent to everyone on the list.

She looked over the list again before returning it to its hiding spot by hitting the memory button. The file disappeared from the screen.

Jane searched the directory again. Several file names intrigued her: "Fincom," "Katmai," "Nataff," and "Skires." The latter seemed like shorthand for ski resort. Did Ellsley hope to have the college lead the bandwagon for such a venture?

She tapped the keys, along with Ellsley's initials, but had no success at entry. She searched the secretary's neat desk for a school catalog, looked up Allen Wilson's name. No middle initial listed. Jane experimented with AJW, ARW, AMW, and ATW. No luck. The code did not have to be a person's initials, it could be a combination of any three letters. The permutations meant there were 17,576 possibilities. Jane gave up trying out new combinations.

She examined every file name. Then she came to two files, "Students A" and "Students B." She typed HCE and hit the enter key, and the file leapt to the screen. Another work sheet file. Nothing more than a list of the students at the school, with 467 entries of names and addresses. Jane hit the print key, thinking that the list might be handy for her during the semester.

She tapped the enter key again to call up the file "Students B." Again the computer purred with compliance, showing yet another list of names and addresses. More students on this list—502. Once again she recognized the names of students from her classes. Also catching her eye was Raino LaQuestion.

A relative of Francesca's, Jane mused. She could only assume that one list showed full-time students and the other showed part-time and full-time. The lists had no labels, no explanations.

She struck the memory key in disgust. Letters and lists of names belonged in a text file and not a work sheet file. She could only assume Ellsley kept such files out of ignorance or to keep his estate-planning program under wraps. Not illegal, but unusual and possibly unethical. She wondered what other work sheet files contained—if any at all contained numbers and mathematical functions.

Would Francesca find Ellsley and his estate planning newsworthy? Would the story rate two minutes or ten minutes of airtime? Francesca could interview an old couple from a small village up north, surrounded by their family heirlooms, broken baskets, and carvings. Ellsley would reiterate the college's desire to preserve the culture. The students would demonstrate how they studied and rehabilitated the pieces and then copied the artifacts for the family. Finally, the camera would watch as Daniel took a hunting mask and reverently placed it at the end of a row of battered masks in the museum. The college would announce expansion of the museum, and each new piece on display would get the space and attention it deserved.

That would be the story if Jane mentioned it to Francesca now. Francesca would ask Jane how she'd found out, and Jane would be too embarrassed to admit she had searched through other people's files on the college's mainframe. Francesca might hate the news story simply because Ellsley was involved.

On the other hand, Bob's story would hit hard and cover the tax implications for both the college and the donors.

The true story was somewhere in between.

No sense in letting either Francesca or Bob know about the estate-planning scheme yet. Not until she searched more in the computer files and discovered the reason Ellsley tried to keep it a secret.

Jane looked at her watch: almost two o'clock. The silence of the building was getting to her, and she was hungry for a real lunch at home.

She switched off the computer and laughed. The only other sound in the gloomy building was the ticking of Lila's clock. She shut the door of the business building and made sure the old lock caught. Walking down the path of the campus, she did not notice the man watching her from the window of another building, talking on a telephone.

JANE TOOK A deep breath. The thermometer touched fifty, and the sky gave a fresh hint of what spring would be like. She walked quickly, thinking about the computer files and what she could do to learn more about Ellsley and his schemes. She'd examine the mainframe later in the week, when the files might be open without codes. Only after she had another chance to study the files would she tell Francesca and, maybe, Bob.

"Jane!" she heard a shout. "Jane, over here!"

Daniel called from the museum.

She waved and smiled but groaned inside. Why did she have to be ravenous and tired when she ran into him?

"Class on Saturday?" he asked.

"No, just writing up an exam," she said.

"I'm glad to see you're still around." He grinned. "So the meeting with Ellsley did not go as badly as you thought."

"I didn't get the job, but you were right—we met again, and I have a job. Not enough to keep me here very long. I guess I'm still searching for the excuse that will keep me in Sitka forever."

"That sounds forlorn."

"This is still not my home. But I want it to be."

"I have an idea," Daniel said. "This museum is empty, and this is the best day I've seen in a while, too nice for anyone to stay inside, and that includes this curator. I can leave a volunteer here, and we can walk through the national park and look at the totem poles."

He did not wait for an answer and returned a moment later with his jeans jacket. She could forget her hunger.

She almost had to run to keep up with him. He wore leather hiking boots and moved surely over the gravel-covered road that led to the park entrance. He had his fists jammed into the pockets, even though it was not cold. He wore no hat, and his black hair lay against his head like the feathers of a raven wing—soft, gleaming, ready to fly. His pace relaxed as they approached the entrance, guarded by a triplet of panels with painted totem faces in stern red, black, and turquoise. Each figure had its right hand over the heart and left hand across the stomach. He took her arm when they reached the trail that wound along the rocky shore. On the right were foamy waves, and on the left was damp forest, with tall trees and plants with massive green leaves, including skunk cabbage and devil's club. It was the kind of place a dinosaur would feel at home in. But adults without children have no reason to contemplate dinosaurs, she reminded herself.

Daniel slowed his gait and interrupted her thoughts. "The poles don't belong here, you know," he said. "This group came from the Haida, the people who lived south of here, closer to Ketchikan."

"The eyes are sad even when the mouth is smiling," Jane said. "Maybe they miss home. Maybe they left something behind."

"They call this Lovers' Lane. Maybe that explains their sadness."

"Love doesn't have to be sad," Jane protested. "You're teasing me; there's nothing about that at the beginning of the trail."

"It's true," he said. "I found some old postcards in town, and that was the name. I suppose someone got embarrassed and decided the name didn't have the right cachet for tourists. Any mention of the name was eliminated from the park."

They walked slowly, and their footsteps were silent on the path lined with cedar chips. Jane liked the light touch of his arm around hers, and she matched the rhythm of his steps.

"It's hard to believe that so beautiful a park can be so close to a town of eight thousand," she said.

"It's my favorite place in the world. So much, it's become the only place where I can think clearly about myself," he said. "Close enough to the museum so I can walk through every day and close enough to town so there's no need to carry a gun to scare off the bears."

"That's good," Jane said. "I don't care how long I live here, you'll never see me packing any pistols."

"That's right," he said, laughing. His eyes were dark, like the sea at night. "You're from Boston. They don't like guns back there, do they? Limit your hikes to Lovers' Lane, then." They laughed and slowed their pace even more.

The light was fading fast in the forest, but the sun was still a full gold ball hanging over the ocean. He guided her to a small bench under the Sitka spruce and next to a totem pole that had turned silvery gray and resembled a piece of driftwood. He let go of her arm and sat close. From the bench they could see down the path that was lined with the totem poles and trees more than two hundred years old. They were alone. In front of them was Silver Bay, and just ahead more than one hundred gulls rode the waves.

"I've never seen so many," Jane said.

"They're celebrating spring," Daniel said. "It's March, and the herring are starting to return. Just about any time you look over the ocean during the next month or two you will see birds, otters, sea lions, even humpback whales, all dancing with the waves, trying to forget the cold and hunger of winter as quickly as they can."

"I knew about the salmon returning; I never heard about the herring."

"The herring were as vital as salmon for the people who lived on these shores." His eyes watched the birds dip at the small fish. "Five species of salmon came at the end of the summer and were almost taken for granted. The arrival of herring meant the end of the winter and the end of hardship. The Tlingit would ride the waves in large canoes, scooping up writhing, silver fish. Herring from the first catch of the season were killed and eaten with a proper ceremony. That way, the souls of the herring could call out for more herring to return."

"If I had known the story, I might have tasted herring," she said.

"Not the same species. The tasty part of this herring is the egg sac or roe. Natives weight boughs of hemlock with rocks in the shallow waters. Herring return by the thousands and spawn—you'll see froth up and down the coastline. Thousands of pale yellow eggs stick to the hemlock branches. But the big market for the herring roe is in Japan.

"Every spring, fifty seine boats go out and net tons of herring. Before the fish are dead, the processors sort the females from the males and slit their bellies open to extract the egg sacs. The season is usually over in less than twenty-four hours, and each captain can walk away with a half million in his pocket—dollars, that is. That happens later this month or next, when the bulk of the population is in and the females are in their prime."

Jane wrinkled her nose in disgust. "Ugh. What happens to the males and the rest of the females?"

"What they can't sell in Asia as a cheap 'fishburger' product or sell as fertilizer, they dump overboard."

"It sounds so bloody and uncivilized."

"Survival of the fittest." Daniel shrugged. "Meanwhile, the gulls are grabbing their share early. Look!"

He pointed at a gull clutching a herring in its beak. The sixteen-inch long fish wiggled and squirmed. Another gull approached to assist, and the first flapped its wings fast to move away from the crowd. The quickness startled the other birds, and they all lifted their wings with nervous shakes followed by steady beats. Together the birds circled high and glided before gently landing farther away from shore. They moved as if following the directions of an invisible conductor. The bird with the fish did not stay with the group but landed on a rock on shore, still tackling the catch. The fish twisted desperately in a useless escape attempt that ended with the gull piercing the tough silver skin with its beak.

Offshore the other gulls floated and waited for their catch. The white bodies sparkled like the whitecaps of the waves.

"When we first met, you insisted you were an amateur," Jane said. "But you know the art and you know this place. Are you...Tlingit?"

He looked quickly at her. His mouth thinned. "I don't know," he said shortly. "My eyes would suggest not, and the hair and cheekbones would suggest yes. I feel like I am, but I really don't know. From what my parents told me, I was abandoned as an infant in Seattle outside their church. St. Jude's."

Jane caught her breath and bit her lip.

"Of course, my adoptive parents had a nicer way of telling the story, but that's what it amounted to. They had been married for nine years and wanted children more than anything. They were not wealthy, and they had been saving for adoption. The priest decided that I could be the answer to their prayers."

"The story has a happy ending," Jane said softly.

"I'm not sure about that," he said as he looked out over the water. "All my life I assumed I was Indian, looking as I did, turning up as I did in Seattle. As a child I imagined my tribe, my people, grandparents singing and talking to me. Needless to say, my parents were not happy when I came up here in the hope that I would find out more about where I came from. Forget the past, they pleaded. There's no reason to look for it, they said. I always wondered if they knew more, but they insisted otherwise."

"You could be from here," Jane said.

"I probably will never know." He shrugged. "Maybe I don't want to meet the people who could leave a baby on the rainy back step of a church in Seattle, the kind of person who could sneak away, afraid of being caught. Maybe I don't want to know. My heart is at home in Alaska, and for now I am content to guess that I belong in this land." His hand reached out to the totem pole as he watched the gulls chase, dive, and fight.

Behind them a breeze whispered through the boughs of the towering spruce and hemlock, the sound of nature breathing. Above, the crisscrossing of branches resembled a dark spiderweb.

Jane reached over and touched his arm. She wanted to take him in her arms and comfort him, but it was too soon.

"Who could do that to a child?" he said bitterly. "I could never live with myself. No, I don't believe there are any children in my future—too many mistakes to be made."

Jane started to cry. He misunderstood the reason for her tears, and he quickly pulled her close and kissed her hard and desperately. She tried to stop her tears. This should be a moment of pleasure, but it wasn't. She leaned into him, laying her cheek against the worn denim of his jacket. She hoped he would keep talking. She was not ready to talk about herself. He gripped her tightly and returned his gaze to the water. The sun was almost down, and the mountains were a dusky violet. A skiff passed by, leaving a bubbling wake that frightened the gulls into flying out of sight. The chase for herring was done for the day.

"I'm not the only one, you know," he said. "Ellsley could be Native, too. At least he knows he's from Alaska. His parents were ashamed and never talked about it.... He found out from an uncle on his father's side, but he didn't have many details, or more important, papers that could prove anything."

"Ellsley's problems are not yours," Jane said. She was disappointed. She didn't want to talk about Ellsley. She didn't want to come out and admit how much she disliked the man.

"He's all right, a good man," Daniel continued, as if he had read her mind. "He knows what he's doing, and he's done a lot to help the people around here, though few recognize his accomplishments. You are lucky that you work for the college instead of the corporation. Non-Natives, people like you, me, and Ellsley, have much to offer. People are willing to listen at the college. The corporation would never allow you, a stranger with no connections, to be an intricate part of politics."

"I suppose I'll never know," Jane said. "I never wanted to go into politics, and I won't be a stranger forever. I wanted to do a job."

"Believe me, you can't really trust a person who doesn't trust you," Daniel said. "You could never trust anyone at the corporation, including Francesca. She undoubtedly was involved with getting you up here on false pretenses."

Jane looked down. How could she explain? Yes, mutual trust was ideal. But when two strangers met, someone had to be the first to take a risk and give friendship and trust a chance to grow.

"The job . . . that wasn't intentional on her part. I'm sure of that. She was kind to let me stay. She didn't have to do that. Yet she asks nothing in return. Her kindness has simply given me time to plan."

He studied her face in silence for a few moments. Her tears and the turn of the conversation to politics and Francesca had ruined the kiss.

"You should use this time to see the rest of Alaska," he said after a long pause. "Late spring or summer is the ideal time for a car trip through the state. Anchorage and Juneau could offer endless opportunities for a woman with your experience. Explore before you bury yourself in work here. Don't make a rash decision after a few weeks in Sitka alone."

"I'm hardly buried in work," Jane said with a wry laugh. She rubbed her fingers nervously. She hadn't thought about moving again. But maybe another move would help her separate from Boston. She should explain to him about herself—and why she had fled to Alaska. But she wasn't sure she could do it without a lot of tears. Now was not the time, she decided. She wanted to change the subject, away from Ellsley, herself, or his own sadness.

"Are there totem poles like this throughout Alaska?"

"You have me there," he said, grinning. "There's a few in Ketchikan. Nothing as elegant or haunting as these."

"Tell me what you know about this one," she said.

"It's the oldest in the park. Back in 1904, it was the newest of the poles sent to a St. Louis fair, the Louisiana Purchase Exposition. The park service commissioned it from a Native man, Nathanial Paul, for the event. He was invited to travel along with the poles to the fair, but his son died two days before the ferry departed. A fishing accident. He committed suicide a month later."

Jane glanced at the stack of faces, the large ones grimacing with stretched mouths and large teeth. The colors were faded, but the cuts were deep, and there was no mistaking the expressions carved by a man capable of many emotions.

"The weather will destroy it," she said.

"Indian carvers never made repairs or tried to protect the poles. A pole was up, the message went out, and then it was left to rot. The park service isn't doing anything different from what the Natives did.''

''What does the pole say?''

''There is the well-to-do Tlingit man, with his only relative, his beautiful Tlingit niece, desired by every eligible man in the tribe. The next face is the young Russian trader who wishes to marry and carry her across the seas. The uncle refuses, and the girl hides in the forest and becomes a frog. The angry uncle mourns the loss of his niece and wonders why small frogs constantly hop about his feet, tripping and confusing him. He kicks at them in frustration, not knowing they are his heirs, croaking over their mother's sadness.''

The largest frog looked downward, directly at Jane, with sad, lonely eyes.

Jane knew that Daniel understood such sadness. She started to speak about herself and why she left Boston, but just then they heard voices and footsteps. Two women laughed as they came around the curve and did not see the quiet couple on the bench among the trees.

''Hi, Nancy,'' Jane said.

The giggles stopped. Nancy's eyes widened, and her mouth opened. She tried to talk, but no words came out, and she pushed at the other woman.

''I didn't mean to startle you,'' Jane said, standing.

''Excuse us,'' said the other woman, her voice shaking. They walked away fast in the direction they had come from. Nancy turned and gave Jane one last terrified, curious glance.

Daniel sat and watched the women hurry down the path. His face was expressionless, his jaw set.

''We were so still—we must have really startled them,'' Jane said, nervously. ''The park is quiet during the winter, but it's safe, isn't it, at this time of day?''

He looked out over the water again and then stood, facing the direction the women had gone. ''Yes, it's safe.''

Turning to her casually, he asked, "Did you know those women?"

"They're students," Jane said. "Not in my class. I've seen the one with long hair. She's shy, afraid to talk. There is something about her that is different. It's difficult for me to imagine her as a college student."

"Talent is not always obvious," he said. "She's an art student. That's a different breed from what you're used to over in the business department."

"True," Jane agreed. "You know, I considered taking an art course and didn't even realize you taught one. But when I went to the art department, I saw students copying what looked like pieces from the museum. Don't you worry that a student could try to misrepresent a copy as the real thing?"

Daniel laughed. "No way. Not with today's technology—X rays and microphotography and pigment analysis. Not a chance. Besides, the copies are never exact."

He studied her face carefully and then smiled. "Let's head back. It's getting dark here." He reached for her hand and held her fingers tightly. "Maybe we could plan a trip up north together."

TWENTY-FOUR

BOB SURPRISED HER by stopping in for breakfast Monday morning. He carried a box of the famous pecan rolls from the coffee shop. "Hope you don't mind," he said. "I haven't seen you in over a week. Missed you."

Jane opened the door wide. "Come in. You're just in time for breakfast."

"Great," he said, cleaning his feet carefully before striding into the living room. "Hey, I noticed your name on the Blotter again—the accident on Harbor Mountain with Mike's Jeep."

She grimaced. "I owe you for not putting my name in the paper. I'm starting to feel like a regular at the police station."

"No names, unless you're arrested. And then there's no way to keep it out. So, don't get arrested."

"I'll do my best. Talking about arrests, what did you find out about that guy at the college? Did you check?"

"Yeah, I checked. Nothing important. No arrest. According to the chief, it was a minor disturbance involving some juveniles and alcohol."

Jane beat the eggs. "I'm telling you, that guy was not a juvenile. There's something strange."

"Do you think it's a big deal? I could press the matter with the police commission, but then the chief wouldn't talk to me for at least a month."

Jane remembered the sadness in Francesca's eyes that night. "No, forget it. But keep your eyes open in the future. So will I. There's something strange about the college, and they certainly manage to keep their 'problems' under wraps."

"They'd rather protect the students' reputations than the students themselves," Bob said. "That's bureaucracy."

She arranged the bulk of the pale yellow eggs on Bob's plate, along with some toast.

"Hey, for short order, this is better than Katlian Café."

She threw her napkin at him.

"I meant it! All right, seriously, there's something I wanted to ask you. It didn't mention this in the report on your accident with Mike—"

"Francesca was there, too," Jane interrupted.

"I wasn't implying anything. You don't need chaperones on top of that icebox. Anyhow, did Michael tell you that he was up Harbor Mountain earlier that morning?"

"No," Jane said. She stopped eating.

"Well, he was. I passed him as I was going up. He was in such a hurry, it's a surprise he didn't have an accident then. There was no mention of it in the report. I was with a buddy who was scouting out some trap sites. What were you guys doing up there, anyway?"

"Trapping? Yuck." Jane sipped her coffee. "That is weird. I have no idea why he didn't mention it."

"What were you guys doing up there, anyway?" he repeated.

Jane paused. She didn't want to ruin the newsbreaking quality of Francesca's ski-resort report. But she couldn't lie to Bob, either. Francesca was almost done.

"We were looking at the mountain, trying to figure if it would make for good skiing or not. Aspen of the North, or so some say."

"What did you decide?"

Jane shrugged. "Like turning Boston Harbor and a coconut into Waikiki?"

AFTER BREAKFAST, Bob offered her a ride downtown.

"Drop me off at the coffee shop," she said. "I can have one more cup before the museum opens."

"You sure go to the museum a lot," complained Bob. "But so do a lot of other women. I would think five minutes would be more than enough to cover a building that size."

"This is only my second visit," Jane said defensively. Actually, she was hoping for another opportunity to be alone with Daniel. "I want a closer look at some of the artifacts."

"Especially the artifact that is about six feet tall and thirty-five years old."

"Now, who's jealous?" Jane teased. "Come with me sometime. There might be an article in some of those carved ravens and frogs."

"I don't think so," he said. "I prefer finding my articles at the police station and the courthouse."

DAN WAS NOWHERE around when she entered the museum about two hours later. She pushed her hair back; it was covered with droplets of mist. A young man waited at the door. He charged her three dollars and then grudgingly offered a tour. Jane declined.

He watched her while she walked from case to case, but when the telephone rang loudly he went into a back office and shut the door. Jane was relieved. If she had to pay, she'd rather be alone with the art and her imagination.

She glanced over the Tlingit section. No new pieces were obvious, and the fine layer of dust was still intact. Ellsley's estate-planning program was not an overwhelming success, she thought as she knelt to examine some old Tlingit baskets dated 1834 to 1957. Her fingers ached as she thought of women painstakingly pulling, twisting, and tightening the strands of spruce root. Some of the hats and bowls were so tightly woven, they were watertight. The baskets were intricate in their weaving, astounding in their tightness, but simple and functional in design.

A large jar-shaped basket caught her eye, or rather the crescent of dustless glass underneath did. The piece had been moved, and she smiled, remembering the day Daniel had pulled a mask from the case and placed it in her hands. Visitors who stayed more than ten minutes discovered a curator who could charm. The large basket had a few simple circular stripes and rectangular shapes around the base. The card read "From Potlatch, circa 1902."

As she stood to move on to other shelves, a figure on one of the basket's lower rectangles caught her eye. She pressed her face against the glass and saw nothing except the berry-stained rectangle. But as she slowly backed away, and the light from the nearby window hit the basket, the figure appeared again—a faint marking, a wavy zigzag. The marking was from the dye and not the weave of the basket.

Strange, Jane thought. Hadn't she seen a similar mark? She walked over to the case labeled "The Tlingit and Raven" and located the raven ladle that had first attracted her.

Again the eyes moved her imagination. The eyes were those not of a prankster such as the raven was said to be, but of a lonely woman in pain. Again Jane wondered about the story behind the spoon. Was it simply a souvenir of a potlatch, given away to show off wealth? Or had a young man carved it as a gift for a special person—a wife, a cousin, or a lover? The ladle had been used and was worn. Maybe the young man had carved the ladle for a woman who was prohibited from wearing showy Tlingit jewelry. Maybe the woman was a slave, and perhaps the only possession she could hold and cherish without detection from a master was a ladle for stirring meals and serving clan members. Maybe her lover met her in the forest on a moonless night. While dressed in only the shadows of the trees, he handed the ladle to her. The two people looked at one another, not knowing how long the secret partnership would last.

Jane took a deep breath as she bent low to examine the wings of the raven. Again she discerned the mark at the tip of the worn left wing. The letter *Z*, she decided. She looked at the label once more. "Circa 1842." Possible that the two pieces were made by the same person. But not likely.

What clan, what family, what moiety, did the figure stand for? she wondered.

TWENTY-FIVE

"I'M NERVOUS," Jane said, munching on stalks of celery. "At last, tonight, I'm meeting Bojack."

Francesca stood at the stove, using two large forks to turn a venison roast from a doe she had shot the previous fall. The browned roast rested in a gently bubbling pool of red wine and filled the house with its aroma. On the counter was a glass of red wine, untouched. Francesca's hair was pinned back, and she looked tired. Lines showed around her mouth. After she returned the roast to the oven, she moved the glass of wine and faced Jane.

"What have other people told you about Bojack?" she asked.

Jane caught her breath in surprise. How could she answer a question like that? Francesca would sense withdrawal. She would not give up.

"Start with Bob," Francesca suggested. "What has he said?"

He was the worst person to start with. Bob had been ruthless with his criticisms of Bojack, had gone down a list of minor police violations committed by the young man. Sure, he had held a steady job for about a year now and avoided trouble with the police, except for three speeding tickets. But he was twenty-two, and he liked a fast crowd. It's only a matter of time before he crosses the law again, Bob had said, shaking his head and stressing that he was only quoting the police. Not dangerous, but trouble. Sad for Francesca, he added.

"Bob didn't say much. Bojack did well at college, got a job right away, and has worked for about a year now, no?" Jane said, trying not to hesitate as she readjusted the silverware at her place setting. She had to say more or Francesca would know she was holding back. "He mentioned Bojack was wild as a teenager but that he had settled down. That's all."

Francesca took a swallow of the wine, then went to the sink and emptied a small brown paper bag. A dozen red potatoes tumbled noisily into the sink. She let the cold water pour, and she quickly washed and chopped the potatoes. Her knuckles turned pink, then red, from gripping the potatoes under the chilled water.

Jane waited for more questions from Francesca. But none came. "Really, Francesca, I should help," she said. "What can I do?"

"No, I enjoy this," Francesca replied. "You do enough all the other nights."

Francesca was tasting her wine when they heard the knock on the door. Jane was closest and went to open it. She fully expected the voice from the threatening telephone call more than two months ago. What she did not expect was feeling more strange about welcoming a man who had once slept in her room and called it his home.

She opened the door wide and was surprised to see the arrogant man from HBC's art department, the one who had told her she could not enroll in the art course.

"You must be Jane McBride," he said briskly as he handed over another bottle of red wine, a cabernet sauvignon from California. His voice was smooth and articulate, so unlike the rough, deep voice of the caller her first night in Sitka.

Bojack probably did not make that telephone call, Jane thought. She could have some other person to fear.

Jane nodded awkwardly, dumbly, and accepted the bottle, grateful to have something to hold. He hadn't telephoned since, Jane told herself. No, but the cottage was vandalized, and Michael's Jeep was almost forced off a cliff after someone deliberately left a trail of ice on Harbor Mountain Road. Maybe Francesca was right after all.

Maybe the incidents, including the telephone call, were designed to target Francesca and hurt her reelection chances in May. Still, Jane wondered if Bojack had known who she was and where she lived the day she had interrupted the women doing beadwork and inquired about the art course.

While Francesca ran into the living room, Jane carried the bottle into the kitchen, placed it on the counter, and watched. Bojack kissed his mother's cheek, and Francesca closed her eyes and held her face against his for a moment.

Francesca's love for Bojack was apparent, and Jane knew how the mother fretted when she did not know what he was doing. Francesca missed him, but she wanted him to have his independence.

Bojack was a younger version of Daniel. He had black hair and deep black eyes to match. His hair was on the long side, and his jeans and plaid flannel shirt were neat but washed to soft pastels.

Francesca returned to the kitchen and gave the roast a final basting. Bojack sat hard on the living room sofa, spreading one leg across the cushions. He picked up a magazine and turned the pages steadily, glancing at the photographs. "Karina said she was sorry she couldn't make it tonight, Mom," he said about his on-and-off-again girlfriend.

Francesca sliced the venison. The meat cut easily, the layers fell away as smoothly as wine-colored Jell-O. "Jane couldn't wait to meet you," she said.

"Bojack and I met one day, but neither of us realized who the other was," Jane said. "Do you remember?"

He finally gave Jane some eye contact. "Yeah. You ever find a course?"

She shook her head. "No, but it's just as well. I have my hands full learning about Sitka."

"That should take all of two days," he scoffed. He went to the counter and quickly transferred food to his plate. Either he was hungry, or he was hinting he did not want to talk to Jane.

"If that were true, I wouldn't have much of a job at the station," Francesca said.

Bojack laughed and quelled the tension as quickly as he had set it on fire. He slowed his fork and poured the wine generously. Smiling at his mother, he lifted his glass.

"To Sitka's beautiful, articulate, and dedicated anchorwoman," he said.

"To Sitka's only anchorwoman," Francesca added, but she tossed her head, pleased that Bojack had complimented her.

"We should also have toasts for the newest financial analyst and the most promising artist," said Francesca.

"Save those for other dinners," said Bojack, refusing to raise his glass. He smiled warmly at his mother.

Attention turned to the venison, the browned potatoes, and the large salad. After a pause, Jane asked him, "Are you teaching a course this semester?"

"One, an introductory drawing course." He did not look at Jane.

"How are your students, Bo?" Francesca questioned, her serving spoon poised. "More potatoes or venison?"

He shrugged. "It depends on dessert, Mom. The students are all right, but I don't think you'll ever see any of their names in a museum. That makes it easier for me, actually."

"You can take some chocolate cake home with you." She went ahead and arranged more meat and potatoes on his plate.

"The HBC Museum is one of Sitka's hidden charms," Jane said, feeling as if she were interrupting. "Strange more people don't go to places like the museum and the national park."

"Most people don't have the time to spend in places like the museum," Bojack said. "One visit, they figure they've seen it all. Who cares if it's one of the finest collections of Indian artifacts in the world? I doubt many Sitkans go more than once."

"I've been twice; the second time was for a story," Francesca admitted. "I don't know what Daniel Greer does. You would think he would do more than the displays or rotate some of the pieces. Doesn't the museum have a warehouse?"

Jane and Bojack both started to protest.

"But he—"

"Dan does—"

They looked at one another, and Jane let Bojack continue.

"Dan does a lot more than take care of the museum, Mom. He's doing more than anyone else in this town to encourage Native art to develop beyond the cage of nineteenth-century styles that tourists and collectors have come to desire. He teaches, he arranges for traveling exhibits to the villages, and he goes along to give lectures. It's sad—this museum is taken for granted here, but when a small exhibit goes to a village of two hundred or so people, the whole town turns out with a reception, a welcoming ceremony, the whole works. Most of the work in that museum should be sent back to the places it came from. If Daniel had his way, that's what he would do."

"That would put him out of a job," Francesca said dryly.

"He'd survive," Bojack said. "He should run the whole college, let alone the museum."

"Anyone would be better than Ellsley," Francesca said, stabbing the roast daintily. "Even Daniel."

"Mom, you don't know him like I do," he said. "All I'm saying is Daniel should be doing more than keeping watch over a bunch of old baskets and masks and artifacts that people don't even look at twice."

"He's right," Jane said. "I always wonder how the people who made the pieces would feel about seeing their work behind glass."

"Behind glass, out of reach from descendants," Bojack said with a hint of bitterness. "Something from my great-great-aunt or uncle could be in that museum or the Smithsonian, and I would never know. Native people were lucky if traders or missionaries offered a pittance for artifacts. Many men of God simply demanded that the heathen objects be turned in. Only later did Native leaders find out that the pieces were sold to collectors in New York or Boston, never to be seen or touched by the Tlingit people again.''

''But there are identifying marks, no?'' Jane asked. ''I noticed an unusual one at the museum, the other day. There was a marking on two different pieces, a carved spoon from 1842 and a basket from 1902.''

''What kind of mark?'' Bojack asked as he poured the last of the wine into the glasses.

''Like a letter, but with wavy lines,'' Jane explained, putting her fork down and using her finger to draw it on the tablecloth. ''Very tiny. Maybe a Z. I'm amazed I noticed.''

''What were the pieces?'' Bojack asked.

''A big basket. The other was on a raven piece. What is it? A signature of some sort? A clan symbol?''

''Pieces weren't signed. It had to be some kind of symbol for the clan or moiety.''

''But why wouldn't the craftsmen or women make a symbol like that more obvious?'' Jane said.

''There's nothing unusual about it,'' Bojack said. The muscles in his neck stiffened. ''A lot of these items were functional. Obviously the pieces were marked to show ownership, age, or specific use. I'd have to see it to know why.'' He took a deep breath, and his tone made it obvious that he thought her question was ignorant. ''The mark is not unusual. Don't go looking for mystery where there isn't any.''

''How can you be so unromantic about mysteries?'' Francesca chided gently. ''Who knows what secret code Jane may have discovered on that basket?''

Bojack threw back his head and laughed. ''Right,'' he said. ''Go ahead, Mom, maybe you can find a story in all of this somewhere.''

She laughed, too. "I don't think so," she said. "Not in the next couple of weeks, at any rate, with the amount of work I have."

"What are you working on? Or is it a secret?"

"No secret," she said. "But if I start talking, you won't be able to stop me. There's better things to talk about tonight."

"It must be good," Bojack commented. "A lot of people have noticed you haven't done much campaigning. The board election's not that far away."

Francesca flashed a smile. "The election, pah! People know what I stand for. Either they like it or they don't. It's too late for me to change anything now. But let's not talk about that tonight, either."

She changed the subject and focused her attention on Bojack. The kitchen was warm, the dinner had been perfect, and her face was flushed with joy.

Jane was warm, too, but her face was flushed with discomfort. Bojack and Francesca were engrossed in conversation about a bay rumored to be good for salmon fishing. Jane wished she hadn't mentioned her observations about the art in the museum. She should have waited to ask Daniel about the Z mark.

AFTER BOJACK LEFT, Fran and Jane packed leftovers, washed the dishes, and did not talk much. Francesca poured more wine—Bojack had insisted on opening the bottle he brought—dimmed the lights, and rocked briskly on her chair by the window.

"What did you think of him?" she asked quietly.

Jane was not sure she had heard, but Francesca was looking her way, waiting for an answer. She straightened the pile of magazines that Bojack had flipped through.

"All boy," she blurted without thinking. She shook her head. That's what people said about rowdy, tough little boys, the kind who were hard to slow down and pick up and cuddle, but so easy to worry about and love. "You're lucky.

He seems like a stable young man. Who could ask for more?'' The words were supposed to be carefree, but she could hear the despondency in her own voice. She exhaled as if she were smoking a cigarette.

"What's the matter?" Francesca asked, stopping her chair.

"Nothing," Jane replied, standing inside the kitchen. She didn't want to join Francesca and start a long discussion of Bojack. She slowly poured some club soda and added a splash of wine. "I'm not sure Bojack thinks much of me."

"Really, Jane, he hardly knows you. He's quiet around strangers."

Jane concentrated on getting some ice for her drink and did not respond. How could she describe Bojack to Francesca from her vantage point? How could she explain the ugliness of the fish left out her first morning in the cottage? How could she tell his mother that Bojack was a person who let others know bluntly that he did not like them, that he would do anything to talk around them, look right through them, while charming everyone else in the room? Wasn't that what sociopaths were so good at?

"Maybe you don't think much of him," Francesca commented coolly.

"I barely know him," Jane protested. "And I don't feel comfortable talking about him with you."

"There's something you're not telling me. I can feel it." Francesca pinched her fingers together as if she were describing something almost invisible to the naked eye. "Well, all I can say is that you don't know him, and you don't know where he comes from. The fact that he's alive and healthy and self-sufficient is a miracle in itself. You can't understand. You don't know what I feel for him or what I would do for him."

"I understand," Jane said. Her mouth tightened to stop the quivering. More than you can imagine, she added to herself. "I also understand that we've had too much to drink." Thanks to heavy pouring by Bojack, she thought.

She drained her drink and filled the glass again, this time just with club soda. She stood in the dark kitchen and drank that, too, trying to shake off the sickening feeling that she was fighting with a spouse over a child.

"Jane...," Francesca began. "Let's not argue. I'm caught between defending him and wanting to know how to handle him differently. His behavior and my reaction to his behavior has always made it difficult for me to get close to other people. What intrigues parents about a child is boring to others. Now, he's an adult. I have no control over him anymore. I can only advise. He doesn't have to listen. I wish I could turn back the clock, but that's futile."

"Doesn't everyone?" Jane said wistfully as she returned to the sofa. "Francesca, all I can say is that he might not be perfect, but he's young. You can love him and be there for him and never give up on him—nothing more. And from all appearances, that's what you do."

Francesca nodded. "I try." She rocked a few moments in silence. "Jane, you are a good friend, and you would be a terrific mother. Now that you've been in Sitka for a while, can you imagine settling here? For the long term, marriage and all that?"

Jane took off her glasses and looked down at her hands. "I like it here. Marriage...if the right person comes along, fine, but I'm not in any panic over that."

"Did something happen in Boston?" Francesca asked softly.

Jane shook her head too quickly. Parenthood was something she could not think or talk about. "No. No, I simply love my work. That's all. If I'm to stay in Sitka, I must find a better job than the one at the college. That place is driving me crazy."

"If I win the election in May, the finance director position will be yours. No question about it. That's if you still want it."

"I do," Jane said. "I'll keep my fingers crossed. I have no desire to return to Boston...."

"Oh, that reminds me." Francesca jumped up and ran to her briefcase. "I had to mail a package today, and there was a letter for you. I'm sorry I didn't remember earlier. Here...."

"Probably a rejection letter from that batch of résumés I sent out last week," Jane said. She studied the fine envelope. No return address, she noticed, so it probably wasn't a letter from a company. The postmark was from Sitka.

She opened it and unfolded the single piece of paper. Her face went pale, and her stomach felt as if she had just stepped off a roller coaster. The paper was a copy of the article that she had lost on the ferry. The headline, CHARGES DROPPED IN TODDLER'S DEATH, had come back to torment her. At the bottom of the page, written in crude block letters, was the warning, "LEAVE THIS WEEKEND OR EVERYONE IN TOWN WILL KNOW YOUR SECRET. A FRIEND."

Jane ripped the paper into tiny pieces and put them in her pocket. Some friend, she thought. She glanced at Francesca, wondering if she already knew. No, she decided, thinking back on the conversation they had had since Bojack left. Francesca could mask her feelings, but she was not downright deceitful. Bojack was a more likely candidate. Had he hoped to see some reaction during the dinner?

Jane bit her lip and wondered how her "friend" would let others know—a few anonymous letters or a phone call to the newspaper? Surely neither Bob nor Francesca would ever be that desperate for news. Somebody clearly wanted Jane out of town—perhaps to keep her away from Francesca. She had to show that she didn't care if people found out about her past. Perhaps the time had come for her to make explanations to people like Bob and Francesca. She also had to figure out what she was doing that bothered this person and apply even more pressure.

"What is it?" Francesca asked.

"A reminder," Jane said lightly. "Nothing important. Francesca, I have a lot of free time on my hands this week. Let me do whatever I can to help with your reelection campaign...."

TWENTY-SIX

JANE SPENT ALL her free time that week compiling more data on Katmai Shee property holdings and preparing one-page analytic responses on various media-raised issues for Francesca to depend on during question-and-answer sessions with Katmai Shee shareholders. Throughout the week she browsed through the bookstore, checked out materials from the library, and searched through back issues of newspapers, making no secret about her research. Her activity prompted no new threats. So when Bob called that weekend and suggested lunch and an afternoon on the water, Jane hesitated only a moment.

"It's spring," Bob insisted. "It doesn't last long in Sitka!"

She decided she could use the break. It was Sunday, she was lonely, and the morning was the most beautiful she had seen in a long time. Besides, she had not been on a boat since the ferry delivered her to Sitka.

"Be sure to check out with Francesca what to wear," was the last thing he advised before hanging up.

Francesca was out, and Jane opened the door to test the air. The sky was blue, and cotton puffs of clouds were tucked behind the mountains. Teal water sparkled in the sun. A carload of teenagers raced down Sawmill Creek Road with the windows down and the radio on high. Dozens of boats zigzagged across the sound. Jane pulled out her oldest clothes—some jeans, a sweatshirt, and socks. She thought about donning her rubber boots, but the day was too gorgeous, no chance of rain, so she settled on old sneakers. When she approached his slip in Sealing Cove Harbor, Bob was bundling a thermos and some plastic bags into waterproof containers. He was covered from head to toe in camouflage rain gear. On his feet were thick, dark green rubber boots. He eyed her up and down.

"That's what Francesca sent you out in?" he asked.

"I'll be fine," Jane answered shortly.

"Like my outfit?" He smiled, some of his fine blond hair falling into his eyes.

"You look like a mercenary."

"I have the complete set. Used to have the camouflage wallet, but I lost that. You ever try searching for a camouflage wallet in the woods?"

He went back to packing the boat. His smile was wicked. Once the skiff was out of the immediate waters of the harbor, he hit speed. Jane tried to relax, but when she wasn't clutching the edge of the boat, she was gritting her teeth. The boat smacked wave after wave, and it felt as if her backbone were trying to drill out the seat of the eighteen-foot aluminum Smoker-Craft.

The air temperature almost touched sixty, an unusual March day in Sitka. But the temperature of the water was in the forties, and because of the spray, Jane's clothes were more wet than dry. The water pooled in the bottom of the boat, and her legs felt like two celery stalks left to chill overnight in ice water.

Her bottom hurt from being slammed over and over against the bottom of a thin metal boat, but despite that, and despite the spray whipping against her face and the salt stinging her eyes and her mouth, Jane looked around. She had to concentrate on something other than discomfort, and the scenery was convenient and spectacular.

The world was different when viewed from the middle of Sitka Sound. The dozens of islands scattered in the water had always been constant, familiar smoky-green lumps from her kitchen window. Now they changed shape with every turn of the boat—and gained feather-fine detail, color, and texture, all in purple, green, and gray. On shore it was easy to be fooled into believing that the focal point of Sitka

Sound was the activity of eight thousand people. On the water, the town was a tiny dent where the sky met the mountains. It was a still-life portrait, a miniature.

"How much longer before we stop?" she shouted to Bob over the sound of the engine, almost biting her tongue after a particularly hard bounce.

He shook his head and put a hand to his ear. He didn't understand. Then he directed the boat into the wind, lifted his head and smiled at the sun. They had to be going more than fifty miles per hour, Jane thought.

When he pulled the boat into a sheltered cove, Jane bit down hard and gritted her teeth. If she tried to talk, her teeth would clatter so hard that one might break. She attempted to clean the spray off her glasses, but the skin on her hands was red and stinging. Her hair was matted, dripping strands.

Bob shut off the engine and dropped the anchor. Even though the cove was protected, the water still pushed the boat about. Jane had never been seasick before in her life, but now that the boat had stopped, her stomach churned.

"Ohhhhh," she gasped, and she bent her head over the side of the boat. The sight of moving water made her dizzy, and she vomited thoroughly.

"I thought you didn't get seasick."

"It's the first time," she groaned. "The moment you stopped and everything got still . . . Ugggh."

Finally it was over. Bob grabbed a thermos and poured steaming tea into a cup. "Drink it slowly," he advised.

She sat up and tried to straighten her hair. Her fingers hurt.

"I've heard of it but never seen it before—you must be one of those people whose equilibrium is fine in rough water, but once the motion stops, your body reacts."

"Let's not talk about it."

"You look miserable."

"I wish I could crawl into the knapsack on the way home. Francesca wasn't around when you called. You hung up too darn fast."

"I might have something that will salvage the rest of the afternoon." He reached in the hatch for a large orange bundle. He unzipped the package and shook out what appeared to be a fluorescent space suit. He stretched the suit across the bottom of the boat.

"Take off your wet clothes and put this on," he ordered. "It's dry, it's waterproof, and it's warm."

She hesitated.

"Go ahead, put it on. I'll look the other way." And he started digging into the cooler and pulling out wrapped packages.

Jane shivered and then stripped off her wet clothes, everything except her underwear. She tackled the orange suit. The legs were long by a foot, the arms by six inches. She couldn't move around much, but she felt warm again. She took off her dripping sneakers, too, and wrapped the extra material from the legs around her bare feet. Her feet stung as the blood rushed back.

"All set," she said. "Now I know how I'd look if I gained about fifty pounds. What is this thing?"

"A survival suit." He pointed to the water surrounding the boat, deceptively shimmering with sunlight. "An absolute necessity whenever you're out on these waters. You fall in here, it would sap all the warmth out of your body, and you wouldn't have more than ten minutes to live. With the suit, you have about three days. Think you can handle lunch?"

"I guess."

"Don't sound so miserable." He laughed. "You don't see scenery like this every day."

Then he passed over a plate with three varieties of cheese, wheat crackers, and slices of apples and pears. The plate was neat and dry. He pulled out a bottle of Chardonnay and looked over at Jane.

"More tea for me," she said, shaking her head.

"We'll save this for the next time," he said, returning it to the cooler.

Jane wrapped her hands around the metal cup. The warm liquid spread through her body. Tea had never tasted so wonderful in all her life. She held the cup against her cheek. Over the water, a pair of eagles skipped along the waves, soared in a circle, and then landed on a dead tree on a nearby small island. Silhouetted against the sunlight, one bird gave a squeal, and the other tilted its head.

"Next time?" Jane said, shaking her head. "I don't know whether to be grateful for the survival suit and the hot tea— or to be furious with you for allowing me to step on a boat so poorly prepared."

"You love it. Getting cold and wet, getting knocked about by the water, feeling miserable, it's what Alaska is all about. You think this is bad, you have to come hiking with me sometime. Spend three days out. My ultimate plan is to cross the island, cut through brush, climb a couple of mountains, and cross the ice fields. Three days before you reach a shower."

"Wait for summer at least," Jane said. She reached for a cracker and bit off a tiny corner. Her stomach did not protest.

"You'd consider it?" he asked in disbelief.

"If you thought I could make it. And if I knew exactly what to wear."

He leaned over and gave her a bear hug. The boat lurched. "There's not enough women like you around!" he shouted in glee.

"Women who are not very bright?" Jane said, laughing. And she gave him a gentle push backward "Bob! Enough— we'll be overboard!"

He sat down and grinned. "You'd need practice," he said. "Walking around the woods can be as dangerous as a boat ride."

"That's what happened to Francesca's husband, no?" Jane reached for more crackers. "She never talks about him."

"I think he was out for the day—hunting. Probably wouldn't have happened if Raino had had company. But people who live here all their lives go out alone all the time. Especially hunters."

"Raino?" she asked. "Did you say Raino?"

"Yeah," Bob said. "Raino lived in Sitka all his life and knew these woods better than some people know their backyards. For him to disappear without a trace was bizarre. Lindsey said there were some whispers about alcohol, but other people were just as adamant that he hadn't been drinking. Poor Francesca."

"Raino," Jane said. "Isn't it an unusual name?"

"I never heard it before. Why do you ask?"

"Oh, a list I saw at the college. That name was on it. Raino LaQuestion."

"He worked there. He was the premier carving instructor. The list you saw must have been an old employee list."

"It said students." Jane absentmindedly picked up and chewed on a slice of sweet pear. The sourness of her stomach disappeared.

"A mix-up."

"You said it. From what I've seen, the staff is not adept with the computers."

"You'll straighten them out." Bob smiled. "Maybe you could straighten Dan out, too? You like him, don't you?"

Jane blushed. "I honestly don't know. I wouldn't mind getting to know him better. Is it that obvious?"

"No, just a guess. But it's hard to imagine. I don't know why. You're both competent, around the same age. Sometimes I'm not sure he's cut out for the long term in Alaska. He's not happy, but I couldn't tell you why."

"I never saw that," Jane said. She wasn't happy, either. Did Bob see that? Not a good common denominator for any couple. But she kept her thoughts to herself.

"How about a slow ride back toward Halibut Point? We'll track down sea lions munching on herring, and then we'll hug the shoreline and check out the houses on the way back."

They packed the lunch and papers in the cooler, and Bob started the engine with a roar.

She was quiet on the return trip, remembering the evening in the park with the totem poles and Daniel. Why didn't he call?

By the time they returned to Sealing Cove Harbor the sun was close to the edge of the sky, turning the shine of the water from gold to silver. The chain of islands, black silhouettes, looked like lumps of onyx set inside a silver bracelet. Bob cut the speed sharply as they approached the harbor.

"Can't let the wake jostle the other boats in the harbor," he explained to Jane.

He aimed the boat for its narrow slot in Sealing Cove and cut the engine. In less than a minute the lines were secure. Jane piled her wet clothes on the dock and then transferred the cooler.

"Keep that on," Bob said. "I'll give you a ride home, and after you change, I'll throw it in the back of the car."

As they walked on the ramp between the boat harbor and the parking lot, Jane compared the boats, hard-worked and weathered, with the cars, metallic and bright. She decided she liked the boats better and wished she could try living on an island, commuting to town through the spray every day.

"Thanks, Bob," she said. "I had fun."

"We'll do it again."

He dropped the cooler and packages on the gravel behind the station wagon while he searched his pockets for the car keys. A man, large, blond, and ruddy and carrying fishing gear, walked by.

"Hi, Russ," Bob called out.

"Catch anything?" Russ asked, stopping by the car.

"Tell you the truth, we didn't drop a hook," Bob said, extracting the keys from an inner rubber pocket.

"You in an accident?" he asked, studying Jane before nodding politely.

"No," Bob said with a laugh. "Just got a little wet. Aren't you heading out a bit late in the day?"

"Busy all last night and this morning," Russ said. Then he took Bob aside.

Jane, blushing, arranged the bundles in the back of the station wagon. The men talked quietly at first, but after a couple of sentences the voices returned to normal and she could hear them clearly.

"Had a nasty death this weekend. At the college. They wanted to keep it under wraps, but it doesn't involve a juvenile, and the department has to do some investigating. Won't amount to much, but it might be a story for you tomorrow."

"What was it?" Bob's glance at Jane warned her to remain quiet. "A student?"

"Yeah, a girl. Indian. Alcohol overdose. Her blood alcohol level tested at point five percent. Five times the state's legal limit for driving. You know how many beers that takes."

"Don't remind me. I'll never forget. That level is damn high," Bob said with a low whistle. "Hard to believe she could swallow that much without passing out."

"It happens," Russ shrugged. "Indians."

The two men stood there a moment, looking out over the water. Jane waited by the station wagon and didn't bother to pretend that she wasn't listening.

"What's the department doing about it?" Bob asked.

"Not much. It was an unattended death, so we have to send the body up to Anchorage for an autopsy. A little woman who partied a little too hard. Sad. The college will probably make a lot of noise and crack down on the drinking for a while. Well, it's an article for you. Not much."

"Sure, Russ," said Bob. "I appreciate the tip. Good luck with fishing—I left you plenty to catch."

"You always do, Bob." He gave them a friendly nod and walked slowly down the ramp, fishing pole in one hand and a beat-up tackle box in the other.

"Thanks, Jane, for loading the car," Bob said, sliding onto the front seat.

Jane felt ridiculous as she stuffed her orange-suited body into the passenger side. "That death sounded horrible," she said. "The way he spoke about her—how could both of you be so...matter-of-fact?"

"I just listen," Bob answered. "And being matter-of-fact is part of the job, particularly for the police. If a cop let a death involving alcohol get to him, Sitka wouldn't have any police."

"What did he mean, you knew how much alcohol that meant?"

"I wrote an article on the Breathalyzer test that the police use on drunk drivers. I rounded up a few volunteers at the Pioneer Bar and thought it would be a fun way for readers to find out how many beers it took to reach the legal limit. Turned out I had to drink six in less than an hour. Never again."

"Still...," Jane said. "You'd think she would have gotten sick."

"A woman wouldn't have to drink as much as a man. It depends on how much you weigh, how fast you drink, and what you have in your stomach. Hey, thanks for keeping quiet. Russ would have shut up like a clam if he knew you worked at HBC."

"You didn't get her name."

"That can wait till tomorrow."

"She could be one of my students."

"I'm sorry," Bob said. "But get used to it."

TWENTY-SEVEN

HALF OF THE students in Jane's Monday class did not attend. The students who did avoided eye contact with Jane and one another. They looked down at their notebooks listlessly, without writing, or out the window at the misty sound.

Students and instructors whispered about the death.

"Who was she?" Jane had earlier asked another instructor in the business school, while both waited for the coffeepot to finish dripping.

"Not one of ours," he'd said, placing three teaspoonfuls of sugar into his cup. "The business school, that is. An art student. Her name was Nancy Nelson." He'd walked away, shaking his head.

Jane did not ask more. Nancy. That was the name of the woman in the art room, the woman who said hi like a child in kindergarten, the woman who wanted red hair for a mask. No, Jane thought, shaking her head. Too much of a coincidence. But how many art students were there?

For the rest of the day Jane looked for the short woman whose long hair tangled with her beaded earrings. She walked through the cafeteria several times during lunch. She walked to the art building. Lights were on, but the doors were locked. As the day went on, she searched faces even more intently, almost in a panic. After class she stood by the doorway of the business school and looked over the smooth lawn of the campus. She wanted to stop a student, grab an arm, and ask, Did Nancy Nelson have long dark hair? Was she short? Were her clothes mannish and worn? The students would understand whom she was asking about but would mistake the question for idle, morbid curiosity. She did not want to be another faculty member, twitching with responsibility and seriousness: "Oh, yes, I knew her. What a bright girl. What a tragedy."

A memo was distributed to all students and instructors. No details about Nancy Nelson or her death, only one sentence that it had happened and another sentence that classes would be canceled for the remainder of the week.

Jane tried to shake the feeling of dread creeping through her. She reminded herself that she had taught at HBC for six weeks and had seen the girl named Nancy three times. The fact that she had not encountered the woman on campus this day was not strange—particularly considering most students chose to handle the death by missing class. Nancy was not an unusual name. The art department must have several women with that name. Jane tapped her fingers as if she were tapping ash from a cigarette.

At the office in the business school she tried telephoning the art department. The line was busy. When she got through, she asked for Bojack.

"I'm sorry, Mr. LaQuestion is not in today," said a harried-sounding woman.

Jane headed for town. She wanted to see a newspaper with Bob's article and didn't want to wait until Francesca's paper was delivered by her young neighbor. The boy was a Tadpole Wrestler. Only during the winter, explained his mother, apologizing for the paper's erratic delivery. On wrestling nights, after dinner the mother drove the boy along his paper route. She stopped at the bottom of each driveway, and the boy jumped out of the car and aimed the newspaper for the doorstep.

Jane did not want to wait three more hours to see the face of Nancy Nelson.

She didn't have to go more than two blocks before she ran into a small boy hugging about twenty papers to his chest— the boy who had fallen in front of the *Record*'s office. Jane thought of her first day in Sitka and smiled.

"Paper, lady?" the boy asked. "Thirty-five cents!" He did not remember her.

"Thank you," Jane said as she put a dollar into the dirty little hand. "You keep the change."

"Thank you," he said, so seriously. He crumpled the bill in his fist and pushed it into his pants pocket before trudging down the street in search of other customers.

Jane stopped and scanned the front page for the article on Nancy Nelson. "Damn," she said. No photo. Just a five-inch block of type under a single-column headline at the bottom left-hand corner of the page.

HBC STUDENT DIES, OVERDOSE SUSPECTED
By *Record* Staff

Nancy Jean Nelson, 26, a Holmes Barrett College junior on scholarship, was found dead in her dormitory Sunday morning. Investigators reported the body had a blood-alcohol level of .5 percent. That level is five times the state legal limit for intoxication.

Nelson, who majored in art at HBC and specialized in traditional Northwest Indian studies, was described as a hardworking and talented student by college officials.

Police found two empty vodka bottles in the room. College officials confirmed that alcohol is not permitted in the dormitories.

Police reported an estimated time of death as early Saturday morning. Witnesses reported Nelson had been alone in her room Friday evening. The body has been sent to Anchorage for an autopsy before being returned to her family in Angoon for burial.

Police said no foul play is suspected.

The article gave Jane no clue about whether or not Nancy Nelson was the Nancy who said hello so strangely.

But in her heart Jane knew. She was sure as she folded the newspaper slowly and tucked it under her arm. She turned around to walk home and had to pass the college campus again.

She walked down Lincoln Street and looked up at the campus, now deserted. The buildings were stern wood frame, stained dark gray with black trim, and together looked like a fort set against the backdrop of a group of steep mountains known as the Sisters. The scene could have been on a postcard. There was no hint that the fortress had failed to protect a young woman from poisoning herself, drinking sip after sip of clear alcohol. The fortress also failed to keep the woman's story, no matter how brief and bare of detail, from the newspaper. Jane wondered if the small story would make a difference.

A cold wind blew in from off the water. As she crossed the street, a battered Toyota pulled alongside.

Michael Benoit rolled down the window and leaned out. "I was hoping I'd see you around. How are you doing?"

"All right," she said, nodding sadly.

"I'm early for an appointment here. Can I give you a lift?"

She was cold. She wondered if Mike was seeing somebody on campus about Nancy's death or if he had known her as a patient. Maybe he knew what Nancy looked like.

"Sure," she said, and climbed into the Toyota. "I appreciate this."

He studied her face. "You look down."

"The girl who died," Jane said. "I thought about her all day. What an awful way to die."

"Alcohol overdose—doesn't happen that often. One of your students?"

She shook her head. "No, but if she's who I think she is, I said hello to her a couple of times." Jane took her eyes off the road and looked at him intently. "I'm not sure it's the same woman. I wish I knew."

"Nancy Nelson was very short, about five inches shorter than you. And she had long hair that looked like it had never been cut. It lay on her like a black silk scarf. Her face was flat and pretty when she smiled.''

"That's her. Damn, I knew it.'' Jane made a fist and hit her knee. ''I don't know her at all, really, but I find it hard to believe that she would drink that much. Not by herself. She didn't seem like the type.''

"Did you talk to her much?'' he asked.

"No,'' Jane said. ''I can't stop thinking about her, though.''

Mike quickly put his hand on Jane's arm. ''Of course you feel terrible. Nancy Nelson was not a stranger—she was a student. Everyone on campus feels some measure of legitimate grief.''

He returned his hand to the wheel to turn into Francesca's driveway. Then he turned off the engine and faced Jane.

"How much conversation did you have with her? What did you think?''

"There was something strange about her,'' Jane said, laying her head against the back of the seat. ''At first I was frightened of her, and then I worried for her. The first time I saw her—it was in the school's art department—she was beading with some other students. She kept saying hello. That was all. She didn't answer my questions. I thought that maybe she was teasing me, trying to make me nervous. When she smiled it was so delightful. But when she spoke it was hollow. Maybe there was more meaning to it than she could articulate. Like a child stuck inside the body of an adult. Oh, I don't know what I'm talking about.''

Big raindrops started falling on the windshield. After a few moments Jane felt as if she were looking at the house and the driveway through a broken kaleidoscope.

"No, your description is accurate,'' Michael said, his hands tight on the steering wheel. ''Precisely on the mark for a woman with an IQ of seventy-three, just a notch away from being diagnosed as mentally retarded.''

"What?'' Jane asked, gripping the collar of her coat and tightening it around her neck. ''That doesn't make sense. How could she be a student at the college?''

"My question exactly," Michael said. "She was not a patient of mine, by the way. The last time I saw her was several years ago, on one of my routine trips to Angoon. That's the village where Nancy grew up. The hospital is responsible for residents in all the villages through Southeast Alaska. Doctors, nurses, travel out to the village periodically for screenings, regular checkups, minor problems. And the villagers fly in to Sitka when they're having babies, surgery, anything serious. I looked up her files. The last notation was from three years ago. Mt. Edgecumbe Hospital has the contract for HBC, but it was strange, she was not listed in the hospital's HBC file at all. There should have been some medical file. Imagine my surprise when I heard she was a scholarship student, no less."

"She was talented," Jane said. "I saw one thing she was working on—a beaded purse—and it was beautiful, meticulous."

"But is that enough to get a degree?" Mike returned quickly. "I don't know the answer to that question."

"Maybe her instructors did not realize," Jane said.

"How could they have helped but notice?" He coughed out a laugh of disbelief. "You did."

"Is that why you're going to HBC this afternoon?"

"Not because of Nancy, no," Michael said. "But I do want to find out why there was a discrepancy in the records. If we had known she was attending HBC, we might have detected a drinking problem. Maybe we could have done something. Maybe not. In the meantime, I want to find out who else isn't in our files."

"What kind of scholarship did she have?" Jane asked.

"Undoubtedly one from the Bureau of Indian Affairs. I'd be surprised if every Native student at the school doesn't have one. That and state loans—which the students must pay back whether they graduate or not. The school recruits the students, helps them file the scholarship or loan application forms, and then sits back and collects the money." He shook his head. "The school is lucky if fifty percent of a class graduates. That's been going on since the BIA and the government have been passing out scholarships. But it's really rotten if they're misleading people with Nancy's IQ. I question how Nancy got accepted at a four-year college. Maybe she deserved it. But maybe she was just another body with money from the BIA. And if that's the case, it's not fair to taxpayers, it's not fair for the BIA, and it sure didn't do Nancy any favors.

"I'm not sure what I'll find out today, though. HBC is private. They don't have to show anyone recruitment, admission, or student background records. But she was Native and entitled to free care at Mt. Edgecumbe. That is my concern."

"Can you wait a minute?" Jane said, opening the door. "I want to show you something I have inside." She gingerly crossed the bridge, slick with rain, and ran to the cottage. She fumbled with the keys, opened the door, and searched her bottom dresser drawer, where she had slipped the printouts with the lists of students from the HBC computer. Mike had started the engine again.

"I don't want to keep you," she said, sliding over onto the passenger seat and shutting the door. "But look these over when you have a chance. Two lists of students—an A list and a B list. The B list is longer, and let me see"—she ran her finger down the two columns of names— "Nancy Nelson is on the B list and not the A list. This might give you an idea of which students are not included in your files.

"There were no labels for these lists," she continued. "For all I know, one's for part-time students and the other's for full-time, or one is a list of students for this year and one from last year."

"How did you get these?" he asked, spreading out the lists. "Were they passed out to the instructors?"

"Ah, no," Jane said. "Please, don't tell anyone where they came from. I found them in the HBC mainframe. A couple weeks ago. I was just fooling around with the computer files. I didn't think much about it at the time."

"But you didn't tell anybody?" Mike asked.

She shook her head.

"Just as well you didn't. These would be tough to explain to Sitkans who've been around for a while."

"Why?"

"Look," he said, pointing to the list with extra names. "There are names of at least three people who are dead. Raino's one. That was Francesca's husband."

"I noticed that name—I thought he was a relative of Francesca's," Jane said. "Then Bob mentioned his name. Maybe it's a mistake. An old employee list got mixed up with the student list. From what I've seen, the staff is timid with the computers."

"I don't know. These other two were not employees."

"What should we do?"

"I'm not sure. Let's think about it. I better hurry. I was supposed to meet Ellsley in five minutes. But I'm not going to show him these lists yet. Don't you say anything, either. My gut feeling is that we talk to someone besides Ellsley. Maybe the BIA, the police, or maybe a journalist like Bob. It would not be unusual for him to go around asking a lot of dumb questions."

"I hate to tell Bob about an article without telling Francesca."

"Her husband's on this list. Maybe it's not fair to put her in the position of having to ask a lot of questions about that. Here, you keep these."

"But she'd want to know," Jane said.

"Yeah," he said, sighing. "Let's think before doing anything rash."

"Michael, I've been wanting to ask you something," Jane said quickly. "When we drove up Harbor Mountain, why didn't you mention you had already been up there that day?"

He sighed. "You talked to Bob."

Jane nodded.

"I felt silly. I drove over to make sure the Jeep could make it up safely before dragging you two along."

"That was thoughtful, but unnecessary."

He looked sheepish. "I felt silly. I was afraid you would get mad and think I was too... patronizing."

Jane laughed. "In hindsight, I'm thrilled you're so cautious. Any news from the police?"

"No. They think I'm delusional."

Jane opened the door and braced herself for a run through pouring rain. "I'm glad you drove by today. I was curious about Harbor Mountain, and I wanted to find out more about Nancy."

"We will," he said. "Hey, I have to leave early in the morning for Angoon. I'll stay overnight. An entire village can go into a slump over a death like this. Especially when the person is young. Why don't you and Francesca consider coming along? Admiralty Island is gorgeous. Angoon is a place from back in time. Don't ask me what time. There's a hotel. Not grand, but comfortable. I promise you'll see more of what the real Alaska is all about."

"We can take the ferry?"

"I'm taking the ferry there, but I have to fly back. If you don't mind staying an extra day by yourself, you can take the ferry both ways. You could be back Thursday afternoon."

Jane didn't have classes and had no reason to stay in Sitka. "I could stand to get away," she said with a smile. "Thanks."

"Good. Keep those lists in a safe spot. After I finish with Ellsley today, those might be the only copies around. Nancy's death alone might have thrown a monkey wrench into whatever scheme is going on over there. I'll call you tonight about when I'll pick you up for the ferry."

Jane shut the car door, stood in the rain, and waved as he backed down the driveway. The papers were dry, tucked in her coat. She ran inside, refolded them, and sealed them in an envelope before returning them to their hiding place. No sense in worrying Francesca. Not until more answers could be found.

TWENTY-EIGHT

THE *LeConte* was a miniature version of the *Matanuska,* and it traveled among the smaller villages in Southeast Alaska. No open waters for the *LeConte.* There were also no staterooms, no bar, and no tourists.

"Bring a sleeping bag," Mike had advised. It was two in the morning when they climbed on board. The floor of the lounge resembled a huge quilt, with stretched-out blocks of red, black, green, and blue sleeping bags. Jane and Michael stepped carefully over the bags to find space. About half the sleeping bags were occupied. The window shades were closed. Sleepy faces emerged and glared at even the smallest noise or bump.

Francesca had stayed in Sitka; she continued to focus more on her reporting than on the Katmai board elections. Her report on the feasibility of a ski resort was almost complete. Jane had declined to be interviewed but put Francesca in touch with several economists and managers familiar with the business. She had thoroughly convinced Francesca that the ski resort for Sitka was absurd.

When Jane awoke at nine a.m. the shades were up and most of the sleeping bags were folded and out of sight. She sat up and looked around. Michael was gone, and his fluffy sleeping bag was stuffed into a sack less than a foot long. Jane stretched. No one paid any attention to the late riser. Though the room was crowded, the general weariness that came from sleeping on the floor of a ferry allowed for an unusual sort of privacy.

Outside the window was an expanse of water and gray mounds of a long island to the east. Fog escaped from every bend and indentation. After looking at a map the night before, Jane knew that she was looking at Chatham Strait and Admiralty Island.

In Angoon the ferry stopped only long enough to discharge and pick up passengers. The short stay and a three-mile dirt road into town ensured seclusion for the village.

A trip to Angoon meant leaving clocks, schedules, and calendars behind. Mike had said they would have a ride waiting for them from the clinic, but the van was not there. An old man in a rusted 1961 Ford Fairlane looked at Mike and nodded. The Ford didn't have a license plate.

"Come on," said Mike. "Let's go with this guy."

"Do you know him?" Jane asked.

"No, but everyone's going in the same direction."

"What about our van?" Jane said, picking up her bag.

"Who knows? We could wait all day. Let's take what we have now. There's only one road to town, and if we pass them, we can ask this guy to honk and let them know."

The man did not speak but pointed to the backseat for both of them. Jane and Michael sat quietly, not speaking to each other as the old Ford bounced down the road between thick stands of trees. The three miles of road were pitted and rough. The Fairlane protested as the speedometer hit thirty-five miles per hour. He pulled over in front of the clinic. They thanked him, and he nodded. His expression did not change.

The van was parked outside the clinic. Inside, the counselor who was supposed to pick them up had his feet on the desk and was talking to an older man. The counselor nodded at Mike. He did not look at the clock or apologize for failing to show. The conversation stopped when the older man walked out without a word.

"Albert, this is Jane McBride. She's from the college in Sitka. And Jane, this is Albert Johnson, Mt. Edgecumbe's contact for Angoon."

Albert stood and shook hands formally. He had a round face, accentuated by a crew cut that was flat on top. He looked like a fighter who had stepped out of a 1940s boxing ring.

"How's everything going?" Michael asked. "Meeting for tonight set up?"

"The meeting is on," Albert said finally. "Nancy's family—they're taking it hard."

"Think I should pay a visit before tonight?" Mike tinkered idly with some pens on a desk in the corner. The desk was covered, not like the desk of a busy person, but as the spot for papers that did not have to be filed and pens that did not work. Jane noticed that the calendar on the office wall showed August of the previous year.

"It might help," Albert said. Then he headed for the door. "I have to meet a few people for tonight's meeting—see you later."

After the door shut, Michael sat down at Albert's desk, and he put his legs up, too. "Albert's my main man in Angoon. The alcohol counselor. He's supposed to set up my appointments, alert me of any crisis situations, provide background on people. I call him, and his stock answer is, 'No problem, chief.' I suggested this meeting. He would be just as happy if I never came to town."

"Fire him?" Jane queried.

"That would be the answer in the real world," Michael said. "But I didn't hire him. The health board here in town has that responsibility. And they feel comfortable with Albert. Medical doctors are like gods in this country. But when it comes to mental health, anybody can play—it's health care by democracy. And so who am I to question?" He wheeled around on the chair and put his briefcase on the desk.

"I have to get over and make sure we have some coffee, cookies, chairs, for that meeting about Nancy," he said. "Maybe check around and find out what people are going to want to talk about. The hotel is right down the hill. Why don't you go on down and check us in? My room should be all set. Ursula always gives me room five. For you, find out if room eight is available. It's comfortable. Leave the bags here. I'll carry them later.''

"All right," Jane said. "Good luck."

He stopped rustling papers and looked up with a warm smile. "Look around. Take it easy."

She stepped outside into a cool breeze of spring. The clouds were thick and low and swirling like smoke but carried no hint of rain. Children played in the dirt of the streets and looked at her with open curiosity. Jane smiled, and they smiled back. The hill was not much of a hill, but the road was rocky and gouged, and she had to watch her step. The houses were wood, some on pilings. Most had small carvings, totem poles or panels, in front.

At the bottom Jane saw only one building large enough to be the hotel. It was a long, dark brown rectangular strip of eight rooms. A small sign in the driveway read "Noowastu Hotel." Jane walked along the strip but saw no office, so she went to the home that was next door. She rang the bell and waited. More than a minute went by, and she tried knocking. Hard. A woman, probably Ursula, opened the door quickly and then dried her hands on a white apron. The light in the kitchen was glaring, and she spoke through the screen door, not inviting Jane inside. Jane could not see the details of her face but guessed that she was in her early twenties. Her hair was short and fine, cut neatly the same length around her head.

"Yes?" she said without a smile.

"I want to check in," Jane said. "Michael Benoit will have one room, and I will have another."

The woman turned away and came back in two minutes. "You have rooms five and seven. Dinner is at six. No later. Let me know before five if you want dinner or not. The TV's in here. Most people wait until after dinner."

"Can I pick up the keys now?" Jane asked. "And is room eight available?"

"It's yours," Ursula said. "No keys. The doors are open." She shrugged as if the question were an odd one. "If

you need me, I'll be here for the rest of the afternoon.''
Then she shut the door firmly.

Jane crossed the yard and went to look for her room.
Each room looked out over the inlet, but trees blocked most
of the view.

She opened the door to eight. The room was small and
looked like a bedroom in a plain house. Better taste than
most motels in rural United States, Jane decided. As a person who hated flying and spent a lot of time on the road, she
had seen purple chenille bedspreads, orange-and-pink
flowered wallpaper from the 1960s, mirrored ceilings, and
mothballs used for air freshener. Here the wallpaper was
simple, the beige bedspread looked clean, and the floor was
tile and covered with braid rugs. Jane threw her bag on the
floor and her coat on the chair, then stretched out on the bed
with her hands behind her head. Coming to Angoon had
been a good idea. She looked at the door. No locks, not even
a bolt.

The village hardly qualified as a town, she thought. The
only stores were a small understocked grocery store, a snack
shop that had irregular hours, and a one-room museum.
There were four churches, a new police station, and a ga-
rage for the one fire truck. No question about it, the people
of Angoon did not want to encourage visitors. The residents went to school, worked for the government, took care
of their homes, fished, gathered shellfish from the tides,
picked berries, and hunted. Any tourism or large business
might interfere with the life-style that had remained intact
for one hundred years. The village had nearly been destroyed by the U.S. Navy in 1882—the only skirmish between Alaska Natives and the U.S. military worth mention.
A Tlingit employee of a whaling operation had been killed
in an accident. The family had seized two employees in retaliation. The navy had attacked. Since then the people of
Angoon fended off interference by creating a perception
that the town was simple, small, and monotonous. The re-

sentiment towards strangers increased if a visitor tried too hard to discover the charm of the village for its five hundred people. Best to observe and not ask too many questions, Michael had warned.

Jane decided to take a walk later. She was tired and wanted to read. After an hour and a nap, she heard soft knocking.

"Yes?" she called.

"It's me," said Mike.

"Come in," she said, sitting up.

She smiled at him as he entered and sat on the edge of her bed. "That didn't take too long."

"No," he said. "Nancy's family is heartbroken, but they're also resigned. I spoke with her great-aunt and uncle. Nancy's mother is dead. They don't know where the father is. And she has a brother in town."

"What will you do tonight?" Jane asked. "Will many people show up?"

"I don't think so, although you never know. Her aunt said something that surprised me. She claimed Nancy did not drink. Said she quit about four years ago. She seemed to know and wasn't being outright defensive."

"At a college, it would be easy to start up again."

"I suggested that. But the great-aunt insisted otherwise. She was adamant in a quiet way, not overdefensive. Nancy came for a visit at Christmas. The aunt says she immersed herself in drawing, carving, all kinds of art. She mentioned Nancy had complained about long hours on school assignments and not enough time to work on her own projects. The stress may have gotten to her. The alcohol overdose may not have been an accident. It might have been a deliberate suicide."

He looked at his watch. "I'll let Ursula know that we'll be at her table. Six sharp."

JANE FELL ASLEEP before Michael returned from the meeting. The sleep was her soundest since the break-in at Francesca's cottage.

The next morning, over a package of powdered doughnuts and instant coffee made with hot tap water, Michael explained the meeting had lasted three hours. Two dozen people had come, and the session had been more memorial service than group therapy.

Fifteen minutes later they heard the buzz overhead of the floatplane. Michael picked up his bags, and Jane walked with him to the dock. The plane did not circle but aimed directly for the center of the inlet. It landed without a splash and motored to the dock. The pilot never turned off the engine.

"Sure you don't want to head back with me now?" Mike asked. "Flying is different in a small plane, and it might not seem so bad as spending a night alone in Angoon."

She smiled and shook her head.

"All right," he concluded. "Yesterday I mentioned to Nancy's great-aunt that you were in town, that you were an instructor at the school and had seen her around during the past month. Don't be surprised if she looks you up."

"That's fine," Jane said.

"And tonight's bingo night," he told her. "Big event of the week for Angoon. You shouldn't miss it."

"Call Francesca when you get back," Jane suggested as she patted his arm.

The pilot stood by the door, waiting for his passenger. Mike gave her a wave, leapt aboard, and bent over as he moved to the back of the plane. The pilot got on and slammed the door, and the engine hummed at a higher note as the propeller turned. The plane left a wide wake and then lifted for the air, water dripping from the bottom. Jane waved and the floatplane banked to the left and flew out of sight.

People who overprotect their privacy risk loneliness, and Jane wondered what happened to towns that valued isolation. She would find out in Angoon.

She had her camera and decided to walk the entire village and take a look at every building, including the churches. She stopped in front of one home with a carved panel that was so weathered, only traces of the original paint showed through. But the cuts were decisive, and the picture was complete—a killer whale opened his mouth and deftly swallowed a canoe full of men.

She climbed a winding dirt road up the hill that overlooked the town. Except for more weathered and rugged homes, the village of Angoon could have been a peaceful mountain hamlet in the Swiss Alps. Streets twisted and turned with the topography. The forest surrounded the town, and ancient trees had been left to stand throughout. A one-room Russian Orthodox church with its two domes, one narrow and one onion shaped, guarded the valley and village from an opposite hilltop. The church intrigued her, and she headed in that direction.

She took photos of the church from several angles. She tried a door and opened it slowly, not wanting to disturb any service or prayer. St. Herman's was stark and small compared with St. Michael's Cathedral in Sitka, which had elegant paintings, gold filigree, and embroidery. St. Herman's walls were white and smooth. The altar was bare. The church had no seats, only kneelers. For those of Russian Orthodox faith, religion was supposed to inspire awe, not comfort.

The church was empty, and Jane went to the old kneeler. The soft cushion covering the kneeler had been thinned long ago by hundreds of knees. The wood was hard on her knees, even through jeans. Jane had just shut her eyes and bowed her head when she heard the door open.

An old woman stepped inside. Her steel-gray hair was rolled into a knot at the back of her neck. She genuflected and went to the kneeler on the other side of the church. From that vantage point she studied Jane unabashedly.

The two women were quiet for about five minutes.

Jane stood to leave, and the woman followed. Jane held the door open for her.

"You are the visitor, the teacher from the college in Sitka," the old woman said.

"Yes," Jane said, and introduced herself. "The business program of HBC."

"My grandniece died in Sitka. I am Esther Vokesh. Dr. Benoit said you had seen her recently. Her name was Nancy Nelson." The woman looked at Jane briefly and then moved her eyes across the valley. The rims of her eyes were red.

"Yes, I did see her a few times," Jane said softly.

"You knew her?" The woman glanced at Jane quickly again, as if she were afraid she was wasting Jane's time.

"I knew who she was. I did not know her well. We said hello a few times. And she asked me for some of my hair. For a mask she was making."

"Nancy never talked very much. Everything she had to say came from her hands and her art."

"I saw some of her work—it was beautiful," Jane said.

"Was she happy?" the woman asked, at last letting go of the question she had been afraid to ask.

Jane hesitated and thought about Nancy. She had seemed relatively content in the art room with her classmates. In downtown Sitka she had giggled and smiled. The last time they'd seen each other, Nancy had run away in fear. Two out of three times Nancy had smiled.

"Yes, she was happy," Jane answered.

The woman sighed, and something close to a smile came to her lips. She made the sign of the cross. "Would you like to see more of what she did?" Esther Vokesh asked shyly.

Jane nodded.

The woman turned, and her heavy legs trudged, her feet not lifting from the ground as she walked. Jane followed slowly.

They stopped at a plain dark-stained wood-frame house, two bedrooms at most. The yard was small and neat. The woman pushed open her door. It was unlocked. Jane went inside and, because of the closed curtains, could not see right away. The woman fumbled with a lamp on one end table, and with a click, a deep golden glow filled the room from a meager twenty-five-watt bulb inside a battered shade.

Jane stood in awe. She was surrounded by drawings, carvings, quilts, and dozens of masks. Sometimes she recognized animals as ravens, salmons, frogs, or killer whales. Others she could not identify. Everything had a face with eerie eyes, full of emotion—laughter, bitterness, or longing. From what she had seen in the Sitka gift stores and galleries, the collection was worth thousands of dollars.

"These are all Nancy's?" Jane asked.

The woman nodded as she turned slowly in a circle. She took off her brown scarf and shook it out before folding it. Then she hung her coat in the closet. It was a man's coat, like Nancy's. She reached for Jane's coat.

"They are all Nancy's except for the mask over there in the corner. That was done by her maternal grandfather."

Jane took in the carved mask. The face was black with red eyes—it was angry, so angry that it appeared to be only half-human. The mouth had three long fangs. Some kind of animal hair was strung along the top and side edges, but the clumps were thin and scattered, which gave the mask a deranged appearance.

Esther Vokesh came over and touched the cheek of the face lightly. "He refused to buy tools. He made his own, wanting to carve the way his own uncle had carved. He died when she was a little thing, but not before he taught her to carve. He was the only one who truly had patience with

Nancy. Had she been like other little girls, we would have chided him for letting her use such sharp tools.'' Esther's voice was low and painful. ''Myself, I loved that girl. But I wept many tears. I couldn't have children. I remember holding her in my arms as a baby and wondering what she could have been had her mother been a different person. As Nancy grew, I came to realize that I respected and marveled at the person she had become. I loved her for what she was. And now I miss her.''

Esther moved away from the angry mask. ''Would you like something warm to drink, tea or coffee?''

Jane said she'd have tea. Then she sat on the small brown sofa, so threadworn and plump that it contrasted violently with the shapes and color of art surrounding it. She closed her eyes a moment, sorting in her mind what she should say and how long she should stay. She did not want to mislead the woman about her relationship with Nancy Nelson. As she knew only too well, what she said and did would either bring comfort or torment. But she longed to stay awhile. She knew there might not ever be a reason to travel to Angoon again.

She heard the old woman moving around the kitchen, the teakettle starting to whine. The woman brought out a tray with cups and Lipton teabags. Jane dipped the bag and watched the color enter the water. She felt the same, as if she was absorbing emotion from the room. She held up the cup—it was a souvenir mug that a tourist might buy. It showed a dog team and a hot dog, with the name of a restaurant and the slogan ''Best Damn Dogs of the North.''

She stirred sugar and milk into the tea and looked around again. There had to be more than one hundred pieces in the room. Her eyes adjusted to the light, and one item in particular made her gasp.

A massive panel hung next to the door where she had come in. The panel was turquoise and black, an eagle soaring over the silhouette of what looked like the village of

Angoon. Inside the eagle's eyes were·small copies of the village. The strain of the eagle's wings made the bird look as though it were in pain.

Prominently etched in the right-hand corner of the panel was the letter she had seen at Holmes Barrett Museum. On a basket and ladle that were supposed to be about one hundred years old. Not a *Z*, though. An *N*. Jane could be certain it was *N,* because the rest of Nancy's name followed in small letters. Other *N*'s were carved, painted, or etched throughout the room.

Jane squeezed her mug. She had planned to listen to Esther Vokesh talk about Nancy. Now, all she could think about were the *N*'s. Why were they all over this room and hidden on pieces at the museum?

"Nancy's initial, the way she drew her *N,*" Jane said as Esther sat. "Is that a tradition in Angoon or from your family?"

Esther looked up and smiled but shook her head. "No, that was how she started writing her name when she was just a small girl in school. She had a lot of trouble in school, but never with her handwriting or later in art classes. She was so proud of what she drew, and she practiced that elaborate signature. Later she signed everything with her *N*. There was so little she could do well at school, but she knew she could draw and carve. She wanted everybody to know what Nancy could do."

"No one else you know uses that *N?*" Jane pressed. "You're sure?"

The woman looked at Jane strangely. "Yes. It's something she always did. Nancy only studied art. It was all she could understand. I'll never forget the schoolteacher telling her to make her signature less flamboyant. 'Don't let the signature interfere with the art,' he had said. He was kind, and she adored him. So she made them smaller, and later she relied only on the *N*. But always the same. Why do you ask about this?"

"I did not realize," Jane said, not sure about mentioning the museum. "I saw *N*'s on some pieces in Sitka."

"Then those were made by Nancy," Esther Vokesh said matter-of-factly. "During the last couple of years—on the few pieces she would send back here—she started hiding the *N*'s. She would challenge me to find them. When she came home for Christmas, she brought me the basket, and I could not find the *N*. Nancy laughed wildly for a few moments, and then she started crying. She couldn't stop. I never understood why."

Mrs. Vokesh stopped drinking her tea. Her voice had gone stern. She wanted to know more about what Jane knew.

Jane shuddered. She wished she had answers for the woman about her niece. The raven ladle, the basket, and God knows what else were not made by Tlingit artists decades ago, passed along in ceremonial potlatches and later to white missionary collectors and traders. No, those two pieces had been made sometime in the past three years in a classroom of Holmes Barrett College. How many pieces in the museum were not old? Worse, Jane had talked about the *N*'s. Before Nancy's death. She thought about the dinner with Francesca and Bojack, the candlelight and the fragrant red wine. Bojack had a glib explanation that the *N* was not uncommon for two pieces that had been made sixty years apart. She had told Bojack about the *N*'s. Bojack was the only person who knew about the *N*'s beside herself or Francesca. Three days later Nancy Nelson died of an overdose. Of alcohol. A woman who did not drink, her aunt insisted. Jane's brain screamed inside. She dropped her tea, and it scalded her hand.

"Oh, my goodness!" Esther Vokesn gasped. She ran into the kitchen and back again, with a towel soaked in ice-cold water. "Here, wrap it with this. Not too tight." She also put a cup of ice cubes within easy reach and a jar of homemade devil's club salve.

Jane murmured an apology as Mrs. Vokesh got to her knees and sopped up the tea from the rug. Jane had asked about *N*'s, and a woman with low intelligence but great talent had died. And now she was in the same room with a woman who had loved Nancy. What could she possibly say? That the young woman had been murdered after Jane had casually pointed out her secret signature? That her grandniece had been murdered because discovery would destroy what would have otherwise been the perfect forgery scheme?

Jane wanted to confide in Esther Vokesh. She wanted to cling to her and tell her everything. But she did not know the whole story yet and had more to sort out. Bojack could have left town by now. Jane had said too much already. She needed more time to think. She would talk to Esther again someday.

"I had seen the *N*'s before and had not realized they were Nancy's work," Jane said weakly.

"Come here," Esther said, smiling and pulling back a curtain to show a view of the inlet. No trees in this view. "I want to show you. Look at the line of the hill, over there."

Against the steamy window Esther traced Nancy's graceful *N* by outlining the shape of the mountain and valley. "When she was a little girl, she played at this window over and over, until the window was filled with her finger marks. Then she would wait a few hours for more frost. And she would do it again and again. Not long ago, she traced her *N* in the frost and said, 'Some things never change.'"

A tear slipped from Esther's eye. And she held her chin high as she looked out the window.

"She was a good girl. She tried so hard. Her mother never loved her, but I did."

The devil's club ointment soothed the stinging pain of her hand. Jane wished it could do the same for her heart. How had she gotten into this mess? How responsible was she for Nancy's death?

"Mrs. Vokesh, I know everything you have said about Nancy is the truth. The police might not believe you, but Dr. Benoit does, and so do I. And I promise you, I plan to do whatever I can to prove it and find out what really happened."

TWENTY-NINE

JANE WOKE UP in panic, as if an alarm had gone off. But no, the room was quiet except for the soft ticking of a clock—and the rumble of tires on gravel outside as several cars passed by.

She had fallen asleep while reading and waiting to catch the four a.m. ferry. The bedside lamp glared into her eyes. She rubbed them and smoothed out her clothes, which were sticking to her body. Then she reached for the alarm clock. Three forty-one a.m. That couldn't be right. She turned the clock over—yes, she had switched the alarm to "on" and set the clock for three a.m. She shook the clock. The bell was gone!

Dropping the clock, she ran to the dresser and scrambled among the change and papers there for her watch. Three forty-two. Any traces of sleep vanished.

Jane swept the clutter on the dresser into her overnight bag. Then she jammed her book, her brush, and camera on top. She slid into her shoes.

She scanned the room for a quick second.

"Forget the shampoo and stuff in the bathroom," she said, and flung open the door.

"Damn, damn, damn," she said as she ran. She stared at the home of the hotel manager. Last night she'd anticipated the hotel would provide rides to the ferry terminal for guests. She had mentioned to Ursula's husband, Odie, that she would be catching the ferry early the next morning. He'd handed over an alarm clock but said nothing. She'd mentioned the need for a ride again.

"You'll get a ride," was all Odie had said. But now the windows of his house were black. Had he handed over his only alarm clock? She didn't want to find out. Knocking on the door would result in more delay. She spotted headlights bouncing along the road. It would be easier to beg a ride from somebody she had never seen and would never see again. She ran from the house to the road.

A truck was coming. She had never hitchhiked, and sticking her thumb out for a ride didn't seem like the right thing to do under the circumstances. She had less than fifteen minutes to make it to the ferry, and she was on a narrow dirt road that was about three miles long. She skipped out to the middle of the road, dropped her bag on the gravel, jumped up and down, and waved her arms frantically.

The truck hit its brakes. Jane picked up her bag and ran to the driver's side. He was middle-aged, thin. His long black hair hung down the front of his face and interfered with his eyelashes. He chewed a toothpick and studied her.

"I'm sorry," she gasped, hoping her hysterics would frighten him into giving her a ride. "The alarm at the hotel, it didn't go off. I have no ride to—"

"Back there," he drawled. The toothpick moved up and down with the words.

"Thank you," she cried as she threw her overnight bag and sleeping bag into the back of the flatbed truck. "Oh, thank you!" She climbed the bumper, put her hands on the floor, and heaved herself up. Toothpick Man hit the accelerator, and pebbles spit from the wheels. Jane fell forward and crawled to her bag.

She wrapped her arms around her knees and noticed the chill in the night air. Except for the two triangular patches of light from the headlights, she could not see much ahead. The sides of the road were black, as black as a forest could get at night. She shivered and glanced at the cab. Two other people were in the front with him, including a heavyset woman. No wonder he'd put her in the back. Hell, she would have agreed to hang on to the bumper.

She looked down at her watch and realized she had swept it into the bag. Don't worry, she said to herself. Toothpick

Man had reason for hitting the gas, too. She laughed again and tossed her head back. It was then she saw the stars, thousands of glorious stars sprinkled across the moonless sky. And spiraling and colliding in the sky over Angoon were streams of pink-and-blue light. Northern lights.

Between the jostling of the truck and the racing lights in the sky, Jane got dizzy. She looked down and then tried looking at the sky again. She spotted another pair of head-lights in the distance before they took a sharp turn. Some-one was aiming to reach the ferry even later than Toothpick Man.

The pickup turned, and a golden halo filled the night, swallowing the stars and the northern lights—the lights of the ferry, the *LeConte*. The engine was in idle. People shouted and pushed carts up the ramp. Toothpick Man parked nearby, where two men were dragging an over-loaded cart. Another pickup passed Toothpick Man's and waited at the bottom of the ramp. A ferry worker accepted a ticket from that driver.

"Damn you, Frank," said the ferry worker. "You know that vehicles are supposed to check in a half hour before departure time."

The man inside must have made some response because the ferry employee laughed and slapped the ticket against the hood, waving the driver aboard.

Jane dropped her two bags and jumped to the ground. The ramp was still down, and ferry employees were on shore. She went to the driver's window of the pickup—still open despite the temperature.

"Thank you." She smiled. "I was frantic that I'd miss the ferry."

He shrugged. The toothpick moved over to the opposite side of his mouth. He dismissed her and turned to his pas-sengers.

Jane did not mind, and she ran aboard. Inside the ferry she found a chair by the window and settled down. But she did not unwrap her sleeping bag. The night, the entire trip to Angoon, had been wild and full of surprises. She wanted to think about her time in the village and the people she had met. If she had been born in Angoon, would she have stayed? Or would she have headed for Sitka or Seattle? Her visit had not been long, and she had not talked with many people, but she had quickly learned the village had a quiet fortitude—a small town not easily forgotten.

The ferry workers boarded and shouted one last call throughout the parking lot. Toothpick Man's truck was still parked near the ramp. Jane started to reach around in her bag for her watch. A man on the seat nearby stirred at the noise, and Jane placed her bag gently on the floor.

Who cares what time it is, she thought, slipping off her shoes and propping her feet on the bag.

The passenger door of Toothpick Man's pickup opened, and a young man hopped out. His hair was uneven and long, but there could never be a doubt that he was a man. His duffel bag was tiny. He walked around the front of the pickup, faced the headlights, and put up his hand in farewell. Then his hand came down, gently, as if he regretted what he was about to do. He stood a moment and then turned and ran up the ramp, the way that only lean, long-legged teenagers can do. The one side of his face shone wet in the light of the *LeConte*.

Jane pressed her face to the window and watched the family, hoping for smiles, a sign that parting would not change their lives forever. The scene reminded her of Nancy, what it must have been like when she said good-bye to her great-aunt before leaving for Sitka. Toothpick Man and the woman hurt saying good-bye to this lanky boy. Leaving was not easy for the young man, either.

THIRTY

JANE STOOD ON DECK, bag at her feet, impatient as the ferry scraped the dock in Sitka. On the dock a crew member grabbed one of the thick ropes and deftly tied it to a metal hook. She couldn't wait to talk to someone about Nancy and wanted to leap the thirty feet from the deck to the dock—the way she had jumped off the pickup truck in Angoon. The minutes dragged.

Somebody shouted that the herring fishery was on and pointed toward Middle Island. Dozens of small craft hovered around fifty seiners. Six planes flew overhead, radioing in code the locations of large shadows that signified a massive school of herring. Each seiner had a skiff that pulled away at high speed, rapidly guiding the floaters of the seine net into a ring over the school of fish. When the circle was completed, the bottom of the seine net was tightened, closing off escape for the herring. The crew brought the squirming catch on board, pulling the net bead by bead.

"I hate sewing beads," Jane remembered Nancy saying.

"There's going to be a party in town tonight!" shouted a laughing red-haired man.

Jane gripped the rail along the deck. The wet metal sent a shiver through her that kept her alert. She had not slept on the ferry. She searched through the crowd waiting by the ferry terminal. The group was small, nothing like the hundreds that gathered when a large ferry came to town.

No sign of Michael. Jane had hoped he would meet her. She wanted to tell him about Nancy and the *N*'s before she went to the police and before she talked with Francesca. She thought about Daniel, too.

A school bus rolled into the parking lot, ready to provide rides to town. After Angoon, Sitka was like a metropolis.

The door to the ferry groaned as it opened, and Jane took off for the stairs that led to the lower deck. There she held her breath against the fumes of running cars. She reached the doorway as the ramp slammed to the ground. Outside she gulped in the fresh air.

In the terminal lot she scanned people waiting at the gate. No one she knew. She thought about calling Daniel or Michael from the pay phone and looked inside the terminal. Six people waited in line at the phone. She realized she would get home faster by taking the bus.

She eased herself through the crowd and boarded. The driver followed her and picked up the sputtering radio.

"How many out there, Mitch?" the voice crackled.

"Not even a full load." The man scowled at the radio. "Over."

"Get back here," the voice said. "Over."

The driver dropped the radio into a pouch and started up the bus with a roar. Jane rested her neck against the back of the hard school-bus seat. She shut her eyes and moved her head back and forth to ease the tension out of her muscles. She missed Michael's Toyota pulling into the parking lot.

JANE PUT HER KEY into the lock and was surprised not to feel the resisting click.

The oil-pot stove sounded like a muttering old man in the corner, and the house was warm. Jane slammed the door hard and dropped her overnight bag on the tile floor in the kitchen rather than on the carpet. She recognized Francesca's footsteps upstairs.

"Hi, I'm back," Jane called. "I'm surprised you're home."

Francesca came down and headed for the coffeepot. "I'm expecting some long-distance calls. It's easier to talk here than at the office. How was your trip?" she asked. "Did you and Michael have fun?"

"Good and bad," Jane said. "Did he call you?"

Francesca shook her head. "He might have tried. I have been so busy. I'm not going on the air this week, so I can finish the ski-resort piece."

She slowly poured black coffee into a fat black mug. She had on tight jeans, and tucked inside was a man's white T-shirt, a simple outfit that provided a sharp contrast to the necklace she wore—a raven pendant hanging from a strand of minute black beads. Wordlessly she offered Jane coffee by holding up the pot. Then she filled a second cup. She put the mugs across from each other on the counter and waited.

Her silence did not make talking about Nancy and Bojack easier for Jane. Taking in the friendly kitchen, the living room with its sofa and pair of rockers, she wondered if the house would ever be so comfortable again for the two of them. But she had waited too long as it was to talk with Francesca about all she suspected about Bojack.

"I don't know where to begin. It's concerning Bojack. And the HBC woman who died."

"The art student? What does she have to do with Bojack? Was she in one of his art classes?"

"Some of the classes he teaches are small. Exclusive. Not many people can enroll. Does he report to Ellsley?"

"Yes," Francesca said, her voice soft and showing no emotion, no concern, as if this were an ordinary conversation. "The head of the art department is out of it. The living example of why tenure should be outlawed. That's what Bojack has always said. Daniel agrees, according to Bojack." Her eyes locked on to Jane's. "That reminds me," she continued. "He telephoned. He wants you to call the minute you return. He said he'd like to see you tonight."

Jane hesitated. Daniel would understand once he found out about Nancy. "He'll wait," she said with confidence. She put her mug on the counter. "Let me see if I can make sense of what I do know about Nancy Nelson's death.

"You remember the night we had dinner with Bojack? It was then I mentioned the marking I had noticed on two pieces in the museum. Do you remember? I said it looked like a Z. That's the only time I ever mentioned it. Here that night. You are the only two people who knew. That was three days before Nancy died. Did you tell anyone?''

"No," Francesca said. "To be honest, I forgot all about it. But what does that have to do with Nancy?''

"When I went to Angoon I never planned to seek out Nancy's family. But I met her great-aunt in this church on a hill all by itself...."

"St. Herman's," Francesca said. "Russian Orthodox."

"Yes, Esther Vokesh," Jane said. "We talked, and she invited me to her home. It was dark, the place was dreary, and I felt so useless for this grieving woman.

"The house is filled with Nancy's art, more than I could ever dream one person capable of. And Francesca, everything in the room had that same mark. Except it's not a Z. It's an N. The exact N that was on the two museum pieces."

"Bojack explained that," Francesca said stonily. "Some clan mark."

"But it's not," Jane whispered. "The mark is how Nancy made an N. It was her signature. Her aunt showed me. She opened the curtains, and there's a sharp little hill across the inlet. Her aunt stood at the window and showed me how Nancy outlined the hill and valley in the window frost when she was a little girl.

"There was only one difference between the N's in Angoon and the ones in the museum. The N's in Angoon were flamboyant, obvious. The two I saw in the museum—on the basket and the ladle—were concealed. Why would anyone hide a clan symbol? Wouldn't more people know about it? Wouldn't you have a symbol like that? And wouldn't there be a lot of symbols on all the artifacts?''

Jane stood and started to pace in the living room. "I'm convinced that this N came from one person. A young woman in college who was proud of what she could do. I mentioned that mark that night, and a few days later, Nancy's body was found."

Jane stopped and went over to Francesca. "I'm so frightened. It's too much of a coincidence."

Francesca shrugged and played with her bracelets, pushing them up and down her wrist, and then she fingered the raven around her neck.

"How do you know the pieces are old?" she asked. "How do you know they are not reproductions or pieces that have been misplaced?"

"I don't think so. They looked old. Some cards identified them. One card said 1902 and the other said 1840-something. I can't remember. Almost sixty years apart."

"You're suggesting that this woman forged the pieces— sold the originals and placed the copies in the museum?"

"She copied them, I'm sure of that. I don't think she was capable of deliberate forgery, selling them and putting the copies in the museum on her own. She was . . . she was retarded."

"Have you told anyone?"

"No," Jane said. "No one. I haven't seen anyone except you since I met with Esther Vokesh."

Jane waited. Francesca drained her coffee and then put the cup in the sink. Jane wanted to do something, call an authority. Telephone the museum, the police. But she waited because the need for haste was gone. Nancy was dead.

"Francesca, I'm sorry to be the one to tell you all this. It might have nothing to do at all with Bojack. Maybe Ellsley . . ." her voice drifted off. "He has a boat. He has a letter hidden in a computer file asking people from the villages all over Alaska to donate artifacts." She no longer had to convince Francesca about some sort of connection between the N's and Nancy's death. Francesca knew more about all the players. The matter involved her son, and Jane left the next move up to her.

"Or Bojack is doing Ellsley's dirty work," Francesca said bitterly, hitting her arm on the counter. The bracelets

clanged. "I knew something was wrong. Bojack called me
this morning and told me he was quitting his job. Then, oh,
not twenty minutes ago, he called again and mentioned he
wanted to borrow *Bluebird,* my skiff. For work, he said. I
didn't ask him, but he said he was taking a short trip—to
Kruzof.

"This morning, he also mentioned something about
leaving town. I got angry. He thinks I don't want him to
leave. But it's not that. I'm angry because I thought he had
no idea about where he wants to go or why. Another Indian
boy off to see the world. I begged him, 'Take your time,
make some plans.' But now I know why he's in such a hurry.
He's leaving because of what happened. He's involved. How
much I don't know. He can be mean, but I know he could
not physically hurt someone. And Ellsley would do anything to get back at me, including manipulate my son."

Francesca looked at Jane, her dark eyes tired and sad.

Jane did not respond. She was not fond of Bojack. But
she also did not know him. What Francesca said could be
true. Still, Jane could not forget that she had told only Bojack and Francesca about the *N*'s.

"Well?" Francesca sighed.

"This involves your son; the next step is up to you," Jane
said, and she reached for Francesca's hand across the
counter.

"All right," Francesca said, determined. "I don't want
to talk to the police yet, or anyone at the school. We don't
have much to go on. Some *N*'s, maybe some forgeries, and
the relative who claims that an Indian woman who died of
an alcohol overdose didn't drink. The story sounds crazy. I
know Bojack. We have to find him, and he will tell us what
he knows about all of this. The truth will make him strong."
Francesca bit her lip and drained the coffeepot.

"All right," Jane said, although she was not comfortable with the thought of confronting a man who may have
killed a woman, quit his job, and was about to leave town.
"Just us?"

"Please understand. I don't want to get Bojack into any more trouble than what he's already in. He may have had nothing to do with this. He may have an explanation. Then we decide together who to talk to next."

Jane was doubtful, but she nodded.

"This boat ride today could have something to do with Nancy. He said he had to tie up a lot of loose ends at work. He mentioned Kruzof Island. That's all he said." Francesca turned to Jane. "I know you just got off the ferry. But how about another boat ride?"

"Kruzof? Out to the volcano?" Jane asked, her eyebrows raised and her finger pointing to Mt. Edgecumbe.

"The wind is down from this morning," Francesca said, pressing against the kitchen sink to look out the window. "It won't take long."

"Wouldn't it be better to wait for him on the dock? Talk to him here?" Jane said.

"But suppose he's hiding something, some evidence, God knows what," Francesca said tensely. "If we wait, we could be too late."

"All right. But if we go out in a boat, we have to call someone," Jane said. "Let them know where we're going and when we plan to get back."

Francesca laughed. "I've never done that. I've been out in worse, that's for sure."

"But what if something happens to the boat, or we get hurt?" Jane insisted.

"Maybe I should just go alone," Francesca said, irritated. "And I can tell you I'm going out on the boat. But that's about all I can tell you, Jane. Because I don't have any idea of where Bojack was headed, other than Kruzof. Kruzof is a big island. Not every person hops into a boat and knows where he's headed. All I can do now is head for Kruzof and see if I can find Bojack. And if I hurry, I might catch him before he leaves the harbor!"

She stomped upstairs.

Jane went into her room and reluctantly kicked off her shoes and reached for her old clothes. She wondered what might happen once Bojack found out they knew about Nancy's forgeries, and she feared Francesca's reaction.

Francesca came back downstairs softly. Any trace of anger had vanished. She had pulled rubber boots over her tight jeans and wore a green slicker. She placed a twin slicker on Jane's bed and waited in the doorway of the bedroom.

"Who would we call? If we telephone the TV station or Michael, they will either try to talk us out of it or ask a lot of questions. We won't be out longer than three, four hours. Look, I'm going to borrow my uncle Gilbert's boat. It's fast, and he won't care. He's at the pulp mill now. We'll drop a note off at Gil's place."

"Let's call Michael. He won't try to talk us out of it. He might join us."

Francesca shut her eyes and shook her head. "I don't want to lay all my troubles with Bojack on him. We can leave a note for him here. On the counter."

"We're locking the door," Jane said. "Call and leave a message that I returned, and to stop by. We'll leave the note on the door. He won't miss it."

Francesca went to the telephone and dialed. Busy. She tried again.

"We'll be back before anyone sees it," Francesca said. "A note will be as good as filing a navigation plan."

"That sounds good. There's more I haven't told you. About HBC giving scholarships away to inappropriate students. Ellsley. I accessed a list of files in the college's mainframe. He had files on Katmai. Even the ski resort. But I couldn't get past the code to read it."

"That bastard."

"Why does Ellsley have to be so sneaky?" Jane asked. "The ski resort is not necessarily good, but not necessarily evil, either. He could argue that it's good economics for Sitka. Why can't he be open?"

"Because I thoroughly embarrassed him another time with one of his development schemes—a large boat harbor, complete with spaces for the massive cruise ships and repair facilities. They wanted to attract boat traffic headed for the Gulf of Alaska. I stopped it with a trick from the mayor of Angoon, of all places."

"What did you do?" Jane asked. She pulled the slicker over two of her warmest sweaters. She planned on staying dry during this boat ride.

"A small trip was planned to view the Katmai property that had been proposed for the project. We were on a yacht from the 1920s. Along for the ride were the developers, Ellsley's people, Katmai executives, and town officials. We were out in the bay, looking over the site, when I asked the captain to cut the motor. Ellsley asked why we had stopped. I asked them all to listen. And they did. Finally Ellsley looks at me and asks, in utter disgust, 'Well, what is it? I don't hear anything.' And I said, 'I know, and that's what's so beautiful.' Needless to say, the project got canned."

"That's great," Jane said, laughing. "I love it!"

Francesca dialed the hospital again and got through. "Is Dr. Benoit in?" she asked. She frowned. "What time do you expect him in?... All right. Please tell him that Francesca LaQuestion called and that Jane McBride is back from Angoon. We'll be back later this afternoon, and we'll leave a message at our house.... Yes, thank you."

"I'll tell you more on the way out to Kruzof," Jane said, standing by the door.

"Jane, I'm sorry I was so stubborn. I don't want to involve too many people now. Not until I know more from Bojack."

"Don't worry about talking to Michael. He would want to help you through this."

"I don't expect you to understand this, but Bojack's my son. My only one. I can't wait a minute longer. I need to see him and talk to him and help him any way I can through this, no matter how he is involved. But I have to know what it's all about, and I have to hear what he has to say. Please try to understand.''

''I do understand,'' Jane said, gritting her teeth in bitterness. ''More than you can imagine. I don't want to interfere. I only want to help you.''

''Jane . . .'' Francesca stopped.

''Come on, let's go, get this over with,'' Jane said, running ahead to the truck.

As Francesca closed the door, the telephone rang. The two women looked at each other.

''Don't answer it,'' Jane said sharply. ''We'll handle this ourselves, and we'll be back by dinner.''

''WHAT DID YOU MEAN back there?'' Francesca asked, gripping the steering wheel with both hands. The needle of the speedometer crept ten, then twenty miles over the speed limit. ''You aren't telling me something. Please, what is it?''

Jane gazed out over Sitka Sound. The water looked rough. On the horizon she could see thick dark clouds, unfolding gray, raggedy curtains of rain. The seiners were returning, and not many other boats were out. Going out was crazy, she thought. But then most mothers would do anything for their children. There was no sense, no fairness, in keeping secrets from Francesca anymore. Not after what she had told Francesca and what it might mean about Bojack. Jane talked and did not look at Francesca; she kept her eyes on the water.

''I left Boston because I divorced my husband of ten years. We had a little boy. Will was three years old, a little red-haired imp, and the easiest boy in the world to love. I stayed with him and worked from home. We were the best of friends.

''It was right before Christmas, a year ago. Glen's department threw a huge party. That morning, Kelly, the babysitter, telephoned and canceled because she didn't feel well. I said I'd stay at home. I didn't mind. But Glen was annoyed and said no.

"He asked his brother to do us the favor. His brother, Craig, was new in town, and I didn't know him well. He was an attorney. Recently divorced, no children. But he was Glen's brother, and I figured he'd be as good as any high school girl.

"We were at that magnificent party. Gowns, ballroom, French champagne. The party was in Newport. We were one of the few couples not staying the night. Glen laughed and said I was overprotective, but he didn't argue. I couldn't bear the thought of my little boy waking up in the morning and not finding his mommy and daddy at home."

Jane stopped to catch her breath. She didn't want to cry. Crying never helped her make it through the memory.

"We were dancing and laughing when Glen's boss came over and tapped him on the shoulder. I'll never forget the look on his face when he said that there was a telephone call for us. I knew then. We ran to the telephone, and the police in Boston told us Craig had been in a car accident. He was headed for the liquor store because we didn't have his brand. Glen never told me that Craig had a drinking problem. The baby was with Craig in the car without his car seat. A truck hit the car. Broadsided it. They said...Willy, my baby, died instantly."

She started crying and put her head down into her hands.

"Oh, Jane, Jane," Francesca said as she whipped the pickup truck into the parking lot of a convenience store. "I'm so sorry. I didn't know. We can go home."

"No!" Jane said fiercely. She sat up. Tears streaked her glasses and face. She took off the glasses. "No. You love Bojack and want to help him. And I'm going with you. You see, Francesca, I do understand. I really do."

Francesca cried, too. She reached over, and the two women held one another.

THIRTY-ONE

THIRTY MINUTES LATER, after discovering that *Bluebird* was already missing from its slip, Francesca and Jane pulled into the narrow ANB harbor parking lot and ran down the dock.

The harbor named for the Alaska Native Brotherhood was a workingman's harbor, and virtually all the boats were registered for commercial fishing. Gil had a forty-five-foot seiner, but the boat they would take out was his old aluminum skiff, scarred with dents. What made it different from other skiffs in the harbor was its width and depth—it looked more like a tub than a boat.

"What kind of boat is this?" Jane asked warily.

"It was custom made for him here in town," Francesca said. "Must have been thirty years ago. I've seen Gil load it with a half ton of halibut. This is a boat for serious fishing."

Francesca stuffed some packages underneath the seats, checked the gas, and rearranged the fishing gear that they would not be using. She searched through a cubbyhole.

"Damn, I forgot. Gil has only one life jacket. But we're not going far, and there's other boats out today...."

"Francesca," Jane warned, pointing to an empty horizon.

"We're not going to need them," Francesca said. "Oh, hell. Do you have a piece of paper? Let's scratch a note out to Marcy. Her boat's a couple of slips down, and we'll borrow her survival suits."

"What if she needs hers?" Jane asked.

"I doubt it. But if she does, she'll borrow them from someone else. People are easy in this harbor."

They picked up Marcy's suits, and Francesca untied the lines. The boat tipped back and forth, but Francesca kept her balance.

"Don't worry," she said. "Gil's engine will rip these waves apart."

"We'll be back before dark?" Jane asked.

"Long before that," Francesca said. She knelt by the engine and tugged at the starter cord. The 150-horsepower engine started on the first pull. Francesca stuffed her hair into a cap from the seafood plant. Some strands escaped. She handed Jane a pair of heavy old binoculars.

"Scan ahead for Bojack," she said. "*Bluebird* is turquoise—there's no mistaking her. There's a cloth inside that case for the binoculars. The spray is going to be wicked, and it's not going to be easy to focus. Give your eyes a break now and then. Now, let's keep our fingers crossed that he's headed for Kruzof, that he didn't mislead me and head someplace else...."

Francesca eased the boat out of the slip and past the other boats. Straggling seiners and skiffs were making a rowdy, jubilant return. Deck hands yelled, and beer cans tossed in the wakes. Not many boats would be out that afternoon. Francesca promised they would not be long. They were going to the island with the volcano and would be within sight of Sitka the entire time. Jane sighed, but she searched for *Bluebird*.

Francesca gave Gil's life jacket a kick. The package had never been opened. "Uncle Gil believes in only the bare necessities." She scowled as she forced the engine to putter, to prevent a wake as they passed the incoming herring fishermen. "He put this on board after getting stopped by the Coast Guard a couple of years ago. They wanted to see his flotation device. He laughed and showed them two king salmon—one seventy-five pounds and the other about ninety. 'Sons,' he told them, 'any man that can haul these on board alone doesn't have to worry about a flotation device, now does he?' The Coasties asked him where he caught the fish, and he lied. They thanked him and told him where to order a cheap life jacket.

"Gil swears those two guys fished that useless cove until the end of their two-year rotation."

Even if her eyes had been shut, Jane would have known the moment the skiff pulled away from the protection of the long rock-wall breakwater. Uneven waves slapped the side of the skiff, but the boat sliced through them neatly as Francesca accelerated and aimed directly for the volcano, Mt. Edgecumbe.

The air and ocean spray stung, but the boat did not beat against her back as it had in the trip with Bob. Either the two boats were different or Francesca had more experience at judging the temperament of the waves. The engine sang, and the boat landed with a gentle, steady beat.

As she looked back toward town, Jane realized how easy it was to forget it was March. A thick mist had settled in around Mt. Verstovia, as if a mother had tucked a soft wool comforter around her child to protect him and keep him warm. Jane had lived in Sitka nearly three months, and so far spring was not much different from winter. The sky and sea were more often gray than blue, snow blanketed the mountaintops, rain came almost daily, and conifers still bent and stretched dark boughs against the winds that blew in from over the ocean.

A winter of rain and sleet had kicked up layer after layer of grit against the vehicles and buildings in town, but the place looked less homely with every skip of the boat over the waves. In a matter of minutes the buildings looked like a pile of toys left out in the rain.

Ahead, the clouds around the volcano resembled thick, twisting smoke. Francesca was right. The water had an ominous metal tinge, but the trip was not rough. Only an occasional wave broke and bubbled into pale froth. As she thought about the water, Jane spotted a speck of turquoise at the southern tip of Kruzof.

"There!" she shouted. "I see him. But he's headed for the outside!"

"Let me see those!" Francesca almost screamed as the boat slid to a near stop. "Yes, that's *Bluebird*. What the hell is he up to?"

"We'll soon find out," Jane said wryly.

Francesca upped the speed and took a hard left to head for the outside of the volcano, and the boat started to thump against the waves, harder, harder.

"It's only a little crazier on the outside of Kruzof than right here," Francesca shouted.

For the first time, Jane saw the other side of Mt. Edgecumbe. A winter's worth of snow covered the volcano and its crater. They were so close she could see trees along the mountain's lower edge. She had always thought that as one got closer to nature it lost its magic. But Edgecumbe was even more majestic. Being this close to the volcano, after seeing it every day from Francesca's kitchen window, Jane knew how bugs felt when they looked up the side of a tree.

Sitka vanished from sight, and any trace of color had disappeared with the town. The world was like a detailed black-and-white photo. White snow, black trees, and a hundred shades of Alaska gray.

Some gusts of wind outroared the engine, and Francesca brought the boat's speed down as they passed a stretch of sand. *Bluebird* was no longer in sight.

"A beach!" Jane shouted. "Is it really a beach?"

Francesca laughed. "Yes, Shelikof is a beach! It came with the volcano, I suppose. Practice keeping an eye out. I don't think he's on Shelikof, though. This bay is too open. *Bluebird* stands out, but if he tied it behind one tree or in one tiny cove, we could miss it."

After about ten minutes they were past Shelikof, and Francesca skipped to the next bay.

"My bet is he's at Gilmer," she said as her hand kept a steady grip on the engine. "That was always a favorite place of his when he was a child—he'd go out hunting with his uncles and cousins, and often they holed up in Gilmer Bay for the night. During summers it was a place to find other boats for a card game. But at this time of year I'm sure he has the place to himself...."

She cut a corner. Once in Gilmer she dropped her speed and peered along the shore. "Just keep scanning," she muttered. "Back and forth. Use different vantage points, looking both ahead and behind."

The boat jolted with a horrible scraping sound. The engine whined.

"Damn—a rock," Francesca said as she pushed out farther from the shoreline.

"I can watch the shore, you look for rocks," Jane said. "Could he have pulled it up on shore?"

Francesca shook her head. "I doubt it. It's too heavy, and he's not going to be here long. If he's here, the skiff is in the water."

They rode in silence for a few minutes. As they approached the inside of the bay, they came on a meadow of long grass.

Francesca tapped Jane on the shoulder and pointed.

Jane followed her finger, expecting to see the turquoise boat. No, two tiny deer stepped carefully through the long grass, then lifted their heads and paused, judging if the skiff meant harm. They did not move until the skiff passed by. Jane kept watching the shoreline, avoiding the temptation to study the deer. She tried hard not to blink. She took a deep breath. They had examined three-quarters of the bay's shoreline and still no sign of the skiff.

She looked ahead, ready to tell Francesca to move on to the next bay, when she noticed a creek roaring out of one fold and two trees down in the water. Between the dying trees she saw *Bluebird*.

"Over there," she hissed to Francesca.

Francesca nodded, took a neat turn, and brought Gil's boat down to a putter, maneuvering close to the skiff. She looked it over.

"Nothing inside," Francesca said. Her voice was wistful. Jane could not tell if the other woman was relieved or disappointed. Francesca cut the engine, dropped anchor, and tied a line to a branch of the fallen tree. She hopped out, and with her backpack dangling from one arm, she pulled the boat in closer for Jane.

The sounds of swirling water and wind in the trees—so much noise, and none of it from living creatures—unnerved Jane. She stepped into the water, no more than a foot deep, and immediately felt its temperature harden the rubber of her boots. The tide was low, and her feet crunched through the thick layer of shells and seaweed. The smell of rot and dead small creatures was in the air. Jane clutched her arms to stop a shiver.

"Bojack must not be near, or he'd be out here, waiting for us," Francesca said. "Here's a trail of sorts. Let's see what we can find."

"How can you be sure he took this trail?" Jane asked, leery about going into the forest. The skiff was the only link with Sitka. "If we wait here, we'll be sure to meet him back at the skiff."

"I want to see him right away," Francesca insisted. "This trail doesn't go far. You can stay with the skiff if you like."

"No way. I'd rather stick with you, thank you. Lead the way."

"We won't go far, no more than a mile," Francesca compromised. "If we don't run into him by then, we can come back and wait at the boat. But before we go. . ." She opened the backpack, took out a plastic grocery bag, and unwrapped an old gun. It looked awkward in her small hands. She dipped into the plastic bag for six bullets and expertly loaded the chamber.

"Lots of bears on Kruzof," she said simply. "This baby's old, but it works." She stuffed the plastic back into the backpack and tossed it against the trunk of a tree that had to be more than two hundred years old.

Francesca started walking at a brisk pace on the thin path, dipping, and dodging limbs and scrub, moving fast with quiet dainty steps. Jane was not as good, and the twigs and branches scraped at her hair and her coat. While trying to avoid mud, she walked right into a stick, which scratched her cheek under her eye and knocked her glasses askew. Rubber boots were not made for hiking an uneven trail. She did not mention any of this to Francesca; she wanted to avoid talking altogether. Every deep breath of cold air hurt inside.

Francesca stopped abruptly and crouched to study a patch of mud. "That's Bojack's heel." She pointed.

Jane didn't bother to get close. Instead she used the minute to lean against a tree. She regretted not sleeping on the ferry. Angoon seemed like something from her distant past, but the thought didn't make her sad. She was starting to feel giddy and shook her head.

"I hope he's close," Jane said. "Let's move slower. I'm tired."

Francesca nodded.

"Francesca, what are you going to say to him?" Jane asked. "Maybe I should hang back when we find him."

"I thought of that," Francesca said. Her face was set, and she paid no mind to the clumps of hair falling from her hat. "I wouldn't have dragged you from Sitka. No, you're part of this. You cared enough about Nancy to visit her home in Angoon, to suspect that there might be more behind the death of an Indian who drank too much alcohol. If it hadn't been for you, I would have been the last person to find out about all of this. Bojack owes an explanation more to you than me."

Francesca stood a moment and put her finger to her lips, listening. "Unless he's meeting someone here," she said. "Then we'll watch and see what happens. The water, we're getting close to shore, around the other side of Point Amelia. Not far now...."

Ten minutes later they could see the wild water of the Pacific through the trees. Francesca walked slowly, then turned and took Jane's arm and put a finger to her lips. She moved her lips to touch Jane's ear.

"Step only on the needles." She breathed the words and, to search the shoreline, moved to a tree that was at the forest edge.

Jane nodded and waited for Francesca to locate Bojack. She shut her eyes and listened to the waves tumble onto the shore. Bojack had probably taken some other trail and had long since climbed into the skiff, returning for the warmth of Sitka.

Jane opened her eyes and knew Francesca had spotted him. Her translucent skin was flushed. Her eyes were tender. Not a muscle moved. Jane stretched her neck to look in that direction. Francesca noticed and, without glancing her way, lifted her arm and pointed a long graceful finger.

"We can talk," she said softly. "He can't hear us. I wish I didn't have to do this. It's like when he was a child, and I'd watch him playing outside, getting into mischief."

Jane searched the rocky beach to find Bojack. A man, tiny against the roaring waves. He was wearing denim pants and a denim coat, both faded to a color indiscernible against the rocky shore. He was pulling in some lines, tugging, tugging, his hands made awkward by his thick gloves. Bojack looked up suddenly, let the ropes go to the waves, and ran back to the trees, about thirty yards away.

Francesca let out a little cry and leaned against Jane. Another sound joined the steady beat of the waves and the chaotic roar of the wind. Jane turned to find the source of the new noise and saw a fishing boat passing by about two hundred yards offshore. She saw two people on board, but they were moving around and paying no attention to the shore. The boat was out of sight in moments. Only when the engine sound had disappeared did Bojack reemerge from the trees. Again he tackled the rope, and this time frustration added to the momentum of his pull. Before long a coil of rope was at his feet, along with what appeared to be two large, rickety crates.

"What are those?" Jane asked.

"Crab traps," Francesca said, "but he's not catching crab. Not here. I don't know what he's doing."

"Do we have time to get back to the boat and town before he knows we were here?" Jane asked.

"Maybe," Francesca said, her eyes not leaving Bojack. "Let us see what he's hiding. I wish we had brought the binoculars from Gil's boat."

Bojack pulled a bundle from the first trap and unwound what looked like dozens of old rags until he had a chunk of wood in his hands. He held out the wood and studied it and then placed it carefully by his feet. Then he unwrapped the next bundle, a larger one. Even from so far away both women could see what Bojack held—a large, blackened carving of a raven.

"I wonder if there's an *N* on that one," Francesca said bitterly, and she held out the gun and pointed to a small lever. "Hold this for me. See, I put the safety on. I'm heading down there now."

"I hate guns," Jane said.

"You'd hate a bear even more," Francesca retorted. "You don't have to shoot a bear. Just aim it in the air to scare him away. I don't dare go down there and talk to Bojack hanging on to a gun. I've read too many police reports about domestic disputes."

Jane watched as Francesca ran lightly over the beach toward Bojack. She looked like a young woman out for a happy run on the beach. Jane stared at the gun, wondering how best to hold it. The beach was covered with round rocks that would slide and roll like a pile of bowling balls. She didn't want to fall holding the gun.

What the hell, she thought, and she slipped it, pointed down, into the deep pocket of her lined slicker.

Bojack spotted Francesca in less than thirty seconds. Then he saw Jane. He paused and then tossed the carving back into the trap in disgust.

Francesca slowed as she got closer to him and stopped about ten feet away, staring at the traps and rags.

Jane wanted her to have a moment alone with Bojack. She stepped back slowly and deliberately, her boots hurting her feet, and looked down at the rocks. She didn't want to see that first look of disappointment and shame that would pass between them.

When Jane looked up again, the two were in a hard embrace. Both had the same expression—a blend of distress for what had passed and determination for the future.

The tide was coming in. The rain was turning south rather than east toward Sitka, but the wind was picking up. The trip home would be choppy, at least until they got around Cape Edgecumbe. Jane was nervous and hoped Francesca and Bojack wanted to do most of the talking by the stove in the cottage. She ground her hands in her pockets, and the smooth metal of the gun surprised her. She wrapped her fingers around the barrel to keep it pointed away from her feet as she joined Francesca and Bojack.

"Jane found out about Nancy," Francesca said. "Did she carve these, too? What did you have to do with her?"

He took a deep breath and then scowled. "All part of the job, Mom. It amounts to nothing. I told you this morning that I'm quitting anyway. I'm through with HBC."

Francesca stared at him and nodded. She kicked a small round stone, sending it rolling to the waterline. A wave struck it head-on. Jane lost sight of it after the water bubbled away.

"That sounds like a good idea," Francesca said. "Maybe there's more you want to tell me. You and I, we have never lied. But we have kept ... unpleasantness from each other. Maybe that was too fine a line to draw." She stopped, and she kicked another stone into the waves.

He bit his lip and looked down. He shrugged his shoulders and shook his head.

"This scam is nothing," he said to her. "How is it going to hurt anyone, really? Students copy pieces from the museum. I choose the best copies and drag them out here. Leave them to soak, put them in an oven at a low temperature for about an hour. Makes them look a hundred years old in less than three weeks.

"People are stupid enough to pay outrageous prices for this. Why should it matter how old it is? Why should a raven carved by a guy nobody even knows be worth so much more than an eagle carved by Nancy? I can tell you, she had a hell of a lot more talent, even if she was not all there, Mom. She could copy any style, any artifact, we gave her—and her own designs were even better. If those collectors down south knew what she had been, you'd be lucky if you could give her stuff away. She'd have been a charity case. It doesn't make a lot of sense, does it? Who around here gives a shit about who we're ripping off down there?" Bojack shot an angry stare at Jane.

"You fool!" Francesca screamed. "You little fool! You silly little fool of a boy!" And then she started crying, tears running down her face. "Damn. Damn you."

She dropped to her knees, not seeming to notice how hard she had hit the rocks. She scrambled and tugged at the second crab trap. Bojack did not stop her, just watching as she extracted a soaking bundle. Francesca wore no gloves but used her fingernails to loosen the wet rags. From the mess tumbled a large bowl, with two somber-faced ravens for handles.

Tears streamed down her face, and she screamed: "Is this why Nancy died?" The wind shook the words like the tail of a kite.

"I don't know, Mom," Bojack said, scared and reaching for his mother. "I really don't know."

Jane couldn't stand it anymore. She bent next to Francesca and took the bowl away. She saw Bojack stare but ignored him.

"Francesca, don't do this to yourself," Jane said. "It's too late for Nancy now. All we can do is find out what happened so it doesn't happen again. Bojack, what do you know? Did you have anything to do with Nancy's death?" She glared at Bojack. "We're not out to get you, so please tell us what you know."

Bojack's shoulders slumped. "No. I don't know. All I knew was that she was copying pieces from the museum. That's been going on for years."

"You didn't kill her?" Jane pressed.

"What?" he snapped. "That's what you thought? Hell, no! I thought maybe the pressure had suddenly broken her down. I feel guilty enough about that. God knows she had to produce a lot in the last few months. But kill her? Go out and buy the alcohol for her? No."

Francesca lifted her tear-streaked face. Her eyes were lined and tired, but still they had a beautiful sparkle.

"So, she and other women, students, made copies. What happened to pieces donated to the college through Ellsley's estate-planning program?" Jane queried.

Bojack looked amazed that she knew about it. "We picked up a few artifacts, but that program never got rolling like Ellsley had planned. That's why we started copying pieces out of the museum."

"Bojack, the pieces made by Nancy and the other students are not going down south," Francesca explained. "They are inside the museum. The original artifacts—Jane thinks those have all been sold down south."

"I'm sure of it," Jane said.

Bojack looked as though he had been slapped. He took an angry turn, as if he wanted to shake or slug some other person. He kicked at the crab trap. It bounced over the rocks, and a section of wood fell off.

"Jane figured it out," Francesca said with a hushed intensity. "First, she saw the *N*'s on the two pieces in the museum. She mentioned it at dinner with us that night, you remember. And she believed what you said about them being some kind of clan marking. I did, too. But then she went to Angoon and was inside Nancy's home. The place was filled with her work, and all of it had *N*'s on it. Nancy's great-aunt told her it was Nancy's signature."

"I'd never have known otherwise, Bojack," Jane said.

"No," he said. "No." His whole body shook. He put his hands to his face, and then he walked to his mother and reached for her raven necklace. Jane could hear his breath catch. "Here's another one. Another *N*. Look." He pounded his fist into his hand and swore.

Francesca took off the necklace and stared at it in disbelief. "Jane thinks Nancy was murdered," she said. "Because of the forgeries. So do I. Did you know the *N*'s were Nancy's marks when Jane told you about them?"

Bojack shook his head, in a daze, unable to speak.

"If not you, then who?" Francesca said, taking hold of his shoulders. "Did Nancy give you this necklace?"

He shook his head.

"Then who?" Francesca questioned, her voice soft. "Jane says she told no one else about those *N*'s. I forgot all about them after that night. Did you tell anyone? Do you remember?"

"One person," Bojack said with a moan. Before he could continue, the three were startled by a deep voice from the trees directly behind them.

"That's right...."

From out of the trees came a man—tall, lean, and dressed only in faded jeans and a dark wool vest. As Daniel Greer sauntered over the rocks, Jane thought how he almost blended in with the forest. He had a smile on his face, and in his hand, ready to fire, was a .357 Magnum.

THIRTY-TWO

"NOW YOU KNOW," Daniel said. He did not get close, and he kept the pistol aimed. "Jane, you never called. But thank you for leaving the note on the door."

He pulled the note from his pocket and smiled as he let it drop to the ground. The scrap fluttered away in the wind.

Jane groaned and looked at Francesca, who was staring at Daniel with a hostile look, too worried to blame anyone for their predicament. All three of them had made a mistake in not getting away from uninhabited Kruzof a lot sooner.

"Daniel," Jane breathed. "You? You killed Nancy? But why?"

"I was good to her, better than anyone had ever been." The words came out slow and smooth, like dripping, dark honey. "You and Francesca, you can talk to those people for a minute or two on the street. You feel sorry for them. But do you ever do anything real for them?

"I got her a job. A real job. Not a token job packing bags at a grocery store. She stopped drinking. I gave her a home. That stupid, stupid bitch. She's lucky she had talent, and she was lucky I found it. And despite what I did for her, she came close to ruining me and everything I worked for. She had to put her signature on her work! Without me, she would have been back to the bottle in less than a week. Without me, she was nothing. A loser. Without me, she's better off dead."

"But you killed her," Jane cried.

Francesca walked over and put her arm around Jane.

"Damn right," Daniel said. "Leave her alone, you bitch. Jane's from the real world. Give her a few minutes to think, and she'll realize how right I am."

He paced in front of them on the beach, never averting his eyes. Never pointing the gun away.

"Yes, I came up with the plan to make copies of museum pieces and sell whatever I could to make a profit. Pump enough money into the right Native groups and Native candidates to get some changes going in this town. You're part of the past, Francesca, and I'm the future. In more ways than one." And he laughed.

"And you broke into our house, too?" Jane asked.

"That wasn't me. Ellsley arranged that. Rash, stupid, I must say. He hired a flunkie, who botched the job. After that, I convinced him that he had to give you a job. That we had to keep an eye on you, and that you could even serve the useful purpose of letting us know what Francesca was up to. What I didn't know was that the jerk followed you up to Harbor Mountain Road and tried to send you guys over the cliff up there. The same idiot who trashed your computer. So you used the college's and started to snoop around. But you didn't find much, did you, Janie?"

"Access codes are only as good as the people who use them. I got into several of Ellsley's files with his initials. And I saw the letter from him to the villages, asking for donations of family treasures to the museum. But none of those pieces ever saw the museum, did they, Dan?"

Daniel did not respond, but the muscles in his neck tightened.

"Which one of you called me that first night?" Jane continued, taking advantage of the silence. Francesca did not hide her surprise, and Bojack was embarrassed.

"That was me," Bojack said sheepishly. He avoided looking at his mother. "I used a tape recorder."

"I convinced him that you would only screw Francesca's chances of getting reelected," Daniel interrupted. "The call, the break-in—none of that shook you. Francesca convinced you that the threats were for her, not you, and you stayed. You were so suspicious of Ellsley that first day in the museum. We figured it was best you had a job on campus so that we could keep an eye on you, while we tried to figure out why you left a good job in Boston for Katmai.

"All it took was a telephone call to a reference librarian in Boston. She was sharp. She scanned the computerized periodical index and sent me a copy of an article on the accident. I found your weak point, Jane. Wasn't Martha great with Tommy that night in the harbor?"

"How could you do that to a little baby? Let him wander alone near the water, looking for his mother?"

Jane lunged at him, ready to slap him. He swung the gun and struck her hand before nimbly backing away. Jane gasped and clutched her hand to her stomach.

"Don't be foolish, Jane," he said with a grin. "Enough of that. What I want to know is, as a financial analyst, what do you think of my little venture?"

"You could have done better if you had represented the copies as reproductions and had catalog sales," Jane snapped at him, pushing mattered red hair away with her good hand. "You could have been a hero in this town."

"Ah, maybe I still can be. And if not here, then somewhere else. You will be in for a surprise I'm afraid. The uproar over what I've done would be far greater if the great rich art collectors got stuck with the forged pieces. Nobody down south will care much that some hick museum in Alaska got ripped off. Outside of Sitka the whole ordeal will be forgotten in less than two weeks."

Jane felt relief sweep through her as she gently rubbed the dark red mark near her knuckles. The hand would be bruised, but it wasn't broken. He was talking as if he planned to let them go. As if he were not going to use the gun.

"Now, let's see what we have here," Daniel said as he scooped up a pistol from behind a rock. During the emotional meeting with Bojack, Jane had not noticed that gun

Good that she hadn't—she would have put the gun inside her pocket down beside it. Not that she knew what to do with the one in her pocket. But maybe...

"Jane, you kneel on the ground. Here. Where I can see you. And hold your hands up, while I search your roommate. I don't want you to be tempted to run. You wouldn't find any help around here, and you wouldn't want to spend the night alone. Be patient.... Bojack, you lie down.... No, not that close. Both of you, your backs toward me."

He gave out orders calmly, as if he were giving directions on how to use the index in the museum. Jane wished he sounded angry. The softness and reason in his voice gave her the creeps.

"Take that jacket off, Francesca," Daniel ordered. "And give me that trinket from Nancy. It would have come in handy for framing Bojack, if the police had realized the truth. Fortunately, their bias could be predicted. The fools never even bothered to dust for fingerprints. If they had, they might have wondered why the vodka bottles had been wiped clean. Now, hold your arms and lovely head high."

Jane turned slowly to see if she could toss Francesca's gun to Bojack. She watched as Daniel moved the barrel of his gun along her chest and thighs, though it was obvious no weapons were hidden. Francesca's face revealed no emotion until he turned away, and then her eyes shot a look of hatred.

"What are you looking at?" He smiled at Jane. "Jealous? Didn't Francesca tell you that we went out a few times? But she didn't like my ideas on Native politics. Or maybe it was because others, like Bojack, preferred my ideas to hers? Which was it, Fran?"

Francesca didn't answer. When Daniel turned away, she glanced at Jane quickly. Almost a hint of a smile there.

"Bojack, I want you to take these traps and rags. Get rid of them in the water. Throw them way out. You don't want to carry them back to the skiffs. Jane and Francesca, you can do me the favor of carrying these carvings. No sense wasting the last skillful endeavors of Nancy Nelson and company. Bojack, here, believed me when I said I was getting a couple hundred dollars each for these pieces. How about thousands for the real thing, old buddy?''

But Bojack did not hear. He stood in the waves, tossing the crab traps and rags away. The wind picked up, howling as if it mourned the end of day. Jane could not hear the splash as the trap hit the water and washed out of sight.

Daniel faced the three of them, still keeping his distance. His smile was gone, but his grip on the Magnum was the same. If he were going to shoot them, it would happen now, Jane fretted. She had never fired a gun before and was certain she would miss if she tried. She wasn't even sure she could unlock the safety and was afraid even the smallest noise or movement inside her pocket would attract his attention. She had to wait until she could put down the raven carving and get close to Francesca.

''Listen, you three. We're headed for the skiffs now. Bojack first, Jane next, and tricky Raven woman in front of me. And no funny business. I know there's three of you and one of me, so stay clear of one another. One wrong step and I won't hesitate. You might be able to take me, but Fran would be gone.''

''Why should we go with you after what you've done? To Nancy and God knows who else. What are your plans for us?'' Bojack blurted out, his voice desperate. ''What's in it for us if we cooperate with you on the trail?''

''Don't worry, you'll be all right. We head back to the boats. I leave you stranded here. I get the hell out of town. People will notice you're gone, and you'll be located in less than a day. By then I won't care what you tell people.''

Bojack grunted. Jane took a deep breath, but she caught herself when she saw Francesca stare hard at her and then at her pocket. Her eyebrows were knitted in a frown. Her eyes moved slightly, as if to signal ''no.'' She stopped the moment Daniel turned his attention away from Bojack. What was she trying to say? Jane wondered. Not to use the gun at all? Apparently Francesca was not through with Daniel yet. She had no plans for him to get away. Jane hoped she would not try something stupid with the gun. It was not worth it at this point, not if he was going to let them go. Jane did not want anyone to get hurt, but for now she would wait.

"Let's move," Daniel said.

Bojack had long legs and started in. Jane trudged. Francesca turned to get her jacket. Daniel poked her hard in the back.

"You won't need that," Jane thought she heard him whisper. Why would he say that? Would they have to cross the trail again tonight to retrieve her jacket? Perhaps Bojack and Francesca knew how to make a fire. Then Jane looked around and thought again—not likely. The wood was so soggy, not even a blowtorch could keep it lit.

Any hope that the walk back would be at a calmer pace was gone. Daniel was irritated and kept shouting at her to keep up with Bojack. Jane stared at her aching feet and just counted to four, to herself, over and over. She could not think or pause, or she felt that she would fall over. Her feet were sweating in the rubber boots, and her sock had loosened. The boots only came in full sizes and had never fit well. Now the ragg-wool sock on her left foot was scraping at every step. She thought about asking Daniel to stop so that she could make an adjustment. But no. She remembered what he had said about any funny moves, and she recalled Francesca's hard look. It was also possible she simply might not be able to stand again once she had sat down. A wrong step. She did not want to take any wrong steps, intentionally or unintentionally. She was numb with weariness and concentrated on getting back to the skiff. She trudged and counted, one-two-three-four, one-two-three-four...

THE SKIFFS. Jane didn't see the skiffs until her feet were almost in the water. She sat on the ground and waited to be told what to do. She was cold, hungry, and aching tired. She looked at her watch—not even five o'clock. Michael probably would not even have come by the house yet. Francesca tried to sit next to Jane, but Daniel yelled for them to move apart. They couldn't talk, and Jane could not slip the gun to Francesca. Damn.

She looked over at Francesca. The woman was tapping her knee. It looked awkward. She must be really on edge, Jane thought. She had never seen Francesca fidget nervously before. Jane picked up pebbles and shells and tossed them into the water.

She had time to study *Bluebird*. The boat was made of planks of wood, curved and carefully molded together. The outside was painted turquoise, covered with a clear thick sealer that looked like a layer of glass. Inside, the cedar was polished to a slick shine. The boat was small, but it was a work of art.

Daniel stepped into his Whaler. The engine was big, bigger than Gil's.

"Bojack, use this line," he shouted. "Tie the three skiffs together. Mine will tow the other two. Let me see the knots you tie. It's getting late. There's a flight out of here at seven-thirty tonight, isn't there, Francesca?"

She didn't answer. She just watched as Bojack tied the boats so that they would ride like a little train. Jane didn't ask questions, she didn't think. She just waited, anxious for Daniel to be on his way and for Francesca and Bojack and her to be alone together again.

"Bojack, get in your mother's boat. Jane and Fran, sit here with me. Each on different seats. Facing me. Remember, no talking. Not a move. And I mean it. This gun is ready." He waited and looked at each of the two women's faces. "Good," he said. And he smiled.

He never let go of the pistol as he pulled the rip cord twice before the boat started. The Whaler strained as it moved out into the middle of the channel. Jane thought about the fishing boat that had passed. Maybe another one come by. Surely two boats being towed by a Whaler would look strange. She sighed. It didn't matter. Daniel would have some explanation for anything that might happen. And she was too worn out to protest. She wished he had left them at Kruzof. She dipped her aching hand in the water collected in the bottom of the skiff and wondered if she could squeeze the trigger with a sore hand. The cold felt good. It numbed the pain and cleared her head.

Daniel turned neither the requisite right nor left for Sitka but took off directly for the open ocean. The engine had a low pitch and groaned in protest with every wave that hit. But he kept pushing, pushing on the throttle, never taking his eyes off his passengers.

When Point Amelia was far enough away that they could no longer distinguish the trees, he took his hand off the throttle.

"Bojack, I want you to chop a hole in that piece of junk you call a boat and then cut the line quick. Before it drags us all down."

Bojack looked at his mother. Jane knew what the two were thinking. His uncle Gil's boat. He had been in that boat since he was a boy. But his mother gave a barely perceptible nod.

"Hurry, before I get trigger-happy," Daniel ordered.

Bojack tugged the metal boat close and stood on the line. He stood, raised the ax, and then swung it down hard, directly on a seam. The boat shook.

"Quick, damn you!" Daniel yelled. He pointed the pistol at Francesca's head.

Bojack hit again. Then a third time. The seam split, and water poured in. Bojack skipped back and tapped the ax against *Bluebird* to sever the line. Then he stood and wa____ the boat disappear silently like the hunk of metal _____ e boat was gone in five minutes. Marcy's survival _____ life jacket, remnants of fishing gear, clothing, _____rs, floated away. Bojack and Francesca _____niel kept his eyes on his captives.

"That boat's been around here for years." Francesca said. "People are going to wonder."

"Shut up," Daniel said.

Jane didn't know how Bojack could remain standing on Francesca's tiny boat. Once Daniel had stopped the engines, the wind tossed the skiffs about in the waves in no particular direction. She felt as if she were going to get sick.

"Toss that ax back over," Daniel called.

Bojack did; the axhead missed Daniel's head by inches. Daniel caught the handle and did not say anything. Jane did not want to imagine the scenario had the ax gone overboard. She kept her mind blank, waiting for some signal for action from Francesca.

Daniel put the ax on the floor and then used his free hand to pull Francesca's boat closer. "Time to join Bojack, you two," he said cheerily.

"But how?" Jane groaned. She could not help it. She was going to get sick all over the place any minute. She hated the water. And she hated being out this far. Tension increased by the minute. None of this was making any sense. Did he expect them just to take off and not report him until he had time to leave on the seven-thirty plane? She looked at her watch again. Five-fifty. How would he ever make that plane? He would have to leave all his belongings behind.

"Easy, Janie," he said. "Crawl. Jump. Fall in. Whatever it takes. But get in the damn boat now!" To compete against the wind and splashing waves, his orders had turned into screams. Jane crawled to the edge, and then she reached with one foot. A wave knocked the two boats together, and she fell in. She had never felt more undignified. But it didn't matter. Whatever it took to get Daniel far away from them.

She rolled against Bojack's feet. He held her for a moment and then helped her sit beside him.

Francesca stood proudly, waited for a wave to hit, kept her balance, and then stepped nimbly over the side. Again, Bojack assisted his mother and sat with his arm around her.

The three of them sat together on one seat, Jane in the middle, with Francesca at her left.

Jane choked back some vomit. Bojack pushed her head down between her legs. The boat was small and sank low in the water. Such a boat would have been adorable in the ponds around Boston. In the Pacific it felt as safe as a toy. While Bojack rubbed her back he pulled on her jacket and arranged it so her back pocket was behind the seat, the heavy load and shape out of Daniel's sight. Somehow Bojack knew she had a gun. Perhaps he would find a way to use it. Jane's stomach felt better.

"What are your plans for Katmai, Daniel?" Francesca asked sharply. She had never sounded more like a veteran television reporter. "Why are you helping Ellsley with the ski resort? Why do you even care?"

Daniel broke out into laughter. "A ski resort—right! Isaac Johnson came up with the idea, and Ellsley and I saw a way to take advantage of it. Ellsley hinted to Johnson that he might be willing to sell his family's holdings for the project. The board tried to keep their plans quiet, but you know what that's like in this town. The rumors have outpaced any plans. People all around Southeast Alaska count on Katmai trying to start a major ski resort—the most glamorous and challenging slopes in the entire Northwest. Real estate prices have already increased by thirty percent. Ellsley and I have undertaken a few transactions to take advantage of the boom stirred by the proposal. Any day he plans to ditch all the worthless land his mother left him. Don't worry, Fran, there's not going to be any ski resort. Your precious Indian land won't be defaced for the pleasure of people from the Lower Forty-eight. All there will be is talk. Lots of talk until May. Because as you have already surmised, thanks to Jane's computer workup, a ski resort in Sitka is not feasible. That's why we had to convince the board members who like development to ditch your financial analyst, Jane, here."

"Katmai could go bankrupt. You don't care about Katmai, you don't care about being Indian."

"You never looked at me as an Indian," he said with a laugh. "Now you see why I can't let you three ruin a scheme that's worth millions. Making money selling artwork was taking too long. Let's see," Daniel mused. "How many jackets do you have?"

What the hell is he talking about? Jane could not help but wonder. He made Francesca leave her jacket at the beach, and now he's counting jackets.

"Two," Francesca called out almost teasingly. "It won't look right unless there's three."

Doubt came over his face. Then he grabbed for a life jacket from under the seat of his Whaler and threw it over. The man had incredible balance, Jane thought.

Reaching over with his foot, Daniel stepped hard on *Bluebird*'s prow. The boat dipped and took on water. He did it again, and his arm with the gun swung wildly in the air. Water swamped their feet, and Jane's stomach churned. She stopped fighting to control her stomach and retched everything, including the fear, overboard.

"You bastard!" Bojack yelled. "What the hell are you trying to do to us?"

"When I told you I was going to strand you, I didn't make any promises about doing it on land," Daniel said, chuckling. "Jane, I was going to try and talk with you tonight, find out how much you knew, and then frame Bojack, if necessary. But meeting the three of you on Kruzof is much more convenient." His face was still handsome, Jane thought, but the sound of his voice was horrible.

Bojack swore bitterly but with an edge of defiance.

Under the sound Francesca muttered, "Not yet." Jane knew what she meant—the gun in her pocket. She felt Francesca's hand around her back and in her pocket, fingering the gun. Jane could feel the click of the safety mechanism. Francesca talked, and Daniel didn't notice her hands.

"All right if we put these on, Daniel?" Francesca said, holding up one of the life jackets in her left hand. "Might look silly if we didn't have them on way out here."

"Sure go ahead—I like to gamble. My bet is you guys will be cold and dead in less than an hour without survival suits. Hypothermia, accidental death. No bullet holes, no sign of confrontation. The perfect way to kill three people. It will be dark soon and nobody's going to notice or find your bodies tonight—if ever. Fran knew what I was doing all along. You're not totally stupid, Fran. Just naive enough to think somehow you could escape out here."

"You're not going to get away, Daniel," Francesca taunted. "We have talked to Michael and Bob. Nancy's great-aunt is pressing for a better investigation of her grandniece's death by the state police."

Francesca smiled serenely, and Jane could see worry and self-doubt cross Daniel's face again. Francesca's lack of fear made him angry and frightened.

"People finding out incidentals has not stopped me before!" Daniel screamed. "What you didn't know, Fran, is that I killed Raino. He stopped by the museum once too often and noticed that some pieces had been replaced with copies. He made the mistake of confronting me. Now it's your turn. Stop smiling. Get real, you bitch! Get ready to die!"

THIRTY-THREE

DANIEL PUSHED against *Bluebird* again with his foot. Waves sloshed into the boat—enough so that the water was around Jane's ankles. The engine was half sunk in the water, and *Bluebird* was starting to drag on Daniel's boat. Jane knew they would be submerged in minutes.

Francesca moved fast. She lifted the gun and aimed. The deafening shot came as a wave hit *Bluebird*. Daniel grabbed a red gasoline can and hurled it at Francesca. She twisted to block the impact, but it hit the side of her head. Her gun splashed into the puddle at the bottom of the boat. Francesca lunged for the gun. As Daniel raised his Magnum, ready to bring it down on Francesca's head, Jane reached for the rope holding the two boats together and yanked it with all her might. The sudden motion combined with the wind, made the Whaler lurch.

Both Daniel and Francesca tumbled overboard. The rope was tangled around Francesca's legs, and she screamed. Daniel thrashed about in silence, still holding his gun, as he drifted away. Bojack pushed Jane aside and tugged on the rope until Francesca was close to the side.

"Help me," Bojack cried. "Thank God she put the jacket on."

He grabbed his mother by the shoulders, and Jane gripped a leg. They pulled her alongside. Francesca's eyes were wide with terror, but she managed to cling to the side of the boat. "Hang on to her," Bojack ordered. "Don't let go! We have to get back in the Whaler!"

Without flinching, he reached into the water, gripped the edge of Daniel's boat, and clambered aboard. The move dipped the Whaler dangerously low. Bojack reached for the ax and cut the line that connected the two boats. The move unleashed Francesca. He took a deep breath and pulled *Bluebird* alongside the Whaler, stretching his arms and straining to keep the boats close but not touching. Francesca's head bobbed in between the two boats.

"Jane, get in here!" he ordered. "Fast!"

Jane hesitated only because she did not want to let go of Francesca. Francesca was shaking and having trouble hanging on to the boat.

"We'll get her," Bojack coaxed. "If you don't fall in. Come on, you can make it."

Jane reached over and tumbled shoulder first into the Whaler. The movement pushed *Bluebird* almost completely under, and Jane's legs were drenched.

The Whaler felt more secure than *Bluebird*. Jane looked over at Francesca and Bojack. *Bluebird* was gone.

Francesca no longer held on to the boat, and the jacket kept only her head out of the water. Her teeth were gritted with pain, and her eyes were shut. Bojack directed Jane to stay at the other end of the boat to maintain some balance. He placed one hand down through the back of Francesca's life jacket for a good grip and the other around her thigh. He waited until the boat was relatively still, and then he heaved the woman to the edge. A wave hit, knocking Francesca back into the water. Jane scrambled and leaned over to grab on to the collar of Francesca's life jacket.

"She can't take much more!" Bojack cried. "Let's try together!"

Jane went to his side and tugged. Bojack gripped the jacket again, and Jane took the leg. She forgot about the pitch of the waves and the wind, and she forgot the precarious position of the Whaler. She remembered Sam, the man from her first ferry trip, stating calmly that a boat could take a lot of stress before it went under. She pulled one leg of Francesca's over the edge and sat on it, before helping Bojack by gripping the life jacket. Another wave hit, and Francesca fell in the boat on top of Bojack. He scrambled out and crawled to the engine. Jane took off her own soaked coat and covered Francesca. Then she scanned the waves.

"Bojack," she said, "what about Daniel?"

The younger man shook his head and looked around. "There's nothing we can do about him. He's gone. We have to get Mom back right away, or she's not going to pull through this. The Coast Guard will start a search, but we have to get back.

Jane got up on her knees and looked around. She saw no sign of Gil's boat or *Bluebird*. The survival suits and other remnants had floated out of sight. Daniel could be a mile away. She moved the raven sculpture under the seat so that it would stop rolling back and forth at the bottom of the boat, and she didn't argue with Bojack.

"We saved her, Jane!" Bojack said. "I was afraid we'd let go, but we did it. Now let me see if I can get this damn motor going." He began to work the starter cord. "The idiot! Stopping the engine out here. We'll be lucky if it doesn't stall on us. Look for flares, Jane. We could use some help."

Jane searched under the seats and in the odd containers. Nothing. The boat looked as though it were never used much.

"How did you know I had the gun?" Jane asked.

"Mom tapped out a message to me when we were back on shore. She warned me you didn't know how to use it and probably wouldn't try. Morse code. I loved it when I was a kid, and she took time to learn it, too. She was the greatest." He looked at his mother with a worried glance. "And she still is. I haven't told her in a long time."

He pulled and pulled at the starter cord. It was futile. The motor coughed.

"We don't even have oars," he said, and made a half-hearted pull.

"Wait," Francesca breathed. Her teeth chattered once she opened her mouth. They sounded as though they could crack. "A minute.... Then pull...*hard*."

Jane drew the other woman onto her lap, retucked the jacket, and then wrapped her arms around her. The swells gently rolled the boat not toward Kruzof, but out to open sea. They were more than an hour away from home, away from warmth, away from life for Francesca.

"I'm worried about her, Bojack," Jane said, holding the shivering woman. "I'm going to take her clothes off and put a survival suit on her. Count to fifteen—no, twenty—before you try that motor."

"Okay." He nodded. "Jane, I owe you. Thanks for being my mother's friend." He turned full attention to the engine.

Looking calmer, more in control of himself, he checked over the various controls and took a deep breath. Then he tore at the cord as if he meant to rip it out of the engine. The motor shook and roared to life.

"All right!" he yelled.

"Yes!" Jane said as she gave Francesca a hug. She had taken off Francesca's sopping T-shirt and jeans and had pulled the survival suit over her legs. The legs no longer felt human. Jane moved Francesca's body so it was stretched out between her and Bojack on the floor of the Whaler. She zipped the suit up to the neck and then tucked the extra material hanging from the hands and legs around the woman's body, the way she had once covered Will when she'd checked him during the middle of the night. "Tuck me up, tuck me up," the little boy would murmur, his voice angelic with sleep. The memory no longer stabbed her like a knife. She draped her own wet coat around her shoulders and then straddled Francesca's body and hovered over her, trying to block the spray and wind.

At full speed, Bojack turned the boat for town. "It's going to be all right, Mom," he said. "Everything is going to be all right from now on."

Francesca opened her eyes. She nodded and smiled. Her body quivered, and she did not talk. Jane held her closer.

"God, I was worried," Bojack said, shaking his head. "No oars, no flares. Nothing. We would have been lucky to have been found tonight. But look, he has a bottle here. Chivas Regal. He was going to celebrate after he got through with us."

"Ever since I moved into Francesca's I imagined owning a skiff and having a drink while watching the sun set," Jane said.

"Some sunset," Bojack said. The sky was filled with dark clouds, and the water was a steely gray that reflected no light. "I suppose it will have to do." He raised it in a toast. "To Jane McBride, thank you." He opened the bottle and passed it to Jane.

"To the three of us," Jane said, lifting the bottle. She bent over and held it gently to Francesca's lips.

Francesca took a sip. "Look." Teeth chattering, she pointed to the west. "Look."

Out over the ocean, the sky that had been dropping dark torrents of rain, cleared, and a patch of light opened in the sky, revealing a far-off miniature rainbow.

"A rainbow, a rainbow for your father," Francesca said as she relaxed against Bojack's leg. Her face was content.

Jane gave Bojack a puzzled glance.

"The Tlingit say that people who die a violent death are trapped above the sky," Bojack explained softly. "If that death is avenged, their soul joins the trail along the rainbow to the world of stars, moon, and sun, the world of happiness."

He put his arm down, brushed his mother's hair from her cheek, and then put his arm around Jane.

"A rainbow for Nancy, too," Jane murmured.

The three people huddled quietly in the Whaler as the boat aimed for the lights of Sitka.

EPILOGUE

May

DEAR GLEN,

You asked me a year ago to consider giving our marriage another try. If the offer still stands, I am ready. But would you consider starting new? Would you consider coming to Sitka?

I must warn you, Alaska has become a part of me. I am a different person. My job and friends are more diverse than ever before. My life is more free than it ever was in Boston. I have many good friends again. I have learned to love them and understand and accept their faults, as they have learned to accept mine. One of my friends, Bob, is like a brother and reminds me of Craig. Please tell Craig that I forgive him, that I have learned to accept what was a tragic mistake, and that I realize he would do anything to go back and change what happened. At last I have moved beyond blame. Blaming him or you. And blaming myself. Underneath is a sadness that is forever, which I know you share. But that does not mean we cannot move on, enjoying life and doing all we can to contribute to a community.

Michael Benoit, a psychiatrist at the hospital and another close friend, has assured me that you would be a welcome addition to the hospital in Sitka. You could make it a sabbatical. We could give this life a year and see if we can make it work.

Michael and Francesca have fallen in love. I found a house on the beach, not far from Francesca, and plan to move out next weekend. My friendship with Francesca is such that we know what the other is thinking and feeling. But now I am the finance director at Katmai Shee, and we are both frantically involved in corporate details. We can't live for the corporation at home as well as at the office. We are two women who value our privacy, but Francesca and I helped each other when each needed it the most. Our friendship will continue to grow.

Bojack is making plans to start studies for his master's degree at the University of Washington. His carvings will be featured at a gallery in New York. He arranged for some of Nancy Nelson's work to be placed there and in other galleries around the country. The money will mean a great deal to her family. But they plan to set most of it aside to start a cultural program in Angoon, in Nancy's name.

The Coast Guard searched for four days, but they never found Daniel Greer's body or any sign of the boats. Everything happened so fast that day. So fast that now it seems like a dream. Maybe if I had talked with Daniel more . . .

I love you. I miss you. I hope to see you soon.

Your wife,

Jane.

Die Dreaming
Terence Faherty

First
Time in
Paperback

An Owen Keane Mystery

ALMA MURDER

Ex-seminarian turned seeker of lost souls—especially his own—Owen Keane attends his tenth high school reunion and finds himself the butt of a practical joke by the old gang. Vengeance being the operative mood in his "morning after" state, he starts asking sticky questions about a decade-old secret that has shadowed the lives of everyone involved.

What he discovers is shocking, but pieces are missing. Not until the twentieth reunion do they fit together. One of the gang has been murdered, and Owen is determined to unravel the tangle of lies that cost a man his life—and now may cost Owen his own.

"Rich and surprising..."—*Publishers Weekly*

Available in July at your favorite retail stores.

Down Among The DEAD Men

GERALDINE EVANS

An Inspector Rafferty/Sergeant Llewellyn Mystery

A FAMILY AFFAIR

When rich and beautiful Barbara Longman is found dead among the meadow flowers, Inspector Rafferty doesn't believe it's the latest grisly offering by the Suffolk killer—though he believes her killer would like him to think so.

Rafferty and Llewellyn suspect someone close to home—someone among the descendants of the family's long-dead patriarch, Maximillian Shore. Everyone, it seems, had a motive: Barbara's weak, ineffectual husband; Henry, her ruthless brother-in-law; as well as Henry's bitter ex-wife. And the police duo discover that Maximillian Shore can wield his influence even from the grave—in a twisted legacy of murder.

"Competent..."—*Kirkus Reviews*

Available in July at your favorite retail stores.

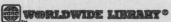

REGINALD HILL
BLOOD SYMPATHY

First Time in Paperback

A Joe Sixsmith Mystery

ALL THIS AND A MATCHMAKING AUNT, TOO...

It is feast or famine for ex-machinist turned private investigator Joe Sixsmith. One minute he's dozing in his office, the next he's been hired by a self-proclaimed dabbler in the dark arts to retrieve a stolen locket. There's also a man who dreams he has murdered his entire family and two thugs who seem to think Joe's in possession of several kilos of heroin. Add to that a meddlesome aunt who wants to fix him up with marriage candidates.

Things are sticky at best. But for a private eye with admittedly more wits than guts, and an alcoholic cat as partner, a bit of luck may just keep him single—and alive.

"Sumptuously plotted..."—*Kirkus Reviews*

Available in August at your favorite retail stores.

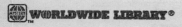

WORLDWIDE LIBRARY®

BLOOD

First Time in Paperback

Jeanne McCafferty

A MacKenzie Griffin Mystery

CLIMBING THE CHARTS IS MURDER...

Murder scenes aren't supposed to look this good. The lighting, the staging, the arrangement of the body, even the clothes are eerie recreations of pop superstar Peter Rossellini's hot music videos. In fact, each victim resembles the sexy singer.

Clearly, the killer is obsessed. But is Peter the next intended victim? Criminologist MacKenzie Griffin fears just that. Mac has no shortage of suspects. And one is setting the stage for a hit that's to die for.

"A highly recommended first novel."

—Susan Rogers Cooper, author of
Dead Moon on the Rise

Available in August at your favorite retail stores.

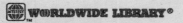 **WORLDWIDE LIBRARY** ®

STAR